CW01095488

TAMING THE WOLFF

DEL ROBERTSON

Affinity
eBook Press
NZ

Taming the Wolff

Copyright © Del Robertson 2008

Affinity E-Book Press NZ LTD.

Canterbury, New Zealand

All rights reserved.

ISBN: 978-0-9922461-2-9

No part of this e-Book may be reproduced in any form without the express permission of the author and publisher. Please note that piracy of copyrighted materials violate the author's rights and is Illegal.

This is a work of fiction. Names, character, places, and incidents are the product of the author's imagination or are used fictitiously and any resemblance to actual persons living or dead, businesses, companies, events, or locales is entirely coincidental.

Editors: Nat Burns
Cover Design: Helen Hayes
Photo Credit: Stoneilse1
http://s487.photobucket.com/profile/stoneisle1

Acknowledgements

Thanks to Erin, Mel and Helen and the rest of Affinity for giving me a new publishing home. Thanks also to BLR, Sherry, Kelly and Mom.

Dedication

For Lee. Always and Forever

Chapter One

THE CAPTAIN

SHIP'S LOG – JULY 17, 1703

Caught an English vessel bound for the Spanish Main. Ordered the men to slash the sails before abandoning the Queen's Navy at sea. We'll be days away before they can repair the damage. I ordered three women bound for Puerto Cabello to be transferred aboard The Wolfsbane. *They should raise a hefty ransom. Their jewelry alone could fetch enough money to feed my crew for six months.*

I closed the logbook, dropped the quill onto my desk, then leaned back in my chair and propped my feet up. I pulled the velvet pouch from my belt and poured its contents onto the table.

I sifted through the assortment of rings and baubles, my fingers deftly gliding across the surface of smooth golden rings and necklaces bejeweled with sapphires and rubies. Seldom had I seen so many treasures come from one booty, let alone from three passengers. Even if the hold of the ship was empty, the bounty from the women would have more than covered the risk of attacking an English naval vessel.

Idly, my fingers toyed with a necklace. The gold cross contrasted sharply against my black glove. I turned the cross in my palm, studying it intently. There was an inscription worn into the metal. I stared intensely, trying to read the faded printing.

Alexis.

I wondered which of my guests it belonged to. Certainly not the mother. Surely, she wouldn't wear such a plain necklace. Not the high and mighty Duchess DeVale.

One of the daughters then. Which one? The sobbing brunette with the pouty lips? Or the blonde? The one who stared at me openly, meeting my gazes squarely, refusing to look away, even as I threatened to reach down the bodice of her dress for the coin purse I was certain she had hidden. Her captivating, verdant eyes held me entranced upon the deck of the burning ship, nearly making me forget my cause.

The door of my cabin creaked open. I quickly looked up, aggravated by the intrusion. A tall man with a sturdy build, a neatly trimmed mustache and with brown graying hair stood just inside my doorway. Vincent.

My quartermaster closed the door and walked the short distance across the cabin. He laid his astrolabe atop our navigational maps on the desk and glanced at the pile of jewelry. I watched as he paced to the open window. He stood silently, staring out to sea, hands clasped behind his back.

My gaze shifted to the necklace I held in my hand. I absently stared at the inscription, my finger tracing Alexis's name etched in the metal. "What troubles you, Vincent?"

He turned his attention away from the window, his hands still clasped behind his back, and a deep frown marred his features. "I don't much appreciate the business of taking women prisoners."

I stared at Vincent, not quite believing what I was hearing. I arched one eyebrow in puzzlement.

"The men could be distracted by them. There could very well be some," he cleared his throat, "complications."

"The crew signed *The Captain's Articles* before coming aboard. The penalty for harming women is death by hanging."

"A slip of paper isn't going to stop a man from doing what comes naturally, Kris. You should realize that better than anybody." His deep baritone voice dropped to a hushed whisper. "What do you suppose would happen if your crew discovered their captain was really a woman?"

My head snapped up, eyes locked with Vincent's. He held my gaze. I felt my gut clench. I knew if my crew discovered my secret, they would turn on me in an instant.

"That's not going to happen. I've taken every precaution."

"Even with every safeguard, the chance of your true identity being discovered is still a consideration." Vincent sat on the edge of my desk, leaning closer. "Thus far, you've evaded detection."

He took my left hand, lifting it in both of his, slipping off my leather glove. "All it takes is one slip—a misplaced glove, a flash of a slender wrist, tender skin too soft to belong to any man." His even gaze met mine as he lulled me with his soft tone. "One mistake, and your deception will be ended."

"If we merely attack for cargo and treasure, we'll never have enough to plan for the inevitable. And as much as I'm loath to admit it, Vincent, you are correct. Eventually, I'll need to end my deception. Not because I fear discovery, but rather because I fear the hangman's noose." I took a deep breath, savoring the smell of the ocean surrounding us. "Governments are taking the events in the region seriously now, and navy warships patrol the seas heavily. We can't outrun the navy forever."

"How do these women concern our future?"

"Look at the valuables they flaunt on a dangerous sea voyage." I gestured toward the jewels laying on my desk, glistening in the sunlight. "Surely, their coffers at home overflow with precious treasures."

"You mean to ransom them." A statement, not a question, said in a disapproving tone.

"Yes. With what we secure from their household, we'll be able to retire. You'll be able to return to England if you wish. I could discreetly disappear, perhaps purchase a plantation, maybe settle down in a new colony. Why, the possibilities are boundless."

"We may never see any of their ransom. As of yet, they refuse all cooperation."

I resumed my pacing. "The mother?"

Vincent nodded. "She has proven to be most difficult."

I rubbed my face. There was always one more obstacle to deal with. "Very well," I said. "Perhaps it's time for The Wolff to pay a social call upon our guests."

"I'll take my leave so that you may prepare." Vincent moved across the cabin and closed the door behind him as he left.

I continued to stare out the window at the ocean beyond. Azure sky met cerulean water on the horizon, rays of sunlight cutting across the surface of the ocean. Sunlight streamed through the window, reflecting off the bounty heaped upon my desk.

I picked up the golden necklace I had fondled earlier, my gaze drawn once again to the inscription.

Alexis.

†

I paused outside the doorway, tapping my knuckles twice on the wooden frame. More of a courtesy rather than a formality. After all, *The Wolfsbane* was my ship. No doors were barred from her captain.

I confidently strode into the cabin. The Duchess DeVale sat in a chair in the center of the room. Near her, seated on the bed, was one of the daughters, the brunette with the pouty lips. The duchess appeared to be consoling her daughter. They both looked up at my intrusion.

Duchess DeVale's face showed unrestrained contempt. Her daughter's was splotched red, her cheeks tear-stained as she fought back her sobs. This was how they had first appeared before me, as well. The mother was strong-willed, utterly defiant in the face of insurmountable odds. She had dared to attempt to dress me down in front of my own crew during what should have been my finest hour. She was indeed fortunate *The Captain's Articles* applied to me, as well.

As for the daughter, she was exactly what I had expected. She was the same as every other noblewoman I had ever encountered. The girl was suitably distressed at being set upon by a horde of ruthless, bloodthirsty pirates, too terribly afraid to do anything other than hide below deck. Then when discovered and dragged kicking and screaming before the pirate captain, she was unable to do anything save weep.

Out of the corner of my eye, I caught a flicker of movement. My gloved hand flew out, catching a slender wrist in my grasp. I instinctively followed through, pulling the assailant's wrist, forcing my attacker to the ground. I knelt there on the deck, straddling my opponent, pinning her wrists down with my strength.

Her deep green eyes, wide with shock, bore into me. Her nostrils flared, her bosom heaved with each ragged breath. Strands of light blonde hair splayed across blue velvet, attempting to hide the soft flesh at the bodice of her dress. My gaze shifted to her full rounded lips and the pink tongue extending to wet them.

My captive squirmed beneath me. I tightened my grip on her wrists in response, leaning in closer with my upper body for leverage. That only served to agitate her further, her struggles increasing. Her lower body arched as she fought, her hipbone connecting between my trousered legs. Lips near her ear, I let out a low, guttural growl. Her struggles beneath me abruptly abated.

"Enough! Unhand her, you cad!" demanded a crisp, English accented voice from somewhere behind my left shoulder.

I rose from my straddling position, pushing myself up from the wooden floor. My hands moved from grabbing wrists to clutching fingers. I pulled my attacker to her feet, gallantly bowing before her.

"My lady." My voice came out deeper, rougher than usual.

I studied the blonde beauty's face. A slight blush colored her cheeks. Yet her jaw remained locked in a determined scowl.

"Captain," she said through clenched teeth.

"I trust your quarters are adequate?" I arched a questioning eyebrow.

"Hardly," the brunette said.

"Really?" I strode across the cabin to another doorway, peering inside. Two more beds, as well as a bureau adorned the room. The ladies' matching travel bags were transferred along with them from the Royal Navy ship onto *The Wolfsbane.* "I went to great lengths to ensure that you'll be comfortable during your stay."

"And, pray tell, how long shall that be?"

"That depends on your cooperation." I looked pointedly at the mother. "Or lack thereof."

"It shall be a cold day indeed when the Duchess DeVale lends her cooperation to a traitorous pirate."

Duchess DeVale turned crimson as she vehemently protested my abduction of her and her daughters. I blocked out most of her tirade as she continued to describe, in vivid detail, my future fate at her husband's hands, including everything from the rack to beheading to hanging.

My attention focused on Duchess DeVale's two daughters. The brunette continued to sit on the edge of the bed, her long dress carefully splayed to cover her legs. She used her handkerchief to dab at her hazel eyes, bloodshot and swollen from her incessant tears.

As the duchess droned on about my crimes, including my abduction of their persons and my subsequent lack of manner thereafter, I shifted my position slightly, so that I could observe her other daughter. . As the mother continued her verbal assault, my eyes subtly assaulted the body of her eldest daughter.

She was tall for a woman, almost equal to my own height. Her posture was rigid, her back ramrod straight, befitting a member of royalty. Her skin was creamy and smooth. Her nose straight and elegant. Her lips full and luscious. Her silken hair fell loosely about her shoulders, past the swell of her breasts. The blonde locks shone brightly in the sunlight, as if spun from pure gold. Smooth, delicate hands clutched at the edge of the table, revealing small veins in each wrist. The porcelain chamber pot she had attempted to strike me with lay on the floor at her feet.

Our gazes locked. Her eyes were filled with a keen intellect, which turned to a fierce glare as she caught me staring. I suddenly realized she too was ignoring her mother's prattling voice and instead was watching me even as I was staring at her.

I felt a sudden flush rise into my cheeks. I turned away quickly, hoping she hadn't seen my reaction. I prayed she hadn't seen the pirate captain blush and risked a sidelong glance at her again. A mocking smile met my gaze, forcing me to turn away. *Damn!* I was suddenly irritated at her, at myself. Fantasy dissipated and I came back to reality. My posture stiffened; I straightened to my full height. Clasping my hands behind my back, I addressed the Duchess DeVale as if she were one of my own crew.

"You will cooperate with the delivery of your ransom if you entertain any hopes of returning to your previous lifestyle. The sooner you cooperate, the sooner the ransom will be delivered, and the sooner you and your daughters shall be free to leave my ship. This evening you will join me at my table for dinner. My quartermaster will escort you come seven bells. Do not disappoint me, ladies." My words were clipped and precise, my tone confident and sure.

The Duchess DeVale huffed and puffed, shocked by the earful I had just given her. "You immoral, uncouth—"

"Duchess DeVale," I cut her off in mid-tirade. "If I were half the scoundrel you imagine me to be, I would have assigned you and your daughters to quarters below deck with my crew, instead of under my protection."

Before any of my captives could protest, I made my way across the cabin. I paused at the door, hand resting on the handle. I looked at them, scanning their faces one by one. Reaching inside my leather glove, I pulled a golden chain from its resting spot in the palm of my hand.

"Alexis," I called, my voice loud in the small room.

The tall blonde looked up, her eyes meeting mine once again. I tossed the chain toward her, then opened the door and turned on my heel to leave. I glimpsed her hand shoot out, catch the chain, and clutch the golden cross in a firm grasp.

†

I sat at the table, sipping my brandy. I picked at the food on my plate. The crew had raided the galley of *The Scorpion* early that morning, taking anything and everything of value. Including fresh fruits, I noted, biting into a slice of succulent melon, feeling the juices dripping down my chin. I swiped at my chin with the back of my hand.

"Save room for the main course, Captain." A voice said loudly.

I twirled around in my chair. The order came from a stocky, muscular man who had long thick red hair trailing down past his waist and a full beard stretching past his belly. Beady eyes watched me, just as they watched hawk-like over his galley. Rufus McGregor.

"Aye," I said, smiling. "Did you cook something special to-night?"

"Of course, Captain," he replied, setting a covered plate in front of me. "The Royal Navy keeps their galleys and holds well stocked. It'll be hearty eating for the lot of us."

My eyes focused on the covered plates being set at the tables. The silver dinnerware was captured from a Dutch vessel nearly a year before. During that time, we'd scarcely used it. And quite frankly, I had almost forgotten it rested in a crate somewhere in the cargo hold of the ship. Obviously, Rufus had not forgotten.

"No more for now," Rufus said, snatching the plate of melons from my grasp. He also grabbed the slice I was about to pop into my mouth. "Ye'll wait for the rest, my Captain."

I frowned, looking up at our cook. "You don't usually stand on such formality."

"We don't usually have such magnificent guests." His gaze transfixed on the door.

My eyes followed his across the room. Duchess DeVale stood inside the doorway, looking every bit as regal as if she'd been the Queen of England. She had changed into a rose-colored dress, complete with matching hat and feathered plumage. She snapped her fan with authority as she, too, surveyed the room.

The daunting Duchess DeVale, as handsome a woman as she may have been, was not what held the undivided attention of my crew, however. That honor belonged to the duchess's two daughters. All heads turned to watch, all conversation ceased, as the women entered the room behind their mother.

The brunette wore a soft blue dress, also with matching hat and handbag. Her breasts were accentuated, riding a little too high in her bodice. Her hair, now curled into tight ringlets, was bouncy and full of life. *In stark contradiction of herself* I thought, ruefully. Elizabeth, I think I heard her mother call her.

I looked at Alexis DeVale. My breath caught in my throat, and my heart stopped. I was pleased. Her blonde locks fell across her shoulders and there was no hat to hide those lovely tresses. A deep burgundy dress clung to her frame. Even from across the room, I could see the sparkle in those lovely green eyes.

My heart stopped yet again as her eyes met mine. We locked gazes. Green eyes staring into gray, neither willing to be the first to look away in a contest of wills, of strength, and courage. I'd let her be the first to avert her eyes; I wouldn't be so weakened by a woman's gaze.

The entourage crossed the room, escorted by Vincent. My men parted a path, allowing their safe passage. Still our eyes remained locked.

"Ladies," I greeted them as they approached my table. Vincent pulled out a chair, seating Elizabeth DeVale. The duchess's discomfort was obvious as my third, Ivan, pulled out a chair for her.

Somehow, my hand found the back of the chair nearest my own, pulled it out from the table. "My lady," I gestured, bowing before Alexis DeVale. As she sat, I gently pushed her chair back in.

Ivan and Vincent uncovered their dishes, encouraging the ladies to do the same. Hesitantly, I lifted mine, wondering what Rufus had managed to concoct in his galley.

Meat, probably venison from the looks of it, carrots, and potatoes. I couldn't remember the last time I'd had a potato. The last batch we'd purchased at Tortuga had gone bad before we'd sailed one hundred leagues.

I cut off a piece of meat with my knife, speared it with my fork, and raised it to my mouth. At Vincent's disapproving glance, I dropped it back onto my plate. Chastised with one look, I meekly cut the pieces into smaller bites.

I casually looked around the room. My crew had also settled down for dinner, with the exception of Darby, who was practicing with his lyre. To my astonishment—and pride—my entire crew were also using their knives and forks, as opposed to fingers. Even Lars, the large warrior who had joined my crew the past spring, was on his best behavior.

My gaze returned to my own table. Ivan and Vincent were engaged in animated conversation with Elizabeth as they ate. The Duchess DeVale picked at her food, eating for sustenance, rather than enjoyment. By my side, Alexis poked at a piece of venison with her fork. I watched intently as she chewed.

"How is it?" I leaned closer.

She smiled politely, swallowed. "It's…unusual. I've never tasted such salty venison."

I smiled at her polite discretion. Obviously, Alexis was unaware that on a sailing vessel, almost all food went bad quickly. Even flour and dried beans spoiled rapidly in a damp hull. Only heavily salted meat lasted more than a few weeks in a cargo hold.

"Would you care for a drink?"

"Water, please."

"Water is a problem." I hesitated. "It spoils quickly in the wooden barrels of a ship. We have brandy, rum, and wine."

It was Lady DeVale's turn to hesitate. She bit her bottom lip in contemplation. "Wine," she said at last, settling on what she must have thought was the lesser of evils.

Rufus appeared at my shoulder with a bottle of red wine. And one of my most prized possessions, I noted ruefully. I turned to motion for Rufus to switch the bottles, but he was already across the room again, fetching a bottle of rum for his own dinner.

I scowled and turned back to my dinner. Alexis waited expectantly. I put on my most charming smile, gallantly passing the bottle to my lovely companion. She held it aloft, carefully inspecting it.

"1492?"

I nodded. "I understand it was a very good year. Legend has it that one of my ancestors attacked a treasure fleet with four ships bound for the Americas. They all sat low in the water, they were so laden with treasure. My ancestor successfully diverted one ship, pillaging it, then sinking it with all hands on board. The hold of that particular ship was filled with cask after cask of fine wines. Also included in the hold were several bottles sealed especially for the voyage of the fleet to America, made from grapes from the queen of Spain's own vineyard. The bottles have been in my family's wine cellars ever since."

"Perhaps you would rather save such a rare wine for a special occasion."

"Of course not." I lied. I was already pouring her a glass, imagining a special occasion with just the two of us and this bottle of wine—and it didn't include a room full of rowdy sailors and Alexis DeVale's captive relatives.

I poured Alexis's glass first, then my own. She brought her glass to her lips, sipping. A delicate hand lowered her glass again. Her fingers stroked up and down, caressing the crystal. Her fingernails clinked against the glass.

I lifted my own goblet. Bumped my front teeth with the rim of the glass—my hand was shaking. I swallowed, gulping down half the contents. I licked my lips, tasting the bittersweet wine, longing for another sweeter wine that wasn't to be found at the bottom of a bottle.

"It's delicious." Alexis took a longer sip. "I don't think I've tasted anything quite so rich."

"Thank you." I poured myself another glass and topped hers off. "You seem surprised."

"Perhaps she's surprised that a mob of barbarians are capable of manners," Duchess DeVale said. "Personally, I imagined you and your crew wallowing on the floor like a drove of hogs at a feeding trough."

Conversation at the table abruptly died. All eyes stared at me, awaiting my reply. Vincent's gaze urged me to proceed with caution, to keep my words—and my temper—at bay.

"Duchess DeVale." I set down my goblet more forcefully than I intended. A loud thunk echoed from the table. "For such a

11

noble lady, it seems that you are the one lacking in manners. Need I remind you that you are guests aboard my vessel, saved at my sole discretion? Lest you forget, spoils go to the victor in any battle."

"Surely, even you do not possess such audacity as to maintain that you had the cunning and resources to overpower Captain Jackson and his crew in a fair fight," she said. "Why, it was only through your trickery and deceit that you were able to capture and board one of Her Majesty's vessels."

"It was rather magnificent, wasn't it?" I smirked, remembering how we had donned an allied flag, lulling the British ship into a false sense of security. Then luring her in until she was too close to use her cannons, attacking with such ferocity that she had no chance to resist.

"Flying under false colors, committing acts of piracy, and endangering a captain loyal to the Crown. Kidnapping!" the Duchess sputtered. "Do you really think Captain Jackson and the Royal Navy will allow your treachery to go unpunished? How I long to see you sentenced to death at Marshalsea Prison."

I scowled at the mention of what was commonly known as Execution Dock. This was exactly the sort of thing I had spoken with Vincent about earlier. I glanced at him. Vincent's face was a mask of indifference. No help from my quartermaster. Also no hindrance, I noted.

"Very well, Duchess DeVale. Since you insist on putting a damper on this evening's festivities, I'll come to the point." I heard music begin playing in the background. "I need a name and location of an individual who will pay the ransom I'm asking for you and your daughters."

The duchess's eyes narrowed to tiny slits. Her upper lip curled in disgust. "You will never live to see a pound note of that ransom."

I jumped up, kicking my chair back, and placing both fists on the table, I leaned across until I was scant inches from the duchess's nose. I snarled, my words rumbling in my throat. "If we don't receive the ransom, we'll sell all our plunder when we dock in port. We may not receive a hefty amount for you, but I'm quite certain both your daughters will fetch a pretty sum."

12

I picked up my glass, swigging down the remaining wine in one gulp. I slammed the goblet on the table with authority, then with a smile and a low bow, I turned to Alexis. "Would you honor me with a dance?"

She was leaning in so close, listening raptly to my conversation with her mother, that she seemed startled when I turned to her. She quickly leaned back in her chair, hand leaping to her throat in shock. I let loose with a grin when I realized she was embarrassed for having been caught listening so intently.

"Y…yes. Of course," Alexis stammered.

I took the Lady DeVale's hand in my own, leading her across the floor. I stopped halfway across the room, turning to face Alexis. One hand grasped firmly with hers, another on her slender waist, we moved to the music.

We began swaying and gliding in the formal dance of Her Majesty's Royal Courts. Hands were properly positioned, mine on her waist, hers on my shoulders. Backs were rigid, posture straight, bodies held a respectable distance apart.

As we turned, I surveyed the room. Around us, my crew continued with their dinner and drink. A few of the more inebriated sailors mimicked the actions of Lady DeVale and me. I laughed as Sven and Brodey glided and swayed in time with the music.

Alexis looked beyond my shoulder, obviously amused as she saw the two burly sailors dancing together. She looked back at me, her green eyes sparkling with delight.

"You have a lovely laugh." I leaned closer, lowering my voice to a husky whisper.

"Thank you." A blush tinted her cheeks.

I pivoted, Alexis following my lead perfectly. "You dance very well," I complimented. "Do you have occasion to practice often at your home in…"

"Canterbury," she volunteered. "I reside at my parents' estate."

"Canterbury." I turned suddenly, causing her to lose her balance, forcing her to clutch me tighter for support. "Do you dance much at Canterbury?" I asked, pretending to be oblivious

13

to my own actions or to the feel of her nails digging into my shoulder.

"Only on formal occasions. Dinner parties. Balls. Entertaining nobility." She adjusted her balance, loosened her grip on my shoulder. "And you?"

"Only rarely do I find myself entertaining nobility of any sort."

Another laugh. Not as joyous as the last but still resplendent to my ears.

"No, Captain Wolff. I meant do you dance much?"

"Not as much as I'd like. As a mater of fact, I entertain members of nobility more often than I find occasion to dance."

As we spun around the floor, I caught sight of the captain's table again. Vincent and Ivan were busy engaging Elizabeth DeVale in conversation. She appeared to be more than eager to divide her attention between the two men. Duchess DeVale sat at the table, fanning herself and sipping from her glass of brandy. She glanced at me, her hard black eyes throwing imaginary daggers.

I grinned, purposely moving my left hand closer upon Alexis's tiny waist. Her mother's jaw clenched, her fan snapped shut. Her face grew red. And my grin grew wider.

"You have an…interesting smile, Captain."

"Thank you," I said. "Would you care to go on deck for some fresh air?"

"Please."

I ended our dance with a sharp bow. Still grasping her hand, I led her toward the door. Across the room, I could see the duchess's face turn a deep crimson.

†

A warm breeze blew across the deck, tugging at our furled sails. Waves lapped at the hull of the ship, gently rocking us to and fro. The anchor chain bumped against the ship as we bobbed in the water.

14

She leaned against the railing, peering over the side of the ship. Her dress clung to her frame, the material shifting with the breeze, accentuating delectable curves. The moonlight played across the night sky, sending luminous waves across the deck, splashing the fair maiden and her deep burgundy dress in images of light and shadow.

I stood just behind her, to her left. Staring. Watching her. I don't think I'd ever seen a sight more beautiful.

Dark shadows played across her features, hiding them from my scrutiny. Her delicate throat was bathed in light, her mouth, her jaw line masked by shadow. Long, blonde locks glowed in the moonlight with the wind softly blowing through her tresses.

"What holds the Lady DeVale's interest so?" I moved closer.

"I can't tell where the night ends and the sea begins."

I looked down into the inky blackness. The darkness was rather disconcerting, even to my experienced eye.

"Try this," I suggested. "Find a place farther out, away from the ship." I pointed a finger, her gaze following my direction. "Pick a spot and focus on it. The horizon will come into view."

She squinted into the darkness.

"Don't try so hard," I advised.

She nodded, still staring. Her mouth tightened and she bit her bottom lip.

"Relax. Let it come to you."

I saw her slowly, tentatively begin to relax. The fine lines around her mouth lessened as she relinquished control, taking a deep breath, exhaling.

"I see it!" she called delightedly.

I smiled. Her enthusiasm was contagious.

"Do you normally anchor your ship at night?"

My gaze followed hers to the bow of the ship. The anchor chain bumped against the hull of the ship with the slick metal disappearing into the wet blackness below.

"No." I turned my gaze back to the Lady DeVale. "Usually, we keep moving, even at night. Unless we find ourselves in unfavorable conditions or unfamiliar waters."

"Nary a cloud in sight. Unfamiliar waters then," she concluded.

I shook my head. "Actually, just the opposite."

She arched one thin eyebrow. The look wasn't lost on me.

"These waters are—" Was that really my voice that squeaked? I coughed, cleared my throat. "These waters are filled with underwater barrier reefs and corals. Jagged rocks lay just below the surface, waiting to tear open the hull of an unsuspecting ship."

Alexis peered over the railing.

"If it's jagged rocks below the surface you're looking for, I'm afraid you won't be able to distinguish them in the darkness." I watched Alexis look from the waterline to the bow of the ship to the horizon far to her left.

"How do you guide your ship at night?" she asked.

I laughed incredulously. "Are you planning on commandeering my ship, my lady?"

She smiled mischievously. "That I might, my dear Captain. Perhaps I'll steal your ship in the middle of the night and sail off to St. Augustine." She gestured widely with her right arm.

I found myself grinning again. It was a habit that was becoming very common with this woman. "St. Augustine is to your port side, Lady DeVale." I pointed in the opposite direction.

"How do you know?" she asked. "It's all ocean out there. And in the middle of the night, it all looks the same. Surely, you can't navigate with charts and maps in the dark."

"During the day, our quartermaster guides us with sun readings from his astrolabe and navigational charts," I explained. "At night, we use the stars to guide our way."

"Show me." She turned to me with her face aglow and her green eyes sparkling as if they held a thousand tiny stars of their own.

"Orion's Belt." I pointed at a cluster.

"Where?" She searched the sky. "I don't see it."

I moved closer behind her. My face was scant inches from hers, my breath on her neck. My gloved hand dwarfed her delicate, petite hand. Gently, I raised her hand within my own, pointing, guiding her movements. "There." I gestured at the cluster again.

"Wh—oh, I see it!" she exclaimed. "What do you call that one?" She pointed to another group of stars.

"The Big Dipper."

She leaned back in my arms, settling against me, staring at the night sky. My left arm covertly circled her waist, marveling at the feel of her in my embrace. Her blonde hairs tickled my nose. I sniffed—strawberries. I closed my eyes and inhaled again.

"That one?" I vaguely heard her ask through the pounding in my ears.

I didn't even look at the sky. "The Little Dipper," I managed to gasp out, my voice low and guttural.

I felt Alexis move out of my grasp. When I opened my eyes again, she was no longer looking at the sky, but rather staring at me. "Thank you for this evening, my Captain. It's been most…illuminating."

"My pleasure, Lady DeVale." I bowed low, once again in formal character.

"Thank you." She was brushing imaginary wrinkles from her velvet dress. She pushed past me, heading for her cabin.

"Oh, Lady DeVale?" I added as an afterthought, as if the matter had only just now crossed my mind. "Urge your mother to reconsider. I'm not sure how long I can continue to offer my…protection from the crew if she doesn't cooperate."

I didn't look at her as I delivered that last statement. Instead, I concentrated my attention on the ocean, as if it held a particular fascination at that precise moment. I couldn't dare risk looking at her for fear that she might realize that perhaps she needn't worry about my protection from the crew so much as she might about protecting herself from Captain Wolff.

Chapter Two

THE LADY

I jumped to my feet, the book I'd been reading landing on the floor with a thud. I snatched it up and tossed it onto a nearby table. I stalked across the room, my heels clicking on the hard wood flooring.

"I can't believe we're having this conversation."

"And I can't believe that my daughter would ever consider associating with such a creature."

"Mother, really." I flicked my wrist dismissively. "I'm engaged to a nobleman. This…roguish pirate holds no interest for me."

"Indeed?" Mother arched a slender eyebrow. "Then why did my eldest daughter spend more than an hour in that roguish pirate's company last evening? And this isn't the first time, I might add."

I bit back my initial answer. *We were on deck.*

I chose my words carefully. "I was attempting to glean as much information about this pirate vessel and its crew as I could. Knowledge is power. The more knowledge we gather, the more power we'll possess."

Her frown curved into a smile. "And the best way to gain that knowledge is to humor the captain."

Mother's smile turned somber. "But be wary whilst in his company, Alexis. Never forget that The Wolff is rumored to be one of the most dangerous pirates to ever sail the seas."

"The captain wishes me to spend time with him on deck today. He's our only protection against the sea—and the crew. It would be foolish to risk his wrath."

"By all means, my precious child, entertain the dear Captain Wolff." She picked up my hat, roughly pushing it atop my head, thrust my handbag at me, and shooed me toward the door. "Learn all you can. Tell me so I may personally use that knowledge to skin The Wolff."

✝

I stepped out of my cabin onto a freshly washed deck. Several sailors were busily scrubbing with hard bristle brushes. Their pants were rolled up to the knees, and their boots were draped across the railing along with their shirts.

One of the seamen had his back to me as he worked. His long hair was tied in a ponytail, his black mane coming halfway down his strong back. The muscles in his arms flexed as he scrubbed the deck.

A smile crept to my lips. "Captain." I reached out, my fingertips brushing his tanned shoulder.

He turned, spinning and standing with the same movement. Astonished, I stepped backward, stumbling. Two strong arms shot out, keeping me from falling.

"Lady DeVale," he said. "Careful, the decks are slippery from the washing."

"My apologies," I mumbled, trying to mask my embarrassment. Was my face crimson? "I thought you were the captain."

That confession earned me a hearty laugh from the sailors. "Hardly, Lady DeVale. But thank ye for the kind words." He flicked a glance at my feet, then lifted his gaze back to my face.

"What?" I prodded.

"Well, my lady," he began, then hesitated. "Perhaps you should remove your footwear." The raucous laughter of the other sailors halted.

"Beg pardon?" Surely, I couldn't have understood correctly.

"Remove your footwear," he repeated, pointing at my boots. "That's what we do to keep from slipping on the wet deck." He pointed at his own feet with toes wriggling.

"You intend for me to bare my feet?" I asked incredulously.

19

He nodded. "'Tis far safer, my lady. It's too easy to slip on a wet deck in footwear."

I looked from one sailor to the next. I exhaled a deep breath. "Very well."

The crewman motioned to one of his shipmates, who turned his water bucket over, spilling its contents across the slippery deck. He ambled toward me, turning the bucket upside down, placing it upon the deck. He nodded, motioning for me to sit atop his makeshift stool.

Oddly enough, I did just that. I bent over, preparing to unfasten my laces. To my astonishment, the pirate knelt before me shooing my fingers aside before he began unlacing my boots. Shocked, I sat and watched as his nimble fingers unlaced one boot, then began on the other.

"What is your name, sailor?"

He stopped long enough to look up at me. His big brown eyes sparkled. "Jon, my lady. Jonathan Fitzpatrick." His response was quick and eager, like a school lad's.

"You have an English accent."

"Yes, ma'am. My parents run a grog shop in Bristol." He bent back to his task of unlacing my boots.

"A grog shop?"

"Yes, ma'am." He didn't look at me this time, instead concentrating upon a knot in my laces. "They specialize in slipping sailors a Mickey Finn, then shanghaiing them into the Royal Navy."

"Were you shanghaied?" I asked, intrigued.

He nodded as he removed my boot. "I served the Royal Navy during the war."

"And now you serve aboard a pirate ship?"

"Yes, ma'am," he said. "I found I don't much like the discipline of the Royal Navy. Someday, I'm going to have my very own fleet of pirate vessels." His face beamed with pride as he helped me to my feet, all the while explaining his cutthroat plans and goals.

"Better?" he asked, as I checked my balance.

"Much." I took a tentative step forward, Jonathan nearby in case I faltered. "Much better," I felt more confident.

"And the length of your dress hides your bare feet." He leaned closer, his voice a strained whisper. "No one need ever know, Lady DeVale."

I looked down. He was correct. I watched as I took a few cautionary steps. My bare flesh remained hidden from view.

"Careful, my lady." a booming voice echoed from across the deck. I looked up to see my captain striding toward me. He wore a pair of black trousers and a loose-fitting white shirt. Like Jonathan, his hair was tied in a ponytail. Seeing the two of them together, the resemblance was remarkable. "They'll have you scrubbing the deck before too long."

"N…no, Captain Wolff." Jonathan backed away, putting a safe distance between the two of us. "We were just showing her how to walk properly on a fresh deck."

I saw the captain's jaw lock and his eyes flash. He saw my boots upon the deck, and his jaw visibly slackened. "No harm, Jon." He bent and retrieved my boots. "Return to your work."

He nodded to where the other sailors were kneeling on the deck. They were raptly watching the exchange between Jonathan and Captain Wolff. When they saw the captain nod in their direction, they immediately bent to their task once again.

Jonathan hastily backed away. "Thank you, Captain Wolff." He rushed to join his comrades. He was practically scrubbing before his knees hit the deck.

"My Lady DeVale." The captain had a smile upon his face once again. "Walk with me." It was an order, not a request.

He extended his elbow, firmly locking my arm beneath his. I matched my stride to his as he guided me across the deck. I cast a quick glance back at Jonathan and the other sailors as I was led away. They were hard at work scrubbing the deck, all traces of conversation and laughter gone as they worked at their task.

†

We walked in silence toward the bow of the ship. The captain's strong stride, which had sped us away from his crew, slowed to a casual stroll. He carried my boots in his left hand. I hung off his right arm. Under better circumstances, we could have been a couple strolling on a stretch of beach along a romantic shoreline.

"I'm glad you decided to come out of your cabin today." His words were soft, his voice carrying a lulling quality.

"I'm hardly the sort to sit idly in my cabin day after day until this ordeal is over."

No answer.

The captain's gaze fixed on the horizon, as if searching the ocean for something elusive. The silence was unbearable.

"Perhaps ordeal was the wrong choice of words," I amended. "It's turning into an interesting voyage. More of an adventure, really. And I'm meeting all sorts of people."

The captain stopped so suddenly that I bumped into him. He turned, cocked his head in my direction. Gray eyes stared at me. He raised one eyebrow, seeming to study me. I noticed the tiny scar above his left eye. It interrupted the natural line of his eyebrow. I couldn't help but wonder how he came by such a scar.

"You were right the first time."

"Pardon me?"

"When you referred to your presence on my ship, you said it was an ordeal."

"I didn't mean to imply—"

He cut me off by placing one gloved finger to my lips. He shook his head. "No, don't apologize. Don't take back the words you meant because you think you've offended me. That would make you seem weak. I don't think of you as a weak woman."

"You don't?"

"No, I don't," he said, his voice low and intimate. "I think you are a strong, competent woman. You've shown courage in the face of adversity. You've shown no fear, meeting your destiny headlong, rather than hiding from it in a dark, dank ship's cabin."

"Like my mother and sister?"

He sighed. "I'd just as soon your mother stayed in her cabin until the ransom is paid and your freedom is at hand. Your sister, on the other hand, I would like the opportunity to better acquaint myself with her. My crew has expressed an interest in her, as well."

"Elizabeth is apt to stay close by my mother's skirts. She is...unsettled by some of your crew."

"Unlike you?"

I caught the tone in his voice. It was sharp and clipped. His gaze was impenetrable.

"You seem disappointed that I find your crew intriguing."

"It's not your interest in my crew that displeases me." He waved that notion off with a flick of his hand. He turned his back on me, looking out at the ocean. This was not the relaxed, playful Wolff of the night before. "What displeases me is the interest my crew has taken in you."

I was stunned. "Your crew has an interest in me?"

Incredulous laughter from the captain. He turned to face me. His eyes were a mask of mirth and irritation. "You act as if you didn't realize." His tone was sarcastic.

"No." I shook my head. "I've only been here eight days. Who could have possibly developed an interest in me?"

"Who? Try my entire crew." He waved his arm wildly, my boots swinging freely through the air. They landed with a dull thunk ten feet away. He gave them a dismissive look, then turned his attention back to me. "Surely, you've noticed how my entire crew follows you with their eyes. How they trip over one another to serve you."

"No!" I felt a hot flush in my cheeks.

"Yes!" The captain leaned toward me, his face scant inches from mine. I could smell his scent; feel his breath on my skin. With his teeth clenched, his voice came out as a low hiss. "What about young Jon Fitzpatrick?"

"He was only trying to help—"

"Himself, you mean."

"Why do you insist on finding harm in every little action, every little gesture?" I demanded, my voice rising.

"Why do you insist on refusing to see the danger you face?"

"Danger." The word came out of my mouth the same way it tasted—flat. "I have been in constant danger from the moment

23

you seized our vessel and disrupted our lives. I hardly see how associating with your crew can put me in further danger."

The captain shook his head, rolled his eyes. "My crew…is a crew of men that have been at sea for quite some time. And while they may have all been sworn to respect prisoners, women in particular, and bring no harm unto them, they are still men. And some may decide…" His fingers somehow found their way into my hair, twisting blonde locks around his fingertips. "That the risk of punishment is worth the pleasure of your affections."

"And what price would you be willing to pay for my affections, my Captain?"

Our eyes locked. My heart pounded in my chest as I awaited his answer.

"I—"

"Captain!" Vincent rushed to his captain's side, preventing The Wolff's answer. "A word, please."

"I…Yes. Of course." He gave me one final wistful look as he allowed his quartermaster to lead him away.

I walked across the deck, the wood sun-warmed beneath my bare feet. I stooped low, retrieving my boots. By the time I straightened, the captain was striding toward me again. He held a parchment in his hand with an excited look on his face.

"We've spied a heavy merchant ship on the seas ahead. We'll be engaging in battle shortly. The offer of good quarter will be given." He thrust the parchment in my hands. "Your mother is to write the duke, convincing him that although captives, you are alive and well."

"Will they accept the parchment?"

He nodded. "If the crew accepts good quarter, the parchment will be given to them and the crew will be free to go."

"It sounds simple." Why couldn't I sound excited?

"I have to prepare for the upcoming battle. Bring the parchment to me as soon as it's ready."

He strode away from me, joining his quartermaster again. I watched as Vincent unfurled a sea chart. My captain stole furtive glances at me over the map, briefly smiling. All too soon, though, his full attention was focused on Vincent, the charts, and the impending battle.

I watched a little longer then wandered back toward my cabin. I knew I should hurry with the parchment. But every step I took seemed slower than the one just past.

†

By the time I returned to the deck, it was blustering with activity. Sailors were everywhere, rushing to prepare for battle. I pressed myself against the cabin wall as a group of men rushed past, brandishing axes and cutlasses.

I crept along, attempting to stay out of their way. More sailors hurried by, carrying muskets. I desperately searched the passing faces for my captain.

"Lady DeVale." A man running by stopped abruptly and grabbed me by the arm. He was wearing a belt with a pistol and short sword, and he was brandishing a long ax. A red scrap of cloth covered his hair, keeping it tied back away from his face.

"Jonathan." I said. "I hardly recognized you."

He pulled me by the arm around a corner between the cabin wall and a large mast just as another dozen men stormed past. "We're preparing for an attack. The deck is no safe place for a lady."

"I need to find the captain—"

"You need to return to your quarters." He cut me off, pulling me by the arm toward my cabin.

"Wait," I protested, dragging my feet. "I must give this parchment to Captain Wolff. He specifically requested I bring it to him."

His nostrils flared. For a moment, I was afraid he intended to drag me back by the hair of my head. "Please, Jonathan."

His face visibly relaxed, his features softened. "Very well. He's on the aft deck."

My face must have given away my dumbfoundedness, for he grabbed me by the hand, leading me in the direction I had just come. "I'll take you."

He led me toward the back of the ship, pushing our way past sailors readying for battle. Most were too busy to pay us any mind, but one had the time to hurl harsh words at Jonathan.

"Ye scurvy dawg, Fitzpatrick! Sneaking away to dally with the wench while we face our deaths in battle!"

Jonathan stopped only long enough to snarl a curse at the seamen. He caught my shocked stare, and his face reddened. "Sorry, my lady," he mumbled, increasing our stride as he led me along.

He rushed me up three wooden steps, past a long wall. He began to round the corner, then stopped. I was following so close, I ran into him from behind, jarring him.

"There," he said, pointing. "I must leave you now."

"Thank you," I said as he rushed off.

I peered around the corner. Captain Wolff was there with Vincent. They were deep in conversation, a map spread before them on a wooden barrel. The captain rubbed his chin, staring at the map.

"Is this really necessary?" the captain asked his quartermaster.

"Yes, Captain. We must careen the ship soon. It's been too long and the hull is starting to drag. We need our speed on the open sea. Surely, you realize that."

The captain shot a reply to Vincent that I couldn't hear. Cautiously, I crept closer, straining my ears. "…don't like careening because it leaves us defenseless. And so soon after battle. "

"We must, Captain."

"Very well," the captain relented. "Here." He pointed to a location on the map. "We'll head to this isle after the attack."

"Brava Island," Vincent confirmed. "Five days journey from here."

Armed with this knowledge, I stole back to my cabin.

†

"Lady DeVale." He bowed before me as I approached.

I smiled at his gentlemanly gesture.

"Is that for me?"

I raised my hand, thrusting the rolled parchment at him.

"Yes, my Captain." My mouth felt unusually dry, my voice hoarse.

Captain Wolff arched an eyebrow. He took the parchment from me, beginning to unroll it. I held my breath.

"Captain, I—" I jumped as a deafening explosion shook me to the very core of my being.

The splintering of wood echoed throughout the ship. Followed by a loud whistling sound as another cannonball was fired from *The Wolfsbane*. Another explosion rocked me as the mainsail of the merchant ship off our side tumbled onto her deck.

"Stay with Vincent, my lady!" the captain shouted above the deafening roar. "He'll see to your safety."

The captain thrust the parchment beneath his belt and charged off toward battle. He ran down the length of the deck, shouting orders as he went.

"Lady DeVale," Vincent said, "we must get you to safety."

I resisted as the quartermaster pulled on my elbow attempting to usher me away from the side of the ship. I protested loudly, "I wish to watch—"

"Then watch from a safe place."

Vincent rushed me toward the aft of the ship. He paused outside a large wooden door, fishing in his pocket for a set of keys. His fingers fumbled as he searched for the correct key.

Pirates were using axes to climb the high wooden sides of the merchant vessel they were boarding. The crew was waiting, swinging their swords wildly at the onslaught of pirates. Several pirates fell as they were struck by shot from flintlock pistols, their axes still firmly embedded in the side of the ship.

The captain clung to his position as a sailor swung with his sword, attempting to swat him away. The captain continued his ascent, firing his own pistol. The sailor fell over the side.

The door opened. Vincent pulled me by the arm, attempting to force me inside. I dragged my feet, looking back at the battle. Another sailor appeared, aiming his pistol.

"The captain—"

"Will be just fine." Vincent pulled me roughly into the room. "Watch the battle from the safety of the captain's own quarters."

I rushed to the window, searching for signs of Captain Wolff. He was on the deck now. He fought fiercely, gaining ground one step at a time. At length, he disappeared from my sight, as did most of the pirates as they swarmed toward the interior of the ship. Only traces of scattered fighting remained visible to my view.

With a sigh, I retreated from the window. Vincent sat at a desk, calmly smoking a pipe. He cast me a sympathetic look and gestured for me to be seated. He took a long draw on his pipe and exhaled. The smoke curled up around his head before dissipating.

"Now," he said, "we wait."

†

I lay in my bed, clutching my stomach. I closed my eyes, hoping that would stop the sensation. It only made it worse. My eyes fluttered open to find my sister staring at me.

"Poor Alexis," she cooed, seating herself on the edge of the bed.

"I'll be fine when the room stops spinning," I assured her, closing my eyes again.

She pressed a damp cloth to my forehead, patting my clammy arms. I took several deep breaths then tried tentatively opening my eyes again. The room wasn't rotating nearly as fast as before.

My eyes focused on Elizabeth's face. Her hair fell about her shoulders, the ringlets loose and unkempt. Her face was taut and weary. Her hazel eyes had lost much of their spark.

"How is she?"

I turned my head stiffly. Mother stood barely inside the doorway. Her face, too, was tired. Her green dress hung loosely on her frame.

"She's seasick, Mother." Elizabeth dabbed at my cheeks with her damp cloth. "Again."

"Really, Alexis." Mother admonished me as she came to my side. "You can't continue to eat the," she curled her lip in disgust, "things these pirates do and not expect to fall ill."

"Mother's right, my sister," Elizabeth said. "Sea turtles soaked with lime juice are hardly suitable dinner fare."

"Better an occasional bout of seasickness brought on by dinner," I closed my eyes as another wave of nausea overtook me, then continued, "than to face starvation." I opened my eyes again, swallowing hard to keep that particular dinner down.

"We'll not eat that filth." Mother fanned herself furiously. "Nor shall we starve, either."

"Look at yourselves." I focused on mother. "You've lost weight. Lots. Your face is noticeably thinner. Your dress hangs off of you now. When we set sail from Canterbury, that dress was tight around your midsection. It scarcely touches your waist now."

I turned to Elizabeth. Her lips were dry and cracked, so much so that they broke open and bled from time to time. The water on board was stale, and she refused to imbibe hard liqueurs. Her face was taut, her cheekbones more pronounced because of the tight flesh.

Like mother, her dress hung loosely. There were several that she was forced to give up wearing because they slid down too far, exposing her bosom. And when she removed her dress at night to prepare for bed, I could count every rib through her thin flesh.

"How long has it been?" Elizabeth asked.

"Not quite a fortnight since our capture," I said. "Three days since the attack on the merchant vessel."

"Two days until we land on Brava Island," Mother finished. She stepped closer to the bed. "You must be well by then." She leaned in close to my ear, whispering so Elizabeth could not hear. "Or you may find yourself left behind."

✝

I picked my way along the beach, carefully stepping between groups of sailors busily working on land. Elizabeth walked with me. We passed a group of men, sitting on the beach, talking and drinking as they repaired the ship's sails, skillfully sewing with long needles.

Another group was carrying fresh fruits and barrels of fresh water to the ship. Rufus was busy taking a short list of inventory, directing the men as to what should be taken straight to the kitchen and what should be stored in the hold for later consumption.

We found the captain among a group of sailors working on the hull of the ship. The ship was tilted to its side at an odd angle, exposing its wooden underbelly. The wood was slick and slimy with wild growing seaweed and barnacles clinging to the hull.

The captain worked side by side with Jonathan Fitzpatrick. They both held long-handled tools that resembled axes but with longer blades. The tools looked heavy, requiring both hands on the handle for swinging. The chisel-like blades chipped off bits of seaweed and barnacles with each swing.

Both men wore their hair tied into ponytails. Sweat poured from their faces. Like most of the men, Jonathan wore no shirt, his sweat rolling down his muscular body, glistening on his bronzed skin.

The captain's shirt was soaked with sweat, yet he made no attempt to remove it. As a matter of fact, he remained fully clothed, all the way down to his gloves, while most of his crew worked half-naked, exposing ample amounts of flesh as they worked without shirts or even shoes.

"Ladies," the captain greeted us. He swung the handle of his tool around, planting it firmly in the sand. He placed both hands on the metal blade, leaning against it as we talked.

"That's an interesting tool, Captain," I said. "Almost like the boarding axes I've seen you use."

The captain spun the tool around on its handle, showing it off. "Almost, Lady DeVale. Actually, this is called an adz. We use it for chipping off barnacles, seaweed, and other assorted nasties that reduce our ship's speed."

Jonathan put down his adz and picked up another tool. "A ramming iron," he explained to me. "We use its broad blade for splitting open rotten seams on the hull."

"Back to work," the captain ordered, turning to his men. Most of them had stopped working with our approach. Still carrying his adz, Captain Wolff led us away from the party of pirates. "You'll have to excuse my men, ladies. They aren't used to having such beautiful guests."

"After nearly a fortnight, Captain Wolff, I'm afraid we're hardly beautiful."

The captain turned to Elizabeth. "You're still both beautiful women." She blushed beneath his flattery. "Perhaps some fresh fruits and water will agree with you."

"Perhaps."

Elizabeth left us, joining Rufus's men. Rufus struck up a conversation with her and before long, he was helping her to select a piece of fruit out of a large net.

"She looks unwell," the captain noted.

"It's been a terrible ordeal for her."

We continued to stroll along the beach in silence. The captain carried the adz in his right hand, the handle dragging a trail in the sand behind us as we walked. He reached out with his left hand, catching my elbow. I found myself spun around to face him.

"You've held up remarkably well through this whole ordeal."

"I'm much stronger than my mother and sister."

"How so?"

"They—" I hesitated. Why was it so easy to say such things, so easy to confide in this stranger? "They are spoiled. They are firmly rooted in the belief that a woman should only do certain things. That a lady should behave properly on all occasions."

"And you're not of that opinion?"

I shook my head. "No. I believe that a woman has a right to behave in much the same manner as a man."

"Really?"

31

"Yes." I nodded toward the group of men working on the hull of the ship. "Given a chance, I would love to learn."

The captain's eyes sparkled with delight. "I would be glad to teach you, my lady." He held out his hand, offering the tool.

I cast a wistful glance at the adz. My quaking fingers caressed the handle. "Mother would die of fright."

He shrugged. "I could teach her to run the scraping boards."

"Scraping boards?"

"A wooden board scarcely a foot wide that runs the length of the ship just above the waterline. Barely wide enough for a scraper's tools," Captain Wolff explained. "On occasion when we can't careen, scrapers work the board. They dive beneath the hull of the vessel, holding their breath as they scrape off the growing barnacles."

"It sounds dangerous."

"It is," he said. "More than one sailor has been caught in the ship's undertow and drowned, unable to reach the surface. It's not the preferred method of cleaning the hulls, but sometimes it becomes necessary."

"And you'd like for my mother to try this?"

He laughed. "Where is the old wench?" He looked up and down the beach.

"Probably reading a book beneath a palm somewhere," I said. "You know, she really doesn't care for you."

"The feeling is mutual, my lady."

"I noticed. You want the duchess to run the scraping boards."

We both laughed. It began as small snickers, then grew in intensity. A smile hung on the captain's lips, a jovial twinkle in his gray eyes. I felt a sudden lurch in the pit of my stomach. Of their own accord, my trembling fingers touched the captain's lips.

I heard a loud pounding and assumed it was the galloping of my own heart. Something closed about my waist, pulling me, snatching me backward, away from the captain.

I heard the captain yelling, shouting orders at his men amongst the chaos and confusion. Around us I saw other riders,

32

soldiers on horseback who were attacking the helpless pirates, slaughtering them.

The soldier who grabbed me galloped away from the fray of the battle, turning his horse toward the inland area. As he rode, one arm was firmly encircling my waist. I saw the captain giving chase on foot, running through the thick sand. Behind him lay a dead soldier in the surf, the captain's bloody adz still firmly protruding from his midsection. Wolff pulled his pistol from his belt, taking aim. I saw the flash of powder.

My abductor fell as the shot ripped through him. I slipped from his grasp, falling on the ground in a heap. The horse ran off, dragging the soldier behind it, his foot still caught in the stirrup.

I scrambled to my feet, running inland. Looking back, I saw The Wolff in pursuit. The sandy beach turned into a clump of trees. I crashed through the dense undergrowth. Branches and twigs held me back, cutting at my face and hands as I stumbled through the thick coverage.

The dense brush gave way to an open field. I heard rustling sounds behind me, turned to see Captain Wolff running after me. I hesitated only momentarily before darting across the field. My shoes quickly became soaked with mud in the marshy mire, weighing me down, slowing my flight.

"Alexis."

His voice called from somewhere behind. Still running, I looked back. The captain was already at the field, chasing me across the mire. His boots were also fast becoming caked with mud.

"Alexis."

I stopped. My heart was pounding in my chest. My breathing ragged, coming in short gasps. I turned around, defeated. He was no more than twenty feet from me. Running would be pointless. I didn't move as he came for me.

†

We ate in silence. The captain had been brooding since our return to the ship. Understandably, for he had suffered heavy losses. More than twenty of his crew had died in the attack. They had barely fought off the soldiers and righted the ship so we could escape to the safety of the open sea.

His mood was reasonable. My presence in his cabin was not. He had asked me to dinner, yet had said scarcely three words to me the entire time.

"Perhaps your sister is better off now," the captain said.

"Perhaps," I agreed. "She wasn't adjusting well to life aboard ship."

The captain nodded. "The soldiers that took her will no doubt make sure she is well-fed before she is escorted home."

I cut off a piece of meat. Roasted chicken, a rare treat indeed. The captain had scarcely eaten anything.

"Perhaps I should count my blessings. That we were able to escape. That I lost only one of my prisoners."

I rose from my chair, skirted around the edge of the table. The captain watched as I approached, mesmerized, unwilling— or unable to look away.

I eased my way onto his lap. "You still have me," I whispered.

My hands draped around his neck as I snuggled closer. My fingernails stroked the back of his neck, softly biting his flesh. I prayed this would distract him enough to quell his suspicions.

My mouth was scant inches from his. I could feel his breath upon my skin. I extended my tongue, licking his lips, barely touching, barely stroking, caressing.

"Perhaps I can improve your mood, my Captain."

His lips parted beneath mine. They were surprisingly soft, teasingly tender. I'd kissed before but never like this. Never with such restrained passion. Abruptly, he caught me by the upper arm, pushing me away. He leaned back as I attempted to pursue the kiss again.

"Those were Spanish soldiers," he said.

I shrugged, removing his hands, replacing them on my hips. "And?"

His hands closed upon my waist, fingers kneading the material of my dress, thumbs drawing lazy circles. "The captain of *The Scorpion* said his ship was bound for Puerto Bello and then Puerto Cabello."

"Yes," I murmured, my mouth at his ear.

"Both—" His voice broke as my teeth lightly nipped at his exposed neck. "Both are on the Spanish Main." His eyes were glazed with lust, but I was convinced his mind was still sharp. I licked the flesh I had just bitten.

Roughly, he grabbed my hands, yanking me off his lap as he jumped up. "You set an ambush." he accused. "You have betrayed me."

I took a step toward him, arms outstretched. "I didn't—"

The blow came hard and fast; the slap echoed in my own head. I fell to my knees. My hand flew to my face, covering the abused flesh. I felt the sting of the slap, tasted blood in my mouth.

"Vincent!" I heard him yell.

I looked up at him through tears. His face was a contorted mask of rage. "Remove her."

The quartermaster appeared at my side, pulling me to my feet. In a daze, I felt him dragging me away.

Chapter Three

THE CAPTAIN

SHIP'S LOG – AUGUST 29, 1703

> *The crew has not been the same since the attack at Brava Island. Neither have I. Twenty-two men died on that island. Four more have died since from infection.*
>
> *In addition to morale being low, supplies are running short. Many of the supplies that Rufus had gathered to outfit* The Wolfsbane *were left behind on Brava as we made our escape. By Vincent's calculations, we still have enough provisions to make it safely into Port Royale. Twelve days away. We'll be able to give the men a well-deserved rest on shore as we refurbish the ship.*
>
> *And it will permit me time to meet with my contact in town. My long-standing arrangement with the tavern keeper will serve me well, for Klaus McBride stocks more than mere rum. He also deals in information. For the right price, he will provide me with not only a safe route virtually free from Navy patrols, but he will also direct me toward a haven where I can ransom off the DeVale women.*

There was quick knock on my door. "Enter," I commanded.

Vincent entered with a tray of food. He kicked the door closed with the toe of his boot and placed the tray on my desk.

Hen eggs. The taste of bile crept into my throat. I pushed the tray to the far edge, as far away as possible. Vincent reached across the desk, taking my journal. He snapped closed my log-book, placing it on the bookcase behind me. He snatched the quill pen out of my hand and dropped it into the inkwell.

He pushed the tray toward me. "You must eat."

"I'd rather not," I said, pushing the tray toward Vincent once again. "Besides, I'm full."

He rubbed the back of his neck, exhaled loudly. "How much have you had?"

I gave him a blank look.

He rolled his eyes. "How many?" he pressed.

I shrugged. "Four."

I leaned over, picking the bottles up off the floor. I lined them up on the desk.

Vincent picked up a bottle and read the label. I watched as he picked up another. And another. And the last. "No wonder you have no appetite, Kris. You've been mixing whiskey, rum, and brandy."

"I like variety." I laughed at my own joke.

My quartermaster stormed to the open window and threw the bottles out. They made a faint splashing sound as they hit the water. "You can't keep going like this."

I arched an eyebrow in response. He paced back and forth, hands clasped behind his back, boots echoing on the hard, wooden floor.

I remained quiet. What was there to say? Vincent was stubborn, like me. Neither of us was apt to give in. It was best just to let him say his piece then kick him out of my cabin.

His brown eyes bored a hole right through me. "You haven't eaten properly since Brava Island."

I began to protest. He held up a hand, silencing me. "You skip meals. And when you do eat, you pick at your food."

I shrugged. "My appetite's been off."

Vincent cast a withering glare at me. He pushed past me, farther into my cabin. He pulled back a black velvet drape separating the cabin from my private chambers. My bed sheets were a tangled mess, strewn about the room.

"When was the last time you slept?"

I shrugged again.

"When?" he pressed.

"Two…no, maybe three days ago."

That same withering glare again. "You don't eat. You don't sleep. You're barely leading your crew."

I rubbed my eyes. Funny. Now that Vincent mentioned sleep, my body craved it. "The massacre at Brava—"

"You've lost men before."

"Never this way." I stood up. My knees buckled; I fought to regain my balance. "Never like this."

"It comes with the territory. You know the risks. We all know the risks. We face death every day, Kristen. The men don't blame you."

I stared out the window, my back to Vincent. I didn't have the courage to face him. "When I sleep, I dream." I paused, gathering my courage. "And with my dreams come the nightmares."

Vincent eyed me suspiciously. "You believe she betrayed you."

"She did," I shouted. "It's clear to me now. She overheard our plans to careen the ship and passed that knowledge along to the vessel we attacked. She—"

"Is our prisoner. Remember that."

For once, I kept quiet and listened.

"She's not here by her own free choice. We've forced her to be here. Therefore, can we fault her for attempting to escape when the opportunity presented itself?"

"But—"

"She owes no allegiance to us. Nor to you, Kristen. To her, you are the notorious Captain Wolff, the most dangerous pirate on the seven seas."

"But—"

"If you want her to view you as anything else, you must go to her. Let her see you for who you really are."

He grabbed my wrist, squeezing, capturing my right hand. He applied pressure, causing me to open my hand, palm up.

"The *captain* she last saw physically abused her, striking her for what was considered to be an act of betrayal. Is that the Captain Wolff you wish to show her?"

"You think she's the reason I can't eat or sleep?"

He shrugged. "I've never seen you behave this way before. She brings out the worst in you."

I scowled.

"And also the best," he added. He snatched up my now cold breakfast tray, carried it to the door. "Go to her if you must. Resolve your feelings for her. But be warned, for, given the opportunity, she will betray you again."

†

I found myself outside her cabin door, my knuckles softly rapping. "Alexis," I called. "Please, open the door."

No answer. I brought my hand up, preparing to knock again. The door abruptly swung open, leaving my hand hanging in midair. Not Alexis, but rather her mother.

"Duchess DeVale." I nodded, making an ill attempt at cordiality.

"To what do I owe the dishonor of your visit, Captain Wolff?" The wording didn't escape my notice. Neither did the way she snapped her fan to emphasize her words.

"I've come to see Lady DeVale." I smiled sweetly, knowing it would gnaw at her insides. "Alexis."

Like a large dog, her jowls flapped. "My daughter, the Lady DeVale, is not presently here."

I pushed my way inside the door. She attempted to bar my entrance, but I easily sidestepped her. I marched into the next room, the Duchess DeVale hot on my heels. I halted dead in my tracks. The room was empty.

She appeared at my elbow. "As I said, the Lady DeVale is not here. Even if she were, I doubt if she'd wish to see you."

"Where is she?"

"I don't know," she spat out. "She left the cabin at dawn as has been her habit since she lost her sister on that dreadful island."

I stared at the woman, barely able to control my anger. My contempt for her at this very moment was unfathomable. My blood was fairly boiling. I felt a nervous twitch start at the corner of my left eye.

"Her sister," I said between clenched teeth, "was rescued by soldiers. She's not lost. As a matter of fact, I'd wager she's on her way back to Canterbury by this time."

I started across the room but turned back to the duchess. "I lost twenty-six of my men. They all died in that ambush you organized. They aren't ever coming back."

"Captain Wolff?" she said, smiling. "Those twenty-six men were lucky. By the time the authorities get through with you, you'll be begging for death." She cracked her fan loudly, the sound reminiscent of the executioner's guillotine. "I'll see to that."

Her whispered words rang in my head as loudly as if she'd screamed them.

✝

I walked briskly, my boots echoing on the wooden planks of the deck. I clenched and unclenched my fists. My breathing came in ragged gasps as I struggled for control.

The duchess had succeeded. She'd managed to needle and goad me until she got my ire up. Logically, I was smart enough to know that my anger would only serve to work against me—and that was what she wanted. Emotionally, I didn't care; I wanted her head.

I stormed along, brooding, paying no heed to my direction. I was vaguely aware of the presence of my crew on deck, busying themselves with various everyday tasks. I felt their gazes following me as they paused in their work, watching their rampaging captain.

I bounded up the stairs leading toward my cabin and froze in my tracks. She was there, standing by the railing, staring out at the ocean. Her back was to me. I hesitated, unsure of what to say, what to do.

She leaned farther over the side, staring at the depths below. This close to Port Royale, the water was pristine clear. You could stand on the deck and see the sand on the ocean floor moving beneath. The sight was breathtaking.

But not as breathtaking as the sight before me. Her hair

40

hung loosely about her shoulders, its length draping down her back. The wind blew her hair wildly. Delicate fingers brushed stray strands away from her face.

She turned, bloodshot eyes focused on me. My mouth opened, closed of its own accord. The words wouldn't come.

"Captain." Her tone was flat, her words tinged with bitterness.

"How's the view?" A poor attempt at conversation.

"I've seen better."

It was days since... The bruise on her right cheek was still very pronounced. I had expected it would have begun to fade by now. Confronted with my own handiwork, I was once again rendered speechless, left searching for the words to express myself. And failing miserably.

"Your face."

Her fingers traced the outline of the bruise. "That's what happens when you displease the captain." Her eyes flashed with anger. She stared at me defiantly.

"I apologize for my behavior."

I stretched my arms out nonthreateningly as I edged my way toward her. "I never should have raised my hand to you."

"No, Captain Wolff, you shouldn't have." Her words were clipped, her voice shaking with barely restrained anger.

"I reacted on sheer instinct." I kept my voice low, my tone soothing. I edged closer as I spoke. "You hurt me."

"I hurt you? What about how you hurt me?" Angry tears threatened to roll down her cheeks.

"It's my own fault," I admitted. "I allowed myself to grow accustomed to you. I enjoyed your company. I forgot you weren't here of your own free will. As soon as you got the chance to leave me, you took it. I saw your actions as a betrayal of my trust."

"You trusted me?" Her voice rang with disbelief.

I nodded. "I gave you free run of my ship, to go where you pleased without escort." I reached out, capturing her hand in mine. "I've given you everything I can."

"Except my freedom."

"You ask for what I cannot give." I let go of her hand, letting it drop. I turned to the sea. I leaned against the railing, balancing myself on my elbows. I shifted my weight, propping my left foot up on the bottom rail. I stared at the ocean, watching as the waves lapped at the hull of my ship.

"Why Spanish troops?" I asked.

"Pardon?"

"The soldiers that tried to rescue you," I clarified. "Those were Spanish soldiers, not English. Why?"

"Did you not wonder why three English women were bound for Puerto Cabello?" she asked. "Traveling aboard one of Her Majesty's Royal Navy vessels rather than a civilian merchant ship?"

"You're a member of aristocracy. Your mother would lead me to believe that your family is powerful enough to own the Queen's Navy."

Incredulous laughter rewarded my sharp wit. "True, my Captain. Mother places a lot of importance on appearances."

"Your trip has something to do with keeping up appearances?"

"My wedding."

My boot slipped; I almost fell off the ship. I clutched at the railing, fingers digging into the wood. "Your wedding?" I mouthed.

"My marriage to Lord Rafael of Puerto Cabello," she said, "will secure a treaty between England and Spain. And open a lucrative trade route for my family."

My stomach churned at the thought of Alexis DeVale marrying. Anyone. "A marriage arrangement."

She nodded. "As part of the agreement, yes."

"Do you wish to be married?"

A thin smile formed on her lips. "Yes. But not now. And not to someone I don't love."

I studied her for a quiet moment. I never would have pictured this woman as being engaged to someone. Let alone a prearranged marriage. She seemed too willful to settle down into something that was not of her own design.

"What?"

I blinked, realizing I'd been caught staring. "It's just suddenly occurred to me that I know so little about you."

A smile, a twinkle in her eye, followed by soft laughter.

"What's so funny?"

"You."

"Me?" My mouth dropped open.

She laughed again. I found myself smiling. I couldn't help it.

"As long as I have been on this vessel, I've never learned your first name."

"And you find that humorous?"

"I only know you as the fearsome Captain Wolff, scourge of the seas. But when you're with me like this, I can't see you as that dangerous pirate."

I shook my head, perplexed. "I'm one of the most feared and hunted pirates on the sea. I've robbed you. I've abducted you." I flicked a glance at her cheek and quickly averted my gaze from the bruised flesh. "I struck you."

"I antagonized you."

"Still, I had no right."

"No, you did not."

My gaze slid from hers once again and returned to the open sea. The sea had always been my first love. She understood my turbulent behavior. She was calm whenever I felt the need to stray toward shore. She was forgiving and always waited with open arms for my return. Best of all, she had no expectations of me.

"Kris."

"Pardon?"

"Kris," I repeated. "My name is Kris."

"Kris," she said. "I like it."

"We land in Port Royale soon. Would you like me to bring you something upon my return?"

"Perhaps."

"And what shall my lady have me bring?"

She looked down at her dress. I followed her gaze. She wore the same deep burgundy dress she'd worn all those long nights before at dinner. That night we first ended up gazing at the stars. I smiled at the memory.

43

Her dress had seen better days. The shoulders were worn and faded from the sun. She was missing a button from her left sleeve. The hem was frayed from countless walks on the deck.

"Is my lady in need of a new dress perhaps?"

"Yes, my Captain. My dress looks a fright. All my dresses do."

I rubbed my chin thoughtfully. I hadn't the faintest notion of how to select proper attire for a lady. "I have an idea." I grabbed Alexis by the hand, pulling her along after me.

†

I slowly descended the staircase, holding a lantern to light my way. I'd already passed the crews' quarters and was on my way to the hold of the ship. With a firm grip on my other hand, Alexis followed closely.

The hold was dank and musty, the air stale. The floor was slimy, which made walking difficult. My right foot slid and I missed the bottom step. Alexis's arms crept about my waist, helping to steady me. I regained my balance and we continued on. I picked my footing carefully, going slowly. She followed close on my heels.

"Scared?" I asked.

"Cautious."

I picked my way through the hold, past furniture and crates of various sizes. Large rolls of material lay in our path; every type from silks to velvet to burlap. I stepped across the rolls then helped Alexis across.

A huge metal chest stood before us. It was as tall as my waist, with metal handles on the sides. Three large locks held the lid closed. I easily slid them off, having broken the locking mechanism long ago. I passed my lantern to Alexis. Using both hands, I lifted the lid. She cautiously leaned closer, peering into the chest.

She gasped out loud. The trunk was filled to the top with colorful French dresses. She lifted a blue crushed velvet gown.

"It's divine!" She held it against her frame excitedly.

"How?"

I shrugged. "Something I came across on one of my—"

She waved a hand, cutting me off, more enthralled with the treasure than with my explanation. She pressed the dress against her, twirling, showing it off for my inspection. "What do you think?"

"Wear this one."

"Pardon?"

"If you would do me the honor, I'd very much like you to have dinner with me upon my return from Port Royale."

I took the dress from Alexis, rolling it and tucking it beneath my arm. I steered her toward the stairs, eager to be out of the stifling heat of the hold. "I can have the rest delivered to your quarters if you like."

We walked back to the stairs, me leading, Alexis following. I inhaled a deep breath of fresh air as we emerged on deck. The sun was already beginning to set, its rays casting an orange glow across the horizon. Even the calm ocean was reflecting the rays from the sun.

All too soon, we came to her cabin door. We continued to talk, her back pressed against the door, hand on the latch. At length, I passed her the newfound dress.

"Thank you, my Captain."

"You're quite welcome."

She seemed so happy with her treasure. As I turned to go, she reached out, capturing my hand, pulling me back and spinning me around. Before I could react, her lips were on mine, kissing me.

My mouth opened and her tongue slipped inside, dueling with mine. My hands clutched her waist, my fingers digging into her hips. I heard a low moan escape her lips. She abruptly pulled back, ending the kiss. Our lips were so close, I could feel her breath. I leaned in for another kiss.

She placed both hands on my shoulders, stopping me. "Until tomorrow, my Captain."

She went inside, closing the door behind her and leaving me standing alone on the deck.

Chapter Four

THE LADY

I studied my reflection in the mirror and ran a brush through my hair, combing the locks back. I had washed it that morning in an odd concoction made from coconut milk that Rufus had created especially for me. Idly, I twirled my hair around my fingers.

The action brought images of Captain Wolff to mind. Several times, he had stroked his fingers through my hair. Always with his gloves on, I thought, ruefully. Why would he tenderly stroke my hair, yet have no desire to feel its softness against his bare fingertips? Perhaps I would pose that very question to him at dinner.

"Really, Alexis."

I caught Mother's reflection in the mirror. She was standing just inside the doorway, leaning against the frame, fanning herself. "I can't see why you put forth such an effort for an uncouth, unscrupulous, ill-bred—"

"I would put forth any effort necessary to secure our freedom, Mother."

She stepped close beside me and reaching around me. Her fingers closing about my perfume bottle, she uncorked it, and passed it to me.

†

The air had the familiar scent of salt water. And fresh fish. And something else that I didn't immediately recognize. I sniffed again and inhaled deeply. Bread. My stomach involuntarily clenched at the smell of baking bread wafting through the air.

I looked around, scanning my surroundings. Our ship was moored securely in its dock, surrounded by other sailing vessels. Outstretched before us, past the docks, I could see the lights of a port city. Squinting my eyes, I could barely make out carts laden with goods being driven from market.

I moved toward the bow of the ship. Sailors were coming and going up a makeshift gangplank that stretched from the edge of the ship to the dock below. Two burly sailors pushed past me on their way down the steep incline. I sidestepped, moving out of their way.

A hand grabbed my elbow, fingers closing about my upper arm. I turned quickly, nearly losing my balance. A second hand shot out, steadying me.

"Jonathan." I said, nodding in gratitude.

"Lady DeVale." He studied me from head to toe. "You look exquisite."

"Thank you. You look… " My gaze settled on his chin, where a beard was sprouting. "Different."

He frowned, then smiled broadly, stroking his fingers through his beard. "You like it?"

I shrugged. "I'm not used to seeing you this way. You look…older."

That statement seemed to please him immensely. He stuck out his chest like a preening peacock. "Just wait'll it gets longer," he said proudly. "I'm going to braid the ends and twirl little pieces of ribbons into it. Then, when we go into battle, I'll light the ribbons."

"Are you coming from town?" I asked, seeking to redirect the conversation.

"Yes." I heard the excitement in his voice as he proceeded to tell me as much as he could in one breath. About Port Royale, its inhabitants, and his day in town. As we spoke, his stomach rumbled. He had the decency to seem embarrassed. "Would you care to have dinner with me?"

"Actually, I'm to have dinner with Captain Wolff upon his return."

"Oh. I didn't realize he… " His voice trailed off and a look I hadn't seen before flitted across his face.

"Jonathan?"

He quickly turned on his heel, his long stride carrying him away from me.

Hurriedly, I pursued him, my shoes echoing upon the deck as I chased him. "Jonathan," I called again.

I heard him sigh. He stopped, turning around to face me.

"Is there something you wish to speak of?" I asked.

He averted his gaze, staring uncomfortably at his boots. I barely heard his mumbled words. "I do not wish to speak ill of my captain."

I arched my brow. "If this has any bearing on my dinner with Captain Wolff, I feel you should inform me."

"I would expect the captain's return to be delayed, Lady DeVale."

"Pray tell, why, Jonathan?"

"It's really not my place to say." He paused momentarily. "But whenever the captain conducts business in Port Royale, he spends the evening with Brandy."

"Is that Captain Wolff's wife?" I held my breath, awaiting his answer.

Jonathan laughed, then suddenly coughed. "A wife?" he managed to choke out.

"I've heard tales of pirates who keep many wives."

"Brandy's not the sort you would marry."

"Pardon?"

"Brandy's not of the same station as you, my lady." Jonathan paused in an attempt to delicately word the situation. "But many men, including the captain, find her other charms more than adequate—"

I raised my hand, silencing him. "No more," I pleaded, already turning on my heel and retreating to the relative safety of my own cabin.

†

I found Vincent on deck with his charts and compasses,

plotting the ship's course, his back to me as he took a sun reading. I watched in silence as he wrote down his readings and gave instructions to another sailor about wind direction and sail settings.

Finally, he turned to me. "I thought you'd be resting in your cabin."

I shook my head. "A lot has been on my mind."

"About your stay on *The Wolfsbane*?"

"About *The Wolfsbane's* captain." I caught the look on Vincent's face, the unspoken question in his eyes. "Does Kris have a woman in every port?"

"Where would you get such a notion from?"

"Vincent, I know about Brandy."

He visibly blanched. "How do you come to know that name, Lady DeVale?"

Dismissive of his question, I continued upon my pursuit of answers. "What is the relationship between this woman and Captain Wolff?"

"I know not what your informant may have intimated, Lady DeVale, but rest assured the captain's relationship with Brandy McBride is one of friendship."

I arched an eyebrow. "A close friendship?"

He nodded. "Whenever business brings us into Port Royale, Captain Wolff often finds occasion to visit with his old friend, Klaus McBride and his daughter. But rest assured, while the relationship he shares with her is a special one, Captain Wolff is not in love with Brandy McBride."

I sighed. "Be that as it may, I'm quite certain he has someone."

"Kris has no one." Vincent folded his navigational charts, tucking them beneath his arm. "Perhaps, though, he already has his eye on a certain young lady. And perhaps that young lady would care to have dinner with him tonight?"

A smile crept onto my lips. "When is dinner, Vincent?"

"I'll arrange it with Rufus. I'm certain I can persuade him to fix something special."

Although I was not yet placated about the captain's failure to return the previous evening, I was somewhat satisfied by Vincent's responses to my questions. And in a few short hours, I would be prepared to address the issue of Kris' trip into Port Royale.

†

I picked my way down the staircase leading to the hold of the ship. I held the lantern tightly in my grasp as I took each step carefully one at a time. The old wood creaked beneath my weight. The lantern cast an eerie light in the hold, menacing shadows seemed to come to life, lurking in the darkness, waiting to attack. My own shadow, cast upon the wall, was bizarre and distorted in the dim lighting.

I picked my way across the slippery floor, lifting the hem of my dress so as not to drag it through the slime and muck. I stepped in a slick spot and lost my footing, nearly falling. I grabbed for a nearby support beam. The rough wood tore at my gloved hand, and I fought to steady myself. I took a deep breath and rested against the beam for a second, trying to reorient myself with my surroundings.

Something small scurried past, brushing my fingertips. I screamed and jumped backwards. My heart leapt into my throat. I raised the lantern, peering into the darkness. A set of beady eyes stared at me from behind a stack of crates. As the light hit it, it turned and ran. I caught a glimpse of its profile silhouetted on the wall before it scurried off. It was a rodent. A huge one.

I stepped back, goose bumps running down my spine. Suddenly, I was no longer so eager to find the trunk filled with dresses that I knew was still somewhere in the hold. I cursed the rampant temper that had rent asunder the dress Captain Wolff had given me. Upon returning to my cabin to prepare for dinner, I was forced to confront my actions from the night before. The dress was ruined beyond repair.

Something brushed against me in the darkness. Something much larger than a rodent. I caught sight of a flash of dark hair tied in a ponytail. The lantern was snatched from my hands and placed on a nearby wooden barrel. Muscular hands gripped my shoulders, fingers pressing into my skin.

"Kris." I breathed a sigh of relief.

His lips were on mine. I could smell liquor on his breath. He pressed his lips harder against mine, and his tongue forced its way into my mouth. I struggled, pushing back, trying to get away. The grip on my upper arms tightened, squeezing. His mouth followed, attempting to resume our kiss. His whiskers scratched at my skin.

I jerked out of his grasp. I bumped against the wooden barrel, the lantern teetering precariously. My hand shot out, snatching it up off the barrel. I held the lantern up, hand shaking, squinting in the dim lighting.

My gaze took in the tall, lean figure. Muscular arms taut with anticipation, fists clenching and unclenching. His bare chest heaved with each breath. His nostrils were flaring, eyes wild with lust.

"Jonathan." I backed away.

He took a step toward me, his long-legged stride eating up the little bit of distance I had managed to put between us. He roughly grabbed my wrist, snatching the lantern from my grasp. He slammed it down on a wooden crate, the lantern wobbling, threatening to topple over.

"Jonathan!" I screamed as his mouth made contact with my neck. My open palm beat upon his back. "Stop!"

I struggled blindly, scratching, clawing at anything I could reach. Jonathan cursed as my nails scratched his skin. He pulled back abruptly, clutching a hand to the side of his face. Blood oozed between his fingers. He drew his hand from his face, staring at the blood on his fingertips. His face contorted with rage.

My head snapped back as the blow connected with my face. A sudden wave of dizziness overtook me. The room spun uncontrollably, my surroundings swimming about my head. I felt myself falling.

A ripping sound echoed throughout the hold. A sudden gust of air blew across my exposed chest. I lifted my lower body, kicking wildly. Jonathan was sent stumbling backwards, slamming against a wooden crate. He fell, long legs sprawled out before him.

I heard a little clinking sound first, then the shattering of glass. I planted my feet firmly on the floor, pushing backwards with my legs and elbows. He was on his feet before me, charging. We both fell, landing on the floor. I struggled, pushing up on my elbows. I peered above Jonathan's shoulder. Behind him, I saw smoke. And flames engulfing several wooden crates.

"Fire!" I shouted. "The ship's on fire!"

Chapter Five

THE CAPTAIN

Sven and Ivan followed me. Vincent suggested I take the two powerful brothers with me to carry up a trunk for Lady DeVale. No doubt the trunk in question was the French one, filled to the top with dresses. I had meant to bring it to her quarters earlier, but I was busy with other matters.

We descended the stairs, lanterns in hand. I sniffed; something odd was in the air.

"Fire." Ivan pointed at smoke rising above some crates at the far end of the hold.

"Get the buckets and men." I jumped the last few stairs. As my feet hit the floor, I slid, caught myself. I scrambled to my feet, rushing toward the smoke.

I heard Ivan running back up the stairs, his heavy boots pounding on the steps. Sven followed me, hot on my heels as we rushed through the hold. I pushed my way past barrels and crates, Sven breathing heavily behind me.

We moved without speaking. There was no need for words. We both knew what was needed. We had to find the source of the fire and attempt to contain it until the crew arrived with water buckets. They would be coming in a matter of minutes, but in a situation like this, every second counted.

A fire on board ship was dangerous enough. But for it to be in the hold of the ship, the danger was two-fold. If it wasn't controlled in time, not only would it spread to the rest of the ship, it would also damage the integrity of the hull. A fire in the hold could cause the whole ship to go down.

Sven coughed loudly. The smoke was more dense in this

part of the hold. An orange glow lit our way, illuminating our path. Wood crackled and popped. I could feel the heat on my skin.

We both saw it at the same time. The fire was licking at wooden crates and cargo nets indiscriminately. Support beams were in danger of being engulfed by flames. And beyond those flames, Jonathan and Alexis. He was on top of her.

It took a few seconds to register. At first, I thought he may have been trying to shield her from the fire but I saw her struggling beneath him. She was kicking, biting, fighting to push him off her. And I saw the blade of the knife he held to her throat.

I shouted for Jon.

He didn't respond to my cries.

Ignoring the heat of the flames, we both rushed the length of the hold.

One of Sven's large hands grabbed Jon by the back of the neck, lifting and throwing him.

Jon landed hard, banging the back of his head on a support beam. The knife fell from his hand. He lay sprawled on the floor, shaking his head, disoriented. His chest heaved as he fought to catch his breath in the smoky room. The shirt around his waist was dirty and torn. His pants were untethered, exposing him.

I was on him in an instant. Punching. Kicking. Cursing. Anger flashed white hot behind my eyes. I punched blindly, not knowing, not caring where my blows landed. I heard him yelp in pain. His cries only served to make me punch him harder.

Hands were on my shoulders, fingers digging into my flesh. I was pulled off of Fitzpatrick. I struggled, fighting to get my hands around his throat. My arms were pinned to my sides. He lay back on the floor, trying to get his breath. His face was a bloody mess; his lip was split open, his left eye swollen shut. I'm sure his nose was broken.

"Captain." I vaguely heard the voice above my own heartbeat pounding in my ears. "Stop."

Still I strained, attempting to break loose from the bear hug that held me captive. I kicked wildly, my boot connecting with his chin. His head snapped back. "Stop before you kill him!" Ivan cautioned me.

That made me stop. I stopped kicking. My arms went limp. Slowly, my breathing calmed. My muscles remained tensed, my jaw clenched. I spit, my saliva hitting him squarely in the face, running down his cheek.

I shifted my gaze away from Fitzpatrick, searching for Alexis. During my madness, the crew had doused the fire, but the hold was still smoky. I found her. Sven was with her, cradling her in his arms.

Her once beautiful dress was now ripped and soiled. One sleeve was torn at the shoulder, the other missing completely. Her tender flesh was already bruising, Fitzpatrick's fingertips clearly defined on her abused arm.

She had a cut just below her right eye. Her lips were swollen. The tender flesh of her neck was bruised, again with Jon's fingertips clearly defined.

My gaze shifted lower, past her collarbone. The bodice of the dress was torn, exposing her flesh. My eyes moved back up, momentarily pausing as her eyes found mine. I couldn't meet her stare, couldn't bear to see the pain in those beautiful eyes.

My eyes met Sven's. The concern, the anger, I saw in that gaze was unfathomable. I subtly nodded. Mutely, he slowly rose to his feet, backing away. I took his place, sliding in next to Alexis, cradling her in my arms.

✝

SHIP'S LOG – SEPTEMBER 11, 1703

The repairs to the hold of The Wolfsbane *have come along quite well. Fortunately, the fire hadn't penetrated our outer hull. However, the damage was still significant enough to force us to divert our route to make repairs, delaying our journey by days.*

The damage to Lady DeVale has been more severe, I'm afraid. She's been very hesitant to leave her cabin of late, spending much of her time in with her mother. On the rare occasion when she does venture forth from her cabin, she has been very selective of the company she keeps. Even on those occasions, it's usually in the presence of the Duchess DeVale. It's apparent that many of the crew would still like to enjoy entertaining Lady DeVale, but few will risk approaching her with her mother around.

Her physical scars are beginning to heal. The emotional ones will take longer. Hopefully, today's action against her attacker will help promote the healing process. Hers, as well as mine.

I stood on the deck of *The Wolfsbane*. The storm clouds were fast accumulating, nearly covering the horizon. Angry waves pounded against the hull of the ship. A wicked wind blew through my hair, chilling me to the bone.

My crew was on deck. Everyone accounted for. I'd never been big on formality, but they all stood at attention. They were a rag tag group, not fit for the queen's elite navy, but they were mine, nevertheless. I doubted if the queen's own navy had men as brave as my crew.

Duchess DeVale was there. She stared straight ahead, refusing to meet my gaze. Still I knew she was eager to be here. I could see it reflected in her eyes. Like a buzzard circling its prey. She no doubt wished it was me instead.

Alexis was beside her. She was wringing her hands, a careful mask of indifference on her face. I studied her intently. The bruises were still prominent on her face, marring her tender flesh. I saw the outline of Fitzpatrick's fingerprints and my blood boiled.

Sven and Ivan flanked Jon, each one holding him by an arm, effectively restraining him. He struggled, but they were more than capable of keeping him held fast. Chains on his wrists and legs rattled loudly with his struggles.

His shirt was ripped in half, hanging off his torso, held in place only by his belt. There were open sores on his chest, red stripes left by Ivan's whip. I knew the same bloody ribbons would also be on his back. Ivan was an expert with a whip. If he had wanted, he could have cleaved the very flesh from Fitzpatrick's bones with only the use of a bolo.

The flesh on his wrists was rubbed raw from the shackles. Dried blood covered his chains. No doubt he had attempted to pull his manacles off by force. I glanced at his feet. His ankles were also rubbed raw, his flesh and chains covered with dried blood.

It was days since he'd been thrown down below in chains. And from the looks of it, he hadn't been cleaned after our fight. Not that he deserved to be.

Dried blood caked his face. Especially around the area of his nose. That was my handiwork. I had felt the bones shatter beneath my fist. That fact was made all the more evident by his breathing solely through his mouth. And judging by his wheezing, I was probably also responsible for breaking at least a few of his ribs.

He had lost his ponytail. His hair hung straight down, an unruly, tangled mess. One eye was swollen shut. The other glared at me, the contempt and hatred shining deeply from the inky black pupil of his eye.

"For violating The Captain's Articles..." My voice was loud and confident, my words strong and sure. "For endangering the safety and welfare of a female, for being the cause of her endangerment... " I paused, pulling my pistol from my belt. "The penalty is your life."

I straightened my arm, aiming my flintlock at Fitzpatrick. He strained against his bonds. Sven and Ivan held him fast. I took a deep breath. And fired.

A loud crack. The smell of gunpowder. A woman's scream. A man's cry of agony. Fitzpatrick's body jerked backwards, his feet flying from beneath him. He would have fallen flat on his backside if Sven and Ivan hadn't had such a tight rein on him.

He slowly raised his head. His jaw clenched in rage. "Damn you, Wolff!" He struggled, trying to escape. Ivan and Sven held him fast. "When I get my hands on you—"

Ivan's fist closed around Fitzpatrick's throat, squeezing. Blood spurted from his shoulder, running down his chest and arm.

I loaded my pistol again, maintaining eye contact with Fitzpatrick the whole time. I raised my weapon, cocking the trigger. I aimed. He was dead in my sights. I snarled, tightening my finger on the trigger.

"Please, Captain Wolff." I blinked, dimly registering Alexis's words. "Please don't do this."

I cast her a wary glance out of the corner of my eye. Her cheeks were tear-stained, her eyes silently pleading.

"Alexis, leave the captain to do his work." The duchess was standing just behind Alexis, a sardonic smile upon her face. "Let him slaughter his entire crew if he wishes."

I nodded subtly.

Two crewmembers moved in, flanking the duchess.

She fairly squawked when they each took an arm, spinning her around. "Am I next, Captain Wolff?" she shouted back at me. "Am I to be made an example of, as well?"

The hand clutching at my arm squeezed, the nails biting through my shirt and into my flesh. "Please," Alexis pleaded once again.

My eyes narrowed. "You would plead for the life of a man that attacked you? Attempted to rape you? He would have slit your gullet open like a fish to keep you quiet as he had his way with you!" My voice had started as a whisper and slowly had grown to an outraged cry.

"Please. Have mercy." She took a deep breath, exhaled loudly. "Killing him would make you no different from him."

I let out the breath I'd been holding. I eased my finger off the trigger, lowering my pistol. Every muscle in my body protested as I relaxed my arm.

"Thank you."

Jonathan Fitzpatrick breathed a sigh of relief. I bit my bottom lip. He smirked, leered at Alexis, and licked his own lips lasciviously.

"Vincent." I called as I turned to my quartermaster. "Is there an island near our present location?"

Vincent cocked his head to one side and peered at the charts lying spread out on a nearby barrel. "As a matter of fact, Captain Wolff, there is." He pointed to a small mass of land on the map. I raised an eyebrow. He quickly added, "As a contingency plan."

I heard murmurs of approval from my crew, cries of protest from Fitzpatrick.

"Very well." I turned to face Fitzpatrick once again. "Time to promote you to governor of an island."

I nodded to Sven. "Do it."

It would be several agonizing hours before we reached the island. I convinced Alexis to return to her cabin to rest and the rest of my crew remained on deck throughout the duration. Anchor was dropped approximately fifteen yards from shore, the metal clanging against the coral reefs below us before securing itself on the ocean floor.

Griffen appeared, presenting a small pine box to Sven. He opened it, inspected it, and showed each item to the crew. "A bottle of powder," he said, holding the small powder horn up. "Halfway full."

He continued on, showing each item in turn. "One bottle of water. One small arm and one shot." Sven showed the pistol and the bullet, placed them back in the box. Sven made a show of locking the box with a key, then throwing the key overboard.

He stood in front of Jon Fitzpatrick, glaring at him before roughly thrusting the pine box into his hands. "More than you deserve, bastard."

With that, Sven moved aside.

Ivan appeared with a key in hand. He stooped over, unlocking Fitzpatrick's leg shackles. Standing, he placed the key in the lock around his wrists.

"Damn you to hell, Wolff. You *and* that cheap whore," Fitzgerald snarled.

Ivan removed the key from Fitzpatrick's manacles before unlocking them. He lifted his hand over the side of the ship and allowed his fingers slowly to let loose. The key fell into the ocean with a tiny splash.

Jon screamed in anger, reaching, as if trying magically to retrieve the key from the briny depths. Ivan pushed, shoving him overboard. He surfaced, sputtering and cursing, all the while trying to tread water, hold his precious pine box and threaten us with manacled arms.

"Away." I turned on my heel, walking away from the side

of the ship.

†

I surveyed the spread before me. Roasted chicken with pota-toes. Breads and fruits. A feast fit for a king. I lifted my mug to my lips, sipping. I reached across the table, turning the bottle around. Just as I thought—one of my prized wines.

Alexis sat across from me, long blonde tresses loose about her shoulders. A new hunter green dress adorned her lovely frame.

"I didn't expect this," I said between bites.

"What?" She paused with her fork halfway to her mouth.

"All of this." I gestured at our surroundings. "The private dinner. The romantic setting."

Alexis offered a shy smile. "I thought the candles would be nice."

I saw a small blush.

"I'm glad you're enjoying our dinner."

"I am, very much so. Thank you."

She returned my smile. "Thank you, my Captain."

"What for?"

"For not killing Jonathan."

My jaw clenched at the mention of that scalawag's name. "I wanted to. But you asked me not to."

She smiled sweetly. Brushed a stray strand of hair back, tucking it behind her ear. She nodded subtly. "I know you did. But it was the compassionate thing to do."

I sputtered, a mouthful of wine flying across the table as I laughed incredulously. "The compassionate thing would have been to kill him."

Her mouth dropped open. "You can't mean that."

"Yes, I can." I nodded. "He hurt you. He would have killed you if we hadn't chanced upon you in the hold."

"But still—"

I held up my hand, cutting her off. How to explain to this woman that I would have gladly shot him limb by limb, one bullet at a time, until he died of blood loss rather than one quick shot through the heart? "I wanted Fitzpatrick to suffer for what he did to you."

"But—"

"And for what he did to me, too."

"It's understandable that Jonathan's betrayal would cause you anguish, Kris. He was a trusted member of your crew, and for him to blatantly disregard your codes and laws is unacceptable." She took my hand within her own.

I shook my head. "This was more than simple anger, Alexis. This was hatred, pure and unadulterated. And, what you may see as an act of kindness and compassion… I can't lie to you. Shooting Jon Fitzpatrick would have been too lenient."

Bewilderment clearly showed on her face.

"I made Fitzpatrick governor of an island."

"You set him off the ship with supplies. You gave him leniency."

"I gave him a death sentence!" I slammed my fist onto the table. My mug jumped, wine spilling onto the wood. I wiped at it with my sleeve.

Alexis reached out, taking my right hand in her grasp, as well. She now held my hands captive within her own. "What do you mean?"

I didn't answer.

"Look at me, Kris."

I refused.

"Look at me!" she demanded, her voice unusually loud.

Slowly, I raised my head, my eyes meeting her gaze.

"What do you mean?" she asked, her voice calm once again.

"When you sentence someone to be governor of an island, you set them off on a deserted island. Away from the normal trade routes," I explained. "The supplies we give are minimal at best. And you'll remember that Sven threw the key to the box of supplies overboard."

Her grip tightened on my fingers. "Surely, he was able to open the box."

"He's wounded," I shrugged. "Even if he somehow got the box open, there's only enough water for one day."

61

"But he may be able to find fresh water," she said. "And you gave him weapons."

"One gun. With one bullet. The smart thing would be for him to use it on himself."

"We have to go back—"

"It's too late."

She got up from the table, slowly walked about the room, arms clutched about her waist. "It's been three days. He's already dead."

I turned the wine bottle up, taking a deep swig. I popped a piece of chicken into my mouth. "I do wish you'd finish your dinner," I said around a mouthful. "It's getting cold."

No response.

"You've been staring at that bookcase for half an hour now," I said some time later. I took my bottle, made my way to the stairs leading to my bedroom. I sat on the top step. "I'm fairly certain there's not a thing there you'd find interesting reading."

Her fingers idly stroked along the top shelf. She lifted, carefully examined several novelties I'd collected from various captured ships. She replaced each one exactly the way she found it. Her nails tapped along the spines of several logbooks. Kneeling, she examined the rolled maps on the bottom shelf.

"You'll find most of the maps have a matching logbook," I offered.

She turned slowly, looking at me. "You certainly have quite a few."

I shrugged. "It's common practice to collect logbooks from captured ships. The information could prove invaluable in unfamiliar waters."

"It must be tedious work sifting through all those books and charts."

"But worth it. You never know what secrets a map and logbook may hold. An unknown island. The potential route of a treasure fleet." I smirked. "Perhaps a lusty tale of a particularly beautiful wench."

Her face went pale.

My smile fell.

She turned her back on me, stalked to the window.

Damn. I thought I was being clever. "I…my apologies, Lady DeVale," I stammered. "I didn't think."

A loud harrumph was her only answer. Hands clasped tightly behind her back, her spine was stiff. Suddenly, I was aware that this was about more than a misspoken word.

I took another swig from the wine bottle. "Alexis—"

If it was possible, she stiffened even more. "Am I included in your logbook, as well, Captain Wolff? Did you write how you came across me in the hold of the ship, flat on my back, Jonathan between my legs?"

"No."

"Did you write of how because of me, he was put off your ship to die?"

I frowned. "Does it really bother you so much?"

She cast me a sidelong glance. "Does it really bother you so little?" she countered. "I know you were close at one time. He tried to emulate you. At one point, I believed you to be brothers."

I laughed. "No relation."

"Still, I should think you would feel for his absence."

I shrugged. "He was a member of my crew. He signed The Captain's Articles before coming aboard my ship. He broke my rules. He suffered my consequences."

"Or rather mine."

"Huh?" It was a brilliant response.

"If I hadn't interfered, he would—"

"Still be dead." I toyed with the wine bottle, dangling the top of it between my fingertips, letting it swing freely.

She now turned from the window, openly staring at me. I felt her eyes upon me, openly assessing me. Judging me. She placed her hands on her hips, tapping her foot. Finally, she rendered her verdict. "I still don't believe you would have killed him."

"Yes, I would have," I said coldly.

"You intentionally missed his heart."

"So I could make him suffer longer." Why did this damn woman have to try to find the good in every little thing? "I'm no hero. I'm no knight in shining armor. I'm no tight-waisted naval officer."

She crossed the room, hands clasped behind the small of her back, taking tiny steps toward where I sat. "You're very gallant. And kind. You returned my necklace." She fingered the cross that lay between her breasts.

"After I stole it."

"You've saved me countless times."

"I'm the one who jeopardized your welfare in the first place."

"You've been a gentleman in every sense of the word." Her own words were much softer now, barely a whisper upon the air.

"I'm a pirate. I'm not a nice person." I lay back, my legs raised, with my back resting against the wooden step. I propped my head up on one arm.

I smelled her perfume, sweetly intoxicating. The material of her dress brushed against my thigh as she climbed the steps. She was leaning above me, her hair falling around her face. Around my face. Her lips touched mine. The lightest of touches. Barely noticeable. Just enough to set my lips on fire. My mouth opened beneath hers.

"To me, you're very nice," she whispered into my mouth. Her lips were upon mine once again, her tongue darting between my lips.

Her hands were on my shoulders, pressing down, fingernails biting at my flesh. My own hands were on her waist, clutching at her dress. When our kiss ended, I was left breathless, torn between taking great gulps of air and attempting to resume our kiss.

The need to continue our kiss won out, and I found my gloved hand on the back of her head. I pulled her to me once again. She resisted. Her tongue flicked out, licking my lips. She playfully bit at the tip of my nose.

Alexis reached out to me, the tip of her index finger tracing above my left eye. I felt her finger follow the bleached white scar in my eyebrow, ruffling the short hairs beneath her fingertip.

I caught my breath. "What is it you've come here for, Alexis?"

"I know you're attracted to me. But you've gone out of your way to be a gentleman. I know you would never do anything to bring me dishonor."

"My lady, you know not what you ask. You must consider the consequences. You are betrothed to a nobleman."

"That I don't love."

"That you don't love," I amended. "But surely...will he still honor the marriage if he discovers that his wife has been soiled?" My fingers stroked along her shoulder, caressing, gently petting. "You risk everything, my lady. You will be outcast. Never able to wed."

She laughed. A deep, throaty laugh. "These are special circumstances, my dear Captain Wolff."

I cocked an eyebrow, prompting her to continue. "I was abducted by bloodthirsty pirates. The captain took me, ravishing me savagely, forcefully taking my maidenhead. I am not to be blamed."

My mouth dropped open. "I'll be hunted down and hanged for raping you."

"They will have you hanged for kidnapping me anyway." She smirked.

I was speechless. We couldn't possibly be sitting here in my cabin discussing this as calmly as one may discuss fashion and politics at afternoon tea.

Her hand was shaking as she reached out to me. Trembling fingers stroked along my neck. Her nails dipped below the collar of my tunic, scratching at my flesh. Her eyes lifted from my neckline, shifted to my face. Verdant eyes intensely burned into mine.

"When I am returned to the English, I shall be sent on to Puerto Cabello." She hesitated and bit her bottom lip. "Before I am resigned to a lifetime of despondency, I deserve to experience one night of passion."

Her lips were on mine once again. I couldn't get enough of her mouth. She was seemingly everywhere. At my ear, my cheek, my jawbone; all fell prey to her touch. My breath came in short, ragged gasps and my heart threatened to beat out of my chest. I felt her tongue licking at the flesh of my neck. I felt her teeth. I gasped as she bit me, then gently sucked the spot she had just bitten.

"You're so soft," she murmured.

I lifted with my hips, using leverage to roll her over. She lay beneath me, hair tousled, eyes filled with lust.

I straddled her on the steps and leaned over, dropping a light kiss on her lips. Her mouth opened beneath mine. I refused to give her my tongue. Instead, I took her bottom lip into my mouth, sucking, scraping her with my teeth.

She lifted with her own hips, attempting to roll me, attempting to regain control. I pressed down, using my weight to keep her from moving me. My legs clamped around her lower body, grinding and squeezing to subdue her.

My head bent low, kissing the little patch of flesh that led to her cleavage. I kissed and licked at the tops of her breasts. The flesh was the softest I'd ever felt. She moaned and stirred beneath me, every little movement she made seemed to connect between my legs, sending white hot flashes shooting through my body.

"Alexis."

Her lids were half-closed, her eyelashes fluttering in what I thought was an attempt to hide them from my view. Nothing could completely hide those eyes, however. Filled with lust, they burned a deep emerald green. I felt as if she was looking not at me, but rather right through me.

My hands were at her shoulders now, pushing the material away. Moving it down her body. Alexis reached behind her back with her left hand. I heard her loosening the ties, working the material open. I pulled hard, exposing her flesh down to her waist.

I was in awe. I had been driven to lust before. But now, seeing all of her, I was mesmerized. She was...magnificent. Soft and firm, inviting my touch. Pink nipples standing proud and erect. The color perfectly matched the shade of her lips at that particular moment.

I reverently kissed her nipples.

She moaned my name, clutching me to her.

That's all it took to send me over the edge. I was on her

again, my mouth, my tongue, my teeth everywhere as I cupped her breasts in both hands.

I roughly yanked off the glove covering my right hand, eager to feel her. I marveled at the touch of her. I'd never felt anything so soft in my entire life. I felt her hands on my body, exploring. My mouth worked her breasts, my hand slipped down lower, beneath her skirts, between her legs. She opened beneath my touch, her thighs parting to grant me access. My fingers grazed her lips, her moisture flowing forth.

Her fingers were on my buttocks, her nails scratching at my flesh through my trousers, squeezing as she moved beneath me. I moved in time with her, my own body grinding into hers. My fingers sought and found her entrance. Her undulating hips gave my finger access, guiding me inside.

Hotness, softness, tightness around my finger. I rested inside her, reveling in the sensation. Her rotating hips slid my finger in farther. She clutched at me with her whole body, holding me to her.

I paused, my middle finger tapping at her maidenhead. She squeezed. I hadn't expected her to be so tight. I would have thought she'd loosened herself with self-exploring fingers deep in the night. I imagined her lying alone in bed on her back, legs spread as one hand fiercely clutched her breast, the other busy between her legs, pulling up her bedclothes, thrusting wildly.

Realization dawned on me. She was a lady, in the truest form of the word. Never before touched. By anyone. The thought went to my head. If I took her, she would never be the same again. Could she live with the consequences? Could I?

"Kris, please." Her lips were at my ear, her voice, husky, pleading with me.

Still, I hesitated. I felt her nimble fingers on the front of my trousers, untethering them. Before I knew it, she had thrust her whole hand inside my pants. I felt her fingers on me, stroking through my hair. Her fingers found my lips. I gasped out loud, thrusting hard against her hand.

Alexis lifted, pushed; I landed several feet away. She openly stared at my crotch. "You son of a bitch," she spat out.

"Alexis, wait." I reached out for her.

She caught my wrist, squeezing it in her grasp. She examined my now gloveless hand. Her nostrils flared, her eyes flashed. Her chest heaved with each ragged breath. "How dare you? To pose as a man—"

"Please, try to understand." I approached her slowly, arms outstretched in what I thought was a non-threatening pose. "I only did it..." My words trailed off, I swallowed, licking my suddenly dry lips. "Please. My crew doesn't know I'm a woman. If they did—"

"They'd get a good laugh, I'm certain." She punched wildly, her fist hitting me in the shoulder. "Go on." She pointed at the door. "Go down to the galley and brag to your crew how Captain Wolff had the proper and refined Lady Alexis DeVale on the floor like a common tavern whore, with her legs spread, begging for you to take her."

The slap came so hard and fast, I had no time to react. Her open palm connected with my cheek, the sound reverberating throughout the cabin. "Bastard." My head snapped back again. I stared at her as she raised her hand to slap me a third time. I didn't flinch, waited for the blow.

It never came. Instead, angry tears rolled unheeded down her cheeks. "Bastard," she repeated. "You bastard."

She adjusted her dress, covering herself before turning on her heel, storming down the steps, across the room and slamming the door behind her with all her might.

Chapter Six

THE LADY

The sunlight streamed in through the window. I blinked, then rolled over and firmly closed my eyes. Burying my face in my pillow, I pulled the sheet above my head. My body slowly began relaxing, slipping back toward slumber.

The door slammed shut. I jerked awake with a start, coming halfway off the bed. A searing pain shot through my entire body and a sudden throbbing reverberated in my temple. I clutched my head, falling back on the bed.

A damp cloth pressed against my forehead, wiping my brow, swiping at my flushed cheeks. I blinked my eyes open, attempted to focus. Mother's visage slowly became clear.

"Are you ill again, my daughter?"

I nodded and closed my eyes against the clamoring in my skull.

"Well, it's small wonder," she chastised. "Out until all hours in the night air. Eating who knows what aboard this disease-ridden ship. You could catch your death of only God knows what."

As always, her words were harsh. But her touch, her fingers were kind. She pulled the sheet from my upper body and wiped at my shoulders and arms.

"It's nearly mid-afternoon. Do you mean to lay in bed all day and into the night?"

I fought back waves of nausea. The wine from the night before boiled in my stomach. It took all my strength to nod.

"Very well. Rest easy, my daughter." Her lips were on my forehead, giving me a tender kiss. I felt her rise from the side of

69

the bed. The sound of her heels echoed on the wooden floor. The door closed as she retreated to her own bedroom.

†

The deck was awash in moonlight when I emerged from my cabin. A soft breeze blew through my hair. Cautiously, I listened. All was quiet. I had not really intended to sleep the entire day and part of the night away. But I was glad for the rest and grateful for the solitude the late hours would bring. I smoothed down my dress and tentatively stepped out on the deck.

Waves crashed and broke against the hull of *The Wolfsbane*. The ship rocked and swayed in the water. I steadied myself, glanced up at the ship's mast. The sails were furled, the ropes securely tied around the rolls of material. Pulleys clanked sharply as they repeatedly struck the fixtures of the masts.

The anchor would also be dropped, I realized. That meant we were either in unfamiliar or dangerous waters. I'd wager that we were traveling through unknown territory.

Wooden boards creaked beneath my weight as I walked the length of the deck. I strode purposefully toward the bow of the ship. I wanted to practice reading the stars. I had learned much during this voyage, and I was eager to apply the knowledge I had gained.

A sudden breeze blew up, whipping my hair around, blocking my vision. I looked away, pushing my hair back into place with my fingers. I turned back toward the bow, continuing to push errant strands away from my face.

Someone was already there. Back to me, muscles flexing as strong arms pulled on the anchor chain. It rattled but didn't give. His profile shadowed by darkness, his stature was overly familiar. He leaned against the rail for support, bent down, yanked off his boots. They landed on the deck with a dull thud. He removed his sword belt, dropping it beside his boots. I gasped as I caught his…her profile in the moonlight. Captain Wolff.

I slowly backed away into the shadows. I had every intention of returning to my cabin, leaving her alone on deck. Once I

70

reached the relative safety of the shadows though, my feet became rooted to the spot. My mind implored my body to leave; my feet steadfastly refused to take another step.

The captain was oblivious to my presence. She stared out to sea as if transfixed by something mysterious upon the waves. She pulled her gloves from her fingers, adding it to the pile at her feet. My heart beat faster as I caught sight of her bare hand, her delicate fingers, and slender wrist. My cheeks flushed as I remembered those fingers upon my flesh. First, in ecstasy as she fueled the flames of my passion, then in anger as she burned me with her betrayal.

She unfastened the buttons on the sleeves of her shirt, rolling the cuffs up to her elbows. Bending low, she pulled her pant legs up, stopping halfway to her knees. There was a flash of muscular calves, yet calves far too supple to belong to anyone but a woman.

She glanced around, taking in her surroundings. I retreated deeper into the shadows. I stood close to the mast, positive she couldn't see me. She had both feet on the railing now, balancing herself. A gust of wind threatened to blow her from her perch. Bending low, she skillfully picked her way up the wooden structure running up from the bow of the ship.

Toes bent, clutching, she darted along the wooden board. She moved cautiously, yet quickly. In seconds, she was out on the maidenhead, standing on the head of the wolf that kept a watchful eye over *The Wolfsbane* and its crew. Perched on the wolf's head, the captain looked out across the water.

Hands moved to her shirt, fingers deftly unfastening buttons. My heart leaped farther into my throat with each button that was undone. When Kris reached the final button, she roughly yanked, pulling her shirt from her trousers.

Now my heart fell from my throat into my chest again, and I thought the captain would surely hear it beating. She cast a wary glance around, checking her surroundings again. Her gaze settled on the mast where I hid. I stood my ground, refusing to move. Her eyes narrowed to tiny slits. I fought the urge to bolt from my hiding place and willed my heart to slow, my breathing to shallow. She couldn't possibly see me in the darkness. I was blended too well with the shadows.

I should have retreated to my cabin and left the captain to her privacy. But curiosity had the better of me. I stayed where I was.

Captain Wolff shrugged out of her shirt. Balling it up, she tossed it. It landed beside her boots on the deck. The white material splayed upon the deck, covering it in silk. I looked back from the pile of clothes to the captain.

She wore a sleeveless shirt, tight, molded to her body. Her stomach was flat and her ribcage defined. And above her ribcage—nowhere near the size of mine—were firm breasts the size of ripe apples. She was stunning.

She stood straight upright, knees together, arms outstretched. She bounced on the balls of her feet. In one fluid motion, she leapt from the wolf's head.

I rushed forward, reaching the railing almost instantly. My initial thought was that I might observe Kris at her swim. But as I scanned the surface of the calm waters, I suddenly felt as if I were intruding. And even though I longed to stay, I resolutely backed away from the railing. This was Kris' time; I would not intrude on her solitude.

†

"And no breakfast for ye today?"

I vaguely registered the voice somewhere in the back of my brain. Odd. I knew the speaker to have a commanding, booming voice. An overwhelming, dominant way of speaking that had initially scared me half to death. So much so that I had wanted to hide behind my mother's skirts like a cowering three-year-old.

That day, though, his voice was calming. I took a sip of my coconut milk and shook my head.

"I've got turtle eggs," he coaxed.

I swiveled on my stool, turning to face Rufus.

He stood at a counter, briskly chopping onions with a knife. In a bowl to his left were a half dozen brown eggs.

"No, I'm fine."

A snort as he continued to chop his onions.

"I take it you don't agree."

There was a slight falter in his chopping. "It's really not my place to say now, is it, Lady DeVale?"

"Why is it not your place?"

A slight shrug of his shoulders. "Well, what with ye being a lady and all and me being nuthin' but—"

I stopped him mid-sentence with a casual wave of my hand. "Tell me," I persisted.

His knife flew fast, his blade biting into the wooden cutting board with each stroke. His blade diced faster than even our master chef back in England. And I was fairly positive that Rufus did not have the formal training of the finest culinary schools as my own chef did.

"All I'm saying, mind ye, is that ye don't act like someone who is fine."

My left eyebrow shot up of its own accord. "Really?" My tone sounded frosty even to my own ears. I tried to sweeten my words and melt the ice a bit. "Why ever would you think such a thing?"

I waited as he rapidly mixed the eggs and onion together. He reached for his spices, randomly choosing one, then another.

"Stop." I caught his hand in my own, feeling his muscles tense beneath my grip. "Tell me."

He dropped the spices and turned to face me. Rufus gripped my hands in his large calloused ones and his gaze met mine.

"I enjoy ye in my galley, helping me work."

"But?" I prompted.

"But…" He shrugged. "But you're young and there must be a hundred other things ye could be doing besides watching an old Scot like me cook."

"I enjoy watching you cook."

Rufus cupped my chin. "And I enjoy ye being here. When ye're here for the right reasons."

"And what would be the proper reason?" I leaned back, his fingers slipping from my chin. I jutted it forward defiantly.

He dared to continue. "Since when does the Lady DeVale spend all of her day in the galley with old Rufus? Ye usually are too busy—all over the ship, doing this and that."

"Perhaps I need a change of pace."

"And I think mayhaps ye're hiding."

I laughed incredulously. "Hiding from what?"

Rufus stroked his beard, running his fingers through its length. "Ye spend all day in here, yet ye tell Sven ye don't have the time for him."

"I—"

"Let me finish."

I was shocked. No servant had ever hushed me before. Then again, Rufus McGregor was no lackey at the DeVale Estates. I permitted him to continue.

"Ye haven't kept up with ye lessons with Vincent."

"Vincent's been too busy. He's always plotting new courses, studying his charts. He has no time for me."

"Harrumph." The sound came from behind him.

Rufus cautiously took a step away from me.

Vincent stood in the doorway.

I pursed my lips. How much had he heard?

Vincent moved into the galley, approaching the counter Rufus was working at.

"Do you have anything ready?" he asked Rufus.

Rufus nodded, produced a metal plate, and passed it to Vincent. "Since early this morning. 'Tis probably cold by now."

"Won't much matter. He hasn't been eating anyway." Vincent took the dish from Rufus and turned to leave. He paused at the door, nodded to me. "Lady DeVale."

"Vincent."

"I believe your mother is searching for you on deck." His tone was frigid.

"Thank you." My reply was just as terse, just as cold.

I watched until he left, closing the door behind him. I turned on my stool, facing Rufus again. He was removing his apron, throwing it in a ball on the counter. He pushed his bowl of egg mixture away. His palms resting on the counter, he pressed down, pushing with all his might. The wooden counter groaned beneath the pressure.

"Rufus?"

Head bowed, back to me, his large shoulders heaved. "He drinks too much and eats too little." A loud sigh. "Of course, 'tis always been that way. Lately, though, 'tis been getting worse."

"Who?" I asked.

"Captain Wolff."

I stiffened at the name. I felt white hot anger flash behind my eyes.

Rufus took a deep breath, turned to face me. His face looked ten years older. "I worry. The crew needs its captain. Yet he treats his body with such reckless abandon. He's practically stopped eating." He frowned. "Like ye."

I bit my bottom lip.

Rufus eyed me suspiciously.

"Come to think of it, ye both lost yer appetites around the same time. And I haven't seen ye two together since I prepared that dinner for—"

I felt myself blush beneath Rufus's piercing gaze. "We had...a disagreement," I said somewhat hesitantly. "Captain Wolff...he's not what I expected."

Rufus straightened to his full height, folded his arms across his broad chest. "In what way?"

"He...pretended to be...something he wasn't." I stumbled on my own tongue, unsure of my words.

"I doubt that."

"Are you saying I lie?" I couldn't believe the audacity of this...this man.

"Nay."

"Yet you doubt my word when I tell you about Captain Wolff?" My eyes narrowed.

"I don't doubt yer word." His voice was light and mirthful.

I glared at him, unable to perceive the humor of the situation.

The grin slipped from his bearded face. "But I believe ye are...mistaken about the captain."

I arched one eyebrow. "Really? How so?"

"Captain Wolff has treated ye far better than anyone else in his position would." Rufus dropped his voice to an almost con-spiratorial whisper. "I've seen the way he looks at ye. How his eyes follow ye from the moment ye enter the room. The way he looks at ye when ye don't know he's there."

I leaned in closer, straining to hear. His voice suddenly rose; I nearly toppled off my stool, he startled me so.

"Most men in his position would take what they want. By force if necessary."

"Rape." The word was out of my mouth as quickly as I thought it. Flat. Distasteful. Ugly.

Rufus let the word hang in the air between us. I studied his face but couldn't read his expression. Finally, he nodded.

"By our laws, it would be his right. Ye are his prisoner. As such, ye belong to him. As captain, he has the right to take what he wants."

"He wouldn't—"

Rufus brought up his left hand angrily, silencing my pro-tests. Anger flashed hot in his eyes.

"Ye try to pretend that he is a gentleman. From yer social circles. Prim and proper and dainty. A sissy boy in faggoty cloth-ing." Rufus cursed, spat on the floor at the very notion. "Ye for-get that Captain Wolff is first and foremost a pirate captain. Scourge of the seas. The English, the French, the Spanish, they all fear the wrath of The Wolff."

I sighed. "He's never shown me that side—"

"Ye've never wanted to see it. It's always been there. But ye've been too busy trying to turn him into something he's not, to notice what's before yer very nose. Ye want to pretend he's yer fantasy lover come to life. Ye tease him and taunt him and lure him with yer feminine wiles and expect him to behave like a gentleman all the while. Ye are like one of the legendary Sirens luring him to his doom."

"Is that what you believe of me, Rufus?"

Rufus glared at me with menacing eyes. "I think ye should freely give what is rightfully his. Maybe once he's had ye, that'll be enough. Enough to dispel the siren song ye've woven 'round his heart. Enough to return our Captain Wolff to us."

I raised my hand and slapped him then I turned on my heel,

racing for the door only to run into Ivan as he appeared in the doorway, coming in with an empty plate in his hand. I shoved him out of my way, storming out of the galley.

†

I carried both shoes in my hand as we strolled upon the deck. The wood was worn smooth beneath my feet and warmed by the afternoon sun. A light breeze swirled around the hem of my summer skirts.

I paused along the port side of *The Wolfsbane*. I leaned against the railing, my shoes dangled over the edge. I surveyed the ocean, the horizon beyond.

"Do you know our location?"

I shook my head, turning to face Mother. She, too, was standing against the railing. I knew she wasn't interested in the scenery, however. I casually looked behind my left shoulder, then my right. The nearest crewmen were working on the sail riggings, a good twenty feet distant.

"I don't know enough about sun readings to tell our position."

I looked at the ocean. Deep blue waters. White caps on blue waves breaking against the hull. Waters too deep to plumb the depths and shadowy secrets hidden from the human eye.

"The quartermaster is taking us through unfamiliar waters. I've seen him with his charts. I've overheard the men talking."

Mother abruptly turned away, staring out at the sea. Ivan and Sven approached, nodding in acknowledgment. We smiled politely, waiting for them to pass. She turned back to me, dropped her voice, and leaned in close. "About what, my daughter?"

"Dissension about the course that Vincent has been plotting. I believe we've been traveling north."

There was a sharp intake of air from Mother. "Are you certain?"

I nodded. "I'll come onto deck again tonight when everyone is abed. I'll attempt to discern our exact location."

"I pray you're mistaken." Mother's face was gray, ashen. With her cheeks sunken from hunger, she was the pallor of death. "North is not good. Not good at all."

"I know. I know." I patted her hands reassuringly. My fingers felt the brittle bones beneath her thin flesh. If rescue did not come soon, she would starve to death.

Mother's own hands clutched at a white handkerchief, wringing it desperately. "I thought they meant to ransom us." Her voice sounded tiny, weak.

"If it's true that we're traveling north," I said, my own voice trembling, "then, we're heading farther and farther away from Puerto Cabello. Soon, I fear, we'll be past the realm of the Spanish Empire. There will be no ransom, no rescue."

"At least your sister has escaped."

I nodded. "With luck, she'll be back at the DeVale Estates by now."

Mother pursed her lips. "If she is indeed safe. There is no guarantee she's in friendly hands."

"Faith, Mother. I lulled them into a false sense of security once. That allowed Elizabeth to escape. I should be able to do the same again."

"Be careful. Remember what happened the last time you were discovered."

Unbidden, my fingers reached for my face, stroking my cheekbone. I remembered the damage inflicted by Captain Wolff for my past betrayal. "Don't worry." I caught her gaze, held it unwaveringly. "I won't rest until I've seen you safely returned to England's shores."

She flashed a weak smile. Her gloved fingers reached out, stroking my cheek. "Why does it sound as if you plan not to return yourself?"

"You've seen how closely guarded we've been since Elizabeth's rescue," I said. "Even if my plan sees fruition, it may not be feasible for both of us to escape."

"Courage, my daughter. Captain Jackson is a very capable British officer. It's his duty to pursue this ship until he rescues us and sees the likes of Captain Wolff swing by his neck."

"I pray that what you say is true, but let us not forget that

Captain Wolff has outmaneuvered Captain Jackson once already. He shan't be easy prey for the likes of the Queen's Navy."

"You must find a way to outfox The Wolff and facilitate our rescue."

My breath caught at the suggestion; my stomach churned. Did I dare risk such betrayal again? I sighed heavily and nodded. "Rest assured, I shall find a way."

Mother reached out, taking my hands in hers. She squeezed gently. Her eyes were misty as they sought out mine. "Careful, Alexis. Our very lives rest in your hands."

I knew not what to say. Never had my mother put such faith in me. Her words served to strengthen my resolve. And I knew was that no matter the personal danger I myself might face, if I incurred The Wolff's wrath, I would not rest until I saw that my mother's freedom was at hand.

†

I marveled at the night sky, staring at the brightest star I'd ever seen in my life. Here, far from civilization, the stars were truly at their best. Once again, there was a decidedly strong wind blowing across the deck. An uncharacteristic chill filled the air.

I glanced at the sky again. Storm clouds were beginning to gather. No matter, I'd already gained the knowledge I sought. The captain herself had unwittingly provided the guidance I needed to learn about ship's navigation. Under her tutelage, I now possessed enough knowledge to discern our position. I dare say, given the opportunity, I would be capable of guiding this ship back to the shores of England.

The deck swayed beneath me, forcing me to reach out blindly to steady myself against the sails' riggings. *The Wolfsbane* bobbed roughly in the water as waves broke harshly against her hull. I struggled to gather my sea legs beneath me.

The ship continued to bob and sway in the choppy waters. The anchor held fast, clanking angrily in its moorings, as if trying to escape its confines. I felt the first large droplets of rain pelt down upon the deck with remarkable force. I flinched from the cold rain and opted to head toward the relative safety of my own cabin.

"Alexis."

I drew up short, recognizing the voice instantly. Heart hammering, I swallowed quickly, willing my body to be calm. I paused, hesitantly turning around, slowly facing Captain Wolff, praying she couldn't sense the guilt I was feeling. I needed to choose my words carefully if I did not wish her to discern the reason I was on deck at that hour.

"You're getting wet," were the only words that came forth from me.

Sharp laughter. "I don't think a few raindrops will matter much."

My eyes narrowed as I took in her appearance. She was clad in much the same way she was when I spied upon her. Her hair was wet, rivulets running off her face. She'd already donned her white shirt, rolled the sleeves down her arms. It remained unbuttoned, contrasting sharply with the black shirt she wore beneath. The midnight material was drenched, clinging to her upper body. I tore my eyes from her torso, forced my gaze to meet hers.

She'd been swimming before the storm came up. She must have thought me daft. Or so addled by her physical form that my sentences were incoherent. My ire quickly grew at her laughter. Gone was my plan to feign ignorance. "Why have you set us upon a northerly course?"

"Since when is ship navigation a concern of yours?"

"Rest assured, it is not my intent to promote myself to any sort of position amongst your crew, Captain Wolff." I noted the twitching at her jaw line. I pushed ahead, daring to risk her wrath. "My sole intent at this point is to complete my voyage to Puerto Cabello."

Her left eyebrow arched. Piercing gray eyes boldly stared at me. "And why are you suddenly in such haste to reach Puerto Cabello?"

"I have a marriage—"

"That you couldn't have given a ship rat's ass about five days ago!"

I willed myself to control my breathing. I forced my voice

to remain calm. I couldn't afford to blurt out the truth in a moment of anger.

"I want to fulfill my obligations," I whispered sweetly.

"I think you don't know what you want." She threw up her hands in frustration. "Five days ago, you wanted me to take that which should have belonged to your betrothed—"

"Until I came to my senses—"

"Until you realized I wasn't—"

"What you pretended to be," I finished.

The sudden proximity was almost too much to bear. We stood scant inches apart. Her breath was upon me, hot and intimate upon my cheek. "At least I can take comfort in the knowledge that I was never that passionate—"

An incredulous laugh. "Shall I drop my breeches and show you the claw marks on my buttocks, my lady?" A wolfish grin mocked me. "I suppose congratulations are in order. Of all my enemies, you are the only one to ever draw first blood." She folded her arms across her chest, leaned back on her heels coolly.

I could have clawed that smug look off her face with my fingernails.

My face remained a neutral mask of indifference. My tone was reasonably civil. "Fortunately, though, I prevented you from drawing my first blood."

"Hah! Keep your precious virginity." Her breath was upon me. She stared fixedly at me. Her bottom lip curled up; her eyes narrowed. A hand was suddenly at the back of my head, pulling me to her. A tongue was on my lips, forcing my teeth to part, burrowing its way into my mouth. She pulled back abruptly, breaking off our kiss. "I wouldn't take it now if you paid me to, little girl."

She made a point of wiping her mouth on the back of her hand. She backed away, stepping into the now pouring rain.

Alone now, angry and hurt, I allowed the tears to come at last, confident that the rain would mask my weakness should Captain Wolff dare cast a glance back at me.

Chapter Seven

THE CAPTAIN

Elbows on my legs, I propped my head up with my left hand. I held my dagger in my right, loosely by the hilt. I swung it back and forth between my fingers, the tip repeatedly poking at my trousers.

I barely flinched beneath the pain. It was merely a distraction. A much needed one. I leaned back, my head resting against the wooden mast. I closed my eyes and ruffled my fingers through my hair.

I'd had the headache for hours now. No doubt brought on by too much thinking, rethinking, and thinking even more. About the present. And the future. And as loath as I was to admit it, the recent past. Specifically, the previous night upon the deck.

I hadn't meant to speak her name out loud. But I was dressing, just returning from a swim when I spied her upon the deck, hair blown by the increasing gale, cheeks flushed from the night air. She was without a doubt the most beautiful sight I'd ever seen. The first raindrops fell and she turned to leave. And her name sprung unbidden to my lips in an instant.

What had I thought—that all would be forgiven and she'd rush into my arms like a lost love? I should have known better. Then again, I should have known better than to do a lot of things I'd found myself doing. Bringing a woman on board ship in the first place was foolishly impulsive. I reasoned my motives away, justifying my actions with an act of piracy, the ransoming of a noble. Risking all for the tempting caresses that I couldn't seem to resist.

What did I expect her reaction to be when she discovered the truth? Had I even considered that before she asked me into her bed? I was careless, reckless with my secret. And even now, my own reaction to her blatant rejection was just as, if not even more so, reckless. Twice now, I was so plagued by my feelings that I had risked all by seeking solace in late night swims. Never mind the danger of the sea at night, the chance of not being able to reboard the ship; I also risked discovery by any crewmember who happened to be on deck.

It was reckless and irresponsible behavior that I could not afford to indulge in. Why then did I feel in my heart that even now I would risk all to capture the heart of Alexis DeVale? Yes, too much thinking.

And not nearly enough fun. I shifted my position, my legs now dangling in midair, feet swinging freely back and forth. Up here, I was free to be myself, safe from prying eyes. I straddled the beam, clutching the wood firmly between powerful thighs. Thirty feet high, I wouldn't want to fall from the mast.

I leaned over, looking at the deck below. From my perch, I could see the length of the ship in all directions. Vincent was at the ship's wheel, steering us ever northward, deeper into unfamiliar waters. Undoubtedly dangerous, but also unusually exciting.

Ivan was on deck, supervising the riggers. I watched as he guided the men using the wooden fids and metal marlinespikes to separate the strands of rope for splicing. A group of men worked at splicing ends of rope together, joining them so they would not unwind. Ten more men worked at patching damaged sails. Soon, the spliced ropes and hemp sails would be joined together to support the ship's rigging.

I heard a sound behind me, turned to find Sven, climbing the mast. He grabbed the main beam in a bear hug, awkwardly swung his torso around. He landed hard on the beam, straddling it. He settled in, throwing his boots across the same beam mine rested on. He dangled his legs over the beam, his feet hanging in midair.

"What are you doing up here?" I asked.

He shrugged. "Thought you might like some company."

"Did you stop to think that perhaps I climbed up the mast because I didn't want company?"

"You haven't wanted company a lot lately." Sven pointed at the deck below. "Ever since she came aboard."

I leaned over, looking down. Alexis and her mother stood near the bow of the ship. "Seems to me you've been keeping some company of your own with the fair Lady DeVale." It hadn't escaped my notice that they'd taken to sharing meals together in the galley.

"I share common interests with Alexis."

"You're on a first name basis?" I cocked an eyebrow.

He suddenly clutched the main mast, pulling himself to his feet. Balancing on the beam, he stared out past the bow.

I turned my head, looking at the horizon and then scrambled to my feet. I crouched, using my fingers and toes to clutch at the beam beneath me. I squinted against the bright sunlight.

"Ship ahoy!" Sven shouted, pointing.

The deck below us was a bustle of activity. The crew scrambled, tossing their equipment down, gathering their weapons. Vincent instantly turned the wheel on an intercept course.

I shielded my eyes, focused on the ship in the distance. It was small, barely noticeable on the horizon. The vessel didn't appear to be manned. The top was covered by some sort of material resembling a tarp. She sat low in the water, barely bobbing upon the waves.

"It's a longboat!" I shimmied down the mast at breakneck speed. "She's sinking."

I let go of the mast, letting myself drop the final few feet. I hit the deck hard, the pain shooting up through my feet and all the way past my knees. I shook off the pain, running toward the port side of *The Wolfsbane*.

Sven landed behind me and hit the deck running. He caught up with me at the port side railing. He thrust my boots at me; we yanked them on as we waited for our own longboat to be lowered by chains.

"There's no sign of crew. No other vessels on the horizon." I pointed at Sven and Ivan. "Strictly a salvage operation."

The two brothers jumped into the longboat, Ivan moving toward the stern, Sven taking up a position at the oars. I grabbed a chain, using it to pull myself up on the railing. I crouched down, preparing to launch myself into the descending longboat.

✝

    The boat was low in the water. Waves were already beginning to lap across her bow. The tarp—no, the ship's sail—that was covering the boat, hung in the water. The edges billowed out, releasing air trapped beneath, almost floating on the water. She would be dragged under soon.

    I motioned for Ivan to pull as near the longboat as possible. Still, I had to lean over, almost falling out of our own boat, to reach it. I grabbed onto the sidewalls with both hands, pulled with all my might. Sven did the same and soon we were alongside the other vessel.

    The water was weighing the material down. It took the three of us to budge it. The sail yanked free so suddenly that we were sent sprawling backwards into the bottom of our own longboat. I scrambled to my knees, anxiously peering over the side of the other boat.

    The water was quickly seeping in across the sides now. But not so fast as to hide the horror from my sight. Klaus was stripped to the waist. His throat had been sliced. And he'd been cut open from neck to belly, gutted like a fish. His left hand was chained, shackled through a bolt placed in the side of the ship, held fast with a padlock. He held a small wooden bowl in his right hand, containing his withered eyeballs and his tongue. I closed my eyes, fought to keep down the taste of bile in my mouth.

    I forced myself to look at the opposite end of the longboat, already fearing what I knew must surely be there. "Brandy."

    The boat jostled sharply beneath me, causing me almost to lose my balance. I instinctively reached out, my hand clutching at the side of the sinking boat. My action caused the boat to tilt farther, sending even more water rushing in. I let loose, willing the boat to right itself.

    Like her father, she too was chained to the side of the boat. Her murderers had obviously taken their time with her, torturing her savagely, bruises mottling her entire body. Her right eye was swollen shut, the left was barely open. Her necklace. It was gone. As I knew it would be. Only the angry bruises from where it was savagely pulled from her neck remained. Her dress was open, her breasts—

The gore was too much; I looked away.

"Captain." Sven's voice was at my ear. "We must go. She'll be under soon."

I cast a final glance at the sinking longboat. "Wait," I ordered.

Leaning over the sidewall, I stretched, reaching into the other boat. My hands worked at Brandy's clutching fingers, prying them open one by one, revealing a gold locket resting in her open palm.

The water was rising rapidly, the boat sinking faster now that the sea had made its way across the sidewalls. The water's own weight hurrying the tiny boat to the waiting depths below.

✝

I stalked the length of the deck, looking for Vincent. To my consternation, I had thus far been unable to locate him. Unusual, for not only was Vincent missing, but so was Rufus and the brothers Ivan and Sven.

The rest of the crew was up on deck, performing their customary duties. Was it a mere coincidence that only my most trusted staff was missing? I quickly looked from bow to stern as I continued my search.

The door to the galley was ajar. As I neared, I heard Vincent's voice. "Was there a marker on the boat, anything that would give us a clue as to their murderers' identity?"

I paused outside the door. He was speaking of Klaus and Brandy. I waited, needing to hear more.

"The boat was too far under by the time we reached it. We had no time to search her," Sven said.

"Surely, there was something on their bodies that may have been a sign?"

"There...was...nothing." It sounded as if he were forcing the words through gritted teeth, one syllable at a time.

"You said they were chained," Rufus jumped in. "Maybe the locks were familiar to you."

"There was nothing." Ivan said. "No clues. No signs. No markers."

"We must do something," Sven added. "We must take revenge for the captain."

"It's rather difficult to take revenge on an unseen enemy." Vincent's voice was amazingly calm.

"So we take revenge on anyone in our path," Ivan said.

I'd heard enough. I pushed open the door, stepping into the galley. I felt all eyes upon me. I returned their gazes one by one. "Leave me with Vincent."

I waited as they hastily retreated out the door, closing it behind them. When I was satisfied they were well out of earshot, I sat beside Vincent.

"What were they doing out here, so far from Port Royale?" he asked immediately. "More importantly, who brought them?"

I placed the gold locket on the table, pushing it toward him.

He glanced at me, then back at the locket. "Brandy?" he asked, already reaching for the chain.

I nodded. "Open it."

I watched as the slip of parchment fell from Vincent's grasp, landed on the table.

"My God, Kris. He knows." Vincent's face went ashen. "He knows our route. He knows who you are."

I looked up, meeting his gaze. "Damn Jackson's hide! When I took his ship, I should have also taken his life. Had I done so, Brandy and Klaus would be alive now."

†

I felt her presence before I saw her. I stood at the ship's wheel, gaze locked on the horizon as I guided *The Wolfsbane* upon her course.

"Kris."

I cocked my head, looked around. Her hair was blowing about her face. She pushed blonde locks away from her eyes, looking at me. Her expression was unfathomable. I turned my attention back to the sea.

She moved beside me, standing near, her hand brushing lightly against the silk of my tunic.

"I'm sorry for the loss of your..." There was a slight hesitation in her voice. "...friend."

"Friends," I corrected. "They were both my friends."

"Of course." She nodded. "I meant no disrespect."

"Of course not." I shook my head wearily. "My apologies, my lady. You were only offering your condolences. You meant no harm."

I felt her hand close upon mine. "Are you well?"

"No."

She squeezed my fingers reassuringly. "We seem to do that a lot lately."

I turned to look at her. "What?"

"Doing...saying things that we need to apologize for."

I nodded. "Have we always fought so much?"

She laughed. "Since the day you stormed into my life."

I raised an eyebrow. "I thought I was very charming when we first met."

"You kidnapped my mother, my sister, and me at swordpoint. Yet you believed yourself to be charming."

I stifled a laugh.

"You find embarrassing the navy, kidnapping women, holding them for ransom amusing?"

"No, I do not find that amusing at all, my lady." The corners of my lips twitched with barely restrained laughter. "However, what I find utterly charming is the way in which your eyes sparkle with passion."

Her smile abruptly fell, the sparkle in her eyes faded. "What happened?" she asked. "Why didn't you tell me before—before we...?"

I winced. She couldn't even complete that sentence. "I didn't realize it would be such a dreadful thing."

"You didn't realize?" She dropped my hand, turned away

from me. "You didn't think you being a woman would be dreadful?"

"I thought being a pirate was far worse."

"No." She looked at me, shook her head. "What is far worse is your deception."

My throat tightened, I averted my gaze. I felt her eyes still upon me, even as I stared out at the sea. The waves churned, much like my emotions. I pondered her words, focusing on the horizon, suddenly clear as to her meaning.

"Captain Wolff." Vincent approached, his presence dispelling the moment. "Lady DeVale."

"Vincent," she acknowledged. "If you'll pardon me." She excused herself.

I turned to watch as she walked away.

"I trust I did not interrupt?" Vincent asked as soon as she was gone.

"She was merely offering her condolences." I turned to my quartermaster. "Nothing more."

"I see."

I felt my irritation grow at his untimely arrival. "What is it you wish, Vincent?" I snapped.

"If it is convenient for the captain," he answered briskly, "I wish to speak with you about your actions as of late. I fear you've allowed your desire for revenge upon Brandy's and Klaus's killers to consume you."

I involuntarily stiffened.

"And I fear that your infatuation with the Lady DeVale has led you to distraction."

I arched an eyebrow. "To what do you refer, Vincent?"

"What of the ransom?" he asked. "When was the last time we spoke of it?"

"What of it?" I countered brusquely. "The plan stands as we arranged it in Port Royale. By the time we reach the Island of Bonaire, the money will be waiting upon a small plantation. We take the ransom, leave the women."

"I wanted to be certain we are in agreement."

"You would question me?" I asked. "And you, have you too been so distracted of late that you have neglected your duties?"

I caught the tightening of his jaw, the sharp glare of his eye. "I've already planned an escape route. We'll travel the north riff past St. Augustine and toward Trepassi Beach. There is a secluded cove near there, uncharted on most maps. No one, not even Captain Jackson, will be able to track us there."

Still irritated at Vincent's interruption and angered by his accusations, I turned my attention back to the sea. He stood beside me momentarily before accepting his apparent dismissal. I steadfastly refused to acknowledge him as he bid me good night before departing.

†

SHIP'S LOG – OCTOBER 18, 1703

We continue to travel north. Ships in these parts have been scarce. The men relish the prey, attacking with such ruthlessness that most surrender their cargo within moments of our initial boarding. Of course, some have refused to cooperate. There have been some instances of bloodshed. In most cases, however, we've managed to come away with little or no resistance.

I think my crew prefers it when our prey resists. It's much more satisfying than merely being given what we desire. It's more thrilling to take our treasures by force. Regardless, my basic order still stands. No harm will come to the women. Noble born or poor. None shall be harmed. None shall be touched.

I remain ever vigil, watchful of an attack by the British Navy. I know not where Captain Jackson is, but I am prepared for whatever may lie ahead.

†

Elbows on my desk, hands clasped together, I closed my eyes. When I opened them again, Alexis was there, seated in a nearby chair. She reached out, picking up the locket from my desk.

"Alexis—" I reached for it but she easily evaded my fingers.

She dangled the necklace from her own fingers. Turning the chain, she carefully studied the locket. "Brandy was your lover." A statement, not a question.

"Yes."

I waited, bracing myself for the verbal assault against Brandy.

"Were you in love with her?" she asked instead.

My answer came without hesitation. "No. But I loved her." There was a slight pause as I gave more thought to my answer. "She may not have been noble born nor afforded the same luxuries as come with a title. That doesn't mean she didn't possess qualities that made her worthy of being loved. She deserved so much more than her station allowed."

Alexis let loose the chain. The locket fell sharply onto the table. She reached out, clasping my hand in hers. "You are not to blame."

"But I am. I could have saved her." I opened the locket, revealing the parchment. I watched as Alexis read the words on the page...*I know. Captain Jackson.*

"What does this mean?"

"A warning. For me," I said. "They were tortured, chained, and set adrift to die upon the open sea."

"And Captain Jackson did this?" Her voice was incredulous. "For what purpose?"

"He was entrusted with the duty of seeing you safely to foreign shores to secure a valuable treaty for the Crown. I impugned his honor, insulting his integrity as a captain of Her Majesty's Navy when I brazenly attacked his vessel, stealing you away in the process."

Alexis fingered the parchment, staring at the scrawled words once again. She pensively bit her bottom lip, eyeing me speculatively. "And he's pursued you so relentlessly because of me," she guessed. "He tortured Brandy until she revealed your secret."

I nodded. "Can you imagine being Captain Jackson and not

only has your ship been invaded, your passengers abducted, your honor compromised, but then to discover that this roguish band of pirates was captained by a woman?"

Alexis's fear was reflected in her eyes. "Given the chance, Captain Jackson will kill you."

"Be assured, he won't stop at merely trying to kill me. His honor will demand so much more. I do not fear what Jackson may do to me. My only concern is what lengths he will go to in his desire to harm those I love." I hesitated before uttering the words that couldn't have possibly come forth from my mouth.

"We reach the Island of Bonaire tomorrow," I said. "There's a small plantation an hour's hike from a secluded cove. I've already seen to the arrangements. You'll be safe until you can board a ship bound for Spain."

"I see."

"Don't tell me you aren't eager to go." Her hesitation made my heart leap for joy. She didn't want to leave. But I couldn't have her stay.

"You presume to know what I feel, Captain Wolff?"

I caught the arch of the eyebrow, the coolness of her tone.

"It's for the best," I said. For her, I told myself. "I won't have what happened to Brandy happen to you, too."

"But—"

"This is not open for discussion." I was suddenly angry. At her. At myself. At having to do this. And her not making it any easier. "I've already told you that Jackson will not stop until he harms everything—everyone—I hold dear to me. Pack your bags. That's my order."

Anger flashed in her eyes. Her chin jutted forward. "I am not—nor shall I ever be—a member of your crew, Captain Wolff! And I am not subject to your orders."

"You will have your freedom."

She fell silent.

"Go now. Pack your things. We land tomorrow morning."

†

I stood on deck. Back rigid. Hands clasped behind my back. Chin jutting defiantly. Wind whipped across the bow, tossing my ponytail. My silk shirt ruffled, billowing beneath the breeze. I glanced skyward. Storm clouds were gathering. Dark, angry clouds covering the horizon. They blotted out the sun, covering my ship in shadows.

"We're in for a squall," Ivan said, following my gaze.

His own ebony hair whipped about his face. Annoyed, he brushed it back with his fingers. His brother was at his side, almost instantly, carrying hair ribbons.

Sven pulled Ivan's long hair back, running his fingers through the black mane. As he worked, his own blonde locks mingled with his brother's dark strands.

A sudden memory flashed in my mind. Of Alexis and me together. Standing on deck late at night, my arms wrapped about her waist. Of her leaning back into my arms as I whispered softly in her ear, my dark locks intertwining with her soft blonde locks. I grimaced. The memory was painfully bittersweet.

I looked away from the two brothers. Open sea was off the port side, water stretching as far as the eye could see. Sandy beach was on the starboard, a lush jungle stretching out beyond that. I wanted to pull up the anchor chain and bolt for the familiar safety of the sea.

"Are we all clear on the plan?" I asked.

My men nodded. "Sven and I will guide the Duchess and Lady DeVale to the plantation. Juan and Isabella will keep them safe until their rescuers come for them."

Ivan nodded. "Vincent and I will take a party west, approximately two and a half miles away from our current position. The ransom will be waiting for us by an old stone well."

"Where is Vincent?" I asked, looking around. No sign of my quartermaster.

"He wanted to check his charts once more," Griffen volunteered. "To make certain we've got the best route out of here."

I rolled my eyes. "He's checked those charts a hundred times already."

"Then once more won't matter any, now will it?" Darby asked. "I'd rather he check them a hundred more times if it'll get us a better route."

"Aye," I agreed. "Ivan, we'll rendezvous with you on the beach. Given the distances, we'll probably meet back here at about the same time."

"But your destination is half a mile closer each way," Ivan protested.

"True. But I have to drag the Duchess DeVale the whole long way. I'd rather go with your group and carry the ransom all the way to *The Wolfsbane* on my back."

A sharp elbow nudged me in the ribs. It was Vincent. I flicked him an annoyed look and was surprised. He wore his best boots and tailored trousers. A button-down white shirt was the final straw. I started to make a crack about expecting the queen when he pointed aft.

Duchess DeVale was gingerly picking her way down the steps leading from the aft deck. She was wearing a velvet blue dress, complete with matching hat and purse. The once tight dress was far too large on her now, but she wore it with as much dignity as she could muster. Her lace-up boots were polished to a high shine. For a trek through the jungle. I smiled at the thought of running the duchess through every puddle and marsh I could find.

I saw the Lady DeVale. And my smile instantly fell. My mouth dropped open, jaw threatening to hit the wooden deck. She was—beautiful. That was the only word that came to mind. The rest of my brain refused to function. Speechless, I stared. Unable to move, unable to look away.

She was a little thinner. But she'd adapted well to life at sea. Her burgundy dress reminded me of my precious 1492 wine. Exquisitely rich. I'd gladly give away every bottle I had to keep her, I knew. That dress clung in all the right places, accentuating her best curves.

Not that she had any bad ones. In all my life, I've never seen a more gorgeous woman. Her blonde locks swirled about her shoulders, blowing with the strong winds. She pushed the hair back from her face, revealing emerald green eyes, deeper than I recalled.

As they approached, my smile returned.

"Alexis." Her name tasted sweet on my lips. The way her own lips had tasted against mine countless times during the past few months.

She returned my smile. "My Captain."

My gut clenched. I fought back the urge to grab Alexis by the arm, drag her back to my cabin, and ravish her. I cursed myself. I had kidnapped Alexis DeVale with the intention of ransoming her. I had never planned on—

I shook the thought from my mind.

"We are quite ready, Captain Wolff." My smile fell. Her annoying mother was pulling on her white gloves, readying her parasol.

I nodded, giving the signal. The gangplank was lowered. Sven and Ivan led the way down the ramp. He was closely followed by Duchess DeVale. I fell in step behind her, beside Alexis. Griffen and Lars followed, carrying the trunks belonging to Alexis and her mother. Vincent trailed behind them. Darby, Felix, and Watkins followed behind, carrying loaded muskets.

The loose sand came across the toes of my boots as we marched. I remembered a day long before in which Alexis and I had strolled upon a similar beach. I glanced in her direction. From the smile she flashed at me, I'd say we shared the same memory.

All too soon, the sandy beach gave way to jungle. I held branches back, motioning for Alexis to proceed. As she passed, I let loose the branch, following her. Stepping through the dense underbrush, I cast a final glance at *The Wolfsbane*.

She was firmly anchored. The crew was still on deck, watching our departure. Rufus was on deck, too. I trusted him to keep things in line and ensure my ship was still there when I returned. I turned, forced myself to look away from *The Wolfsbane,* and continue to push through the underbrush.

Chapter Eight

THE LADY

The woods were suffocating, perhaps because the entire area was so overgrown, and we had to pick our way through the underbrush.

There was a path, a small, trodden-down footpath that we followed. It was so overgrown with greenery that it was difficult to traverse. The dirt was packed down, but there were large ruts worn into the ground. I soon discovered that walking was made much easier by stepping into one of those ruts and staying there, rather than attempting to step back out onto higher ground.

Another identical set of ruts ran the opposite side of the path, spaced an equal distance apart. Realization dawned on me. A wagon was run down to the secret cove at the beach, weighed down so heavily as to leave ruts in the path. Probably loaded with supplies for pirate crews. No doubt loaded only with pirate coin on the return trip.

"Will you be returning to the DeVale Estates or continuing on to the Spanish Main?"

Captain Wolff's question caught me off-guard. I stopped dead in my tracks, staring at her. Griffen and the others stepped around us, continuing on.

"I had not considered what would happen after—"

She nodded, clasped her hands behind her back. She continued to trail slowly behind our party, kicking loose pebbles with the toe of her boot as she walked. I strolled alongside her, matching her pace.

"I imagine you'll join your sister, Elizabeth."

I nodded. "Surely, she's returned to the DeVale Estates. She'd have no reason to continue on to the Spanish Main."

The captain cocked an eyebrow. "You sound as if you're hoping she's returned to England because you don't want to travel on to Puerto Cabello."

"Would you if you knew what fate awaited you there?"

"You mean if I were you?"

"Yes." I nodded. "If you were me."

She stopped, turned, stared at me. I felt a shiver run up my spine at her cool appraisal.

"If I were you, my lady," her voice was smooth, even. "I'd shoot the bastard."

Her delivery was flat, her tone serious. I had no doubt that she would just as soon kill my fiancée as look at him.

"Well." I forced a laugh, "I'm afraid that's one luxury that I don't have."

A frown. "You'll end up marrying him."

I nodded. "If the trade agreement is still set. After all these months, some other lucky noblewoman may be bound for marriage to Lord Rafael."

"If not marriage to Lord Rafael, someone else then."

I heard the disappointment in her voice. She quickly turned away and began walking down the makeshift trail again. I fell in step beside her. Looking down the trail, I could just make out our party in the distance. We'd soon be left behind. Still I couldn't bring myself to pick up the pace.

I reached out and rested my hand on her shoulder. She didn't break her stride and easily shrugged me off. My hand fell to her elbow, fingers straying down the sleeve of her silk shirt. My hand came to rest within hers.

She stopped so suddenly that I ran into her, jostling her. I took a step back, putting some distance between us. Her feelings were written on her face, changing from hurt to agitation in an instant. Thunder rumbled overhead, almost identically matching the timbre in her voice.

"You've been doing that a lot lately."

"What?" I asked, perplexed.

She cocked her head to one side, her eyes flicked between us. My gaze followed hers. Realization finally dawned on me as I caught sight of our intertwined fingers.

97

"Not that I mind the affection," she said, "but I find it odd considering you wish to have me hanged for doing to you what Jonathan had attempted."

"At least he didn't hide what he was—or what he wanted."

My words hung in the air between us. We barely moved, scarcely breathed. The only movement was the twitching of Captain Wolff's left eye.

"That's what I mean." Her tone was rough.

Once again, thunder rumbled overhead as she spoke. "You're still angry with me. So much so that you can't control it sometimes."

She was as tall as any man I'd ever seen. The cleft chin, the scar above her eyebrow, the posture and attitude. It was easy to imagine that Captain Wolff was quite a formidable man.

However—

The hair on her head, soft as any babe's, the barely noticeable bulge beneath her loose shirt, the slender fingers that I knew were beneath those leather gloves she always wore and the tender touch of her lips upon mine.

"I cannot believe I didn't realize you were a woman."

"And that's where the anger stems from."

Not a question. Rather, a statement.

How had this woman come to know me so well? Finally, conceding, I nodded.

"I can't change what I am."

"Neither can I."

Silence.

She resumed walking.

I fell in step beside her, careful not to touch her.

"Then why the sudden show of affection?"

"In truth, I'm unsure. I hate you for your deception. When I think of what you've done, I feel such rage. I look at you now and I see you for who you really are."

Her mouth dropped open.

I waved off her protests with a flick of my hand. "I see beneath your façade. Behind the mask you wear. You are not the ruthless pirate you portray yourself to be."

"Then you don't wish to leave me?"

"I enjoy your company." I was surprised at how easily the admission slipped from my lips. "At times, I forget the reasons why I can't be with you."

I reached out, fingertips barely brushing her cheek. "It would be so easy to give in to you."

Her hand went up, intending to capture my fingers within hers.

I forced myself to let my hand drop, evading her searching fingers.

She reached for me.

I took a deliberate step back. If she touched me now, I would not have the will to resist.

I forced the next words from my lips. "But you're a woman. And so am I."

"That doesn't mean—"

"And you're a pirate. And I'm a noble." I rushed ahead, not giving her a chance to continue her objections. "I should not be in any sort of a relationship with you."

"That didn't seem to be an issue when you were lying on top of me in my cabin."

"That was an…." The word lodged in my throat, not wanting to come out. "Indiscretion on my part. And I do apologize to you for that."

"You apologize?" She turned to me, anger flashing in her eyes.

"Let me finish. Please."

She bristled but grudgingly acquiesced.

The woods suddenly grew darker, and I glanced skyward. The clouds had moved in quickly, darkening the horizon. I heard another rumble of thunder. Lightning flashed across the sky.

"I know you feel an attraction toward me."

"And you feel it…"

I cast her a stern look. Her words trailed off.

"The only relationship I can offer you is one of friendship."

"Friendship." Her lip curled in disgust.

"You make it sound like something loathsome."

I felt the first raindrops upon my flesh.

Kris grabbed me by the arm, attempting to hurry me along.

I stood my ground, refusing to move until we resolved this. She finally relented and waited for me to finish.

"Do you find my friendship so undesirable?"

"No." Her eyes shifted from a light gray to dark, growing murky in color. "But you only offer your friendship because your freedom is at hand."

"That's not true."

"Isn't it? After today, you'll be well on your way back to England's shores. You'll be a proper lady at Her Majesty's courts again. And I'll still be a pirate upon the open sea, hunted by your Queen's Navy. And I shan't ever see you again."

"No matter where I am," I said, "I shall always be your friend. And," I relented, "you shall always hold a special place in my heart."

She said nothing. Merely stared.

"Would you not be my friend?"

Still she stared at me. When she spoke, I could scarcely believe my ears.

"I would be anything to you that you would allow me to be."

"Friends then," I said.

"Friends," she agreed.

She turned and trudged down the road. I hurried to catch up with her, my boots weighing me down. I lifted my legs higher, fighting to loosen some of the mud from my shoes. As I fell in beside her, she reached out, taking my hand in hers once again. Her grip was relaxed, easy. I sighed and settled into the pace.

"And by the way, my lady..." She leaned toward me, her words softly spoken in my ear. Her breath tickled as she whispered huskily, "...I never hid from you what I wanted, either."

†

The wood soon gave way to lush countryside. We caught up to our party resting in a clearing by an old oak tree. Ivan was sitting on a boulder, using his knife to scrape mud from the soles of his boots. His shirt was gone, his body bare from the waist up.

100

His muscles glistened, raindrops running down his bare torso. Griffen and Lars were nearby, checking their muskets, speaking softly. Mother sat on a tree stump, using Ivan's shirt as a cushion. She adjusted her parasol, attempting to block the rain from herself and our baggage. As we approached, Mother looked up. Her eyes narrowed to tiny slits. I quickly pulled my hand back, disentangling my fingers from Kris'. Her frown deepened. She didn't even attempt to disguise her disdain.

"I was beginning to worry, Alexis." She looked pointedly at Kris. "I thought perhaps you'd been kidnapped."

Kris forced a smile but let it fall quickly into a frown, then into a ruthless sneer. Without uttering a word, she turned her back on Mother. She stalked to where Ivan sat, talked with him animatedly. Ivan was nodding, listening intently to the captain. Ivan jumped to his feet, wiping his blade on his pants. The reddish mud left coarse stains across the thigh of his white trousers. I held my breath in anticipation as the large pirate approached.

He loomed above us, blade still in his hand as he addressed Mother. "Come, Duchess, the plantation is just over the next rise."

He aided Mother to her feet, motioned for his colleagues. They immediately slung their muskets over their shoulders and adjusted their shoulder straps. Griffen and Lars picked our luggage up. They struggled to get all the baggage situated between the two of them. Ivan led the way down the road, Mother at his side, Lars and Griffen close behind.

Captain Wolff strolled back to where I sat. "Shall we?"

I rose, taking her proffered arm. We stayed to the edge of the road, keeping well away from the muddy ruts.

†

Ivan was crouched low, hiding behind the ridge of the hill. We peered across the edge, staring at the plantation below us. Rows of sugarcane grew straight and tall, beginning at the bottom of the embankment and stretching to within twenty feet of the front door of a country farmhouse.

101

The farmhouse appeared to be in a state of disrepair. Paint was peeling off the shingles, leaving white flakes embedded in the mud. The screen door was hanging from its hinges, barely on the frame. I counted at least five broken windows. And the ones that weren't broken were so filthy they couldn't be seen through.

Captain Wolff knelt beside Ivan. "Report."

"I saw movement." Ivan pointed to his left. "Near the corner window."

Kris focused on the window. She moved subtly, muscles flexing as her body tensed.

"A blue gingham dress," Ivan clarified.

"Isabella." The captain visibly relaxed. "Any sign of Juan?"

"None."

"He's probably in another field with the workers." She half crouched, still watching the farmhouse below. "Juan owns several acres of land. No doubt he's tending his crops."

Kris motioned for Griffen and Lars. They left our baggage on the ground and swiftly moved to their captain's side. Lars and Griffen checked their weapons, pushing down the gunpowder in the barrels. As did Ivan and Captain Wolff with their own pistols. The captain cautiously set forth down the embankment, weapon at the ready, motioning for us to follow. Ivan fell in five paces behind Captain Wolff. Griffen nodded for us to go next.

"Our bags—"

"Carry them yourselves," Lars said.

"Well!" Mother stamped her foot on the ground, mud spattering halfway up her boots and onto the hem of her dress. "To think that you would actually expect—"

"Carry them yourselves or leave them here," Lars said. He towered taller than Mother, arms folded across his barrel chest. He looked every bit the ruthless pirate.

I grabbed one bag with my left hand, another with my right. Balancing my weight on one leg, I was able to tuck another beneath my left arm. For her part, Mother lifted one small overnight bag and proceeded to carry it down the embankment, acting for all the world as if she carried the weight of her entire estate within that bag. I followed as best I could, juggling my cargo from side to side to retain my balance. Lars and Griffen brought up the rear, covering our flank with their loaded muskets.

We crossed the sugarcane field cautiously. Weaving in and out of the rows, the tall stalks camouflaged our movements. I picked my way through the field, hurrying as best I could. Head lowered, I trudged ahead, pushing wet stalks out of my way as I went.

I looked up and was surprised to see Captain Wolff making her way toward me. I slowed as she approached. Mother passed me, continuing on. Likewise, Lars and Griffen made their way around us, rushing to join Ivan. Kris took two of the bags from my grasp.

"My apologies, my lady. It was never my intent for you to pack mule your own belongings."

"Thank you for your assistance, my Captain," I allowed a small smirk to appear on my lips. "A true gentleman to the end."

An arched brow was her only response. Wordlessly, she held several stalks aside, motioning for me to go ahead. By the time we neared the edge of the field, Mother was roughly twenty paces ahead of us, still feigning struggle with the bag she was carrying. Griffen and Lars flanked each side of her. Ten paces beyond my Mother, Ivan was at the front door of the farmhouse.

Ivan raised his hand, knuckles rapped on the wooden door-frame. He knocked louder, longer this time. He stepped back, watching the windows for movement.

"Hello!" he called out. "Isabella!"

Mother dropped her bag by the door and stood at the front stoop, hands on hips, foot tapping impatiently. The door abruptly opened. There was a flash of gunpowder, the barrel of a musket, the retort of gunfire. Ivan fell backwards from the force of the musket ball plowing into his chest. Griffen raised his musket, taking aim at the open doorway.

The first soldier through was cut down by the shot from Griffen's gun. A second soldier in a navy blue uniform managed to rush out the door, crouched down by my Mother, who was huddled in a protective ball at the edge of the doorframe. He shielded her with his body as he rushed her inside the farmhouse. The heavy wooden door slammed shut behind them.

Griffen and Lars, caught in the open, retreated toward the

field. A volley of gunfire erupted from the open windows. Griffen, caught in a hail of musket balls, fell to the ground. Blood poured from his mouth, and he fought to keep from choking on the crimson tide as it rushed forth. It poured down his chin and neck, soaking his shirt, mixing with the rain and mud.

"Go!" the captain shouted, pulling Lars into the sugarcane field with us. "Back to *The Wolfsbane!*"

Lars yelled above the repeated gunfire. "What about Griffen?"

"Go," she yelled at Lars again. "On my order."

Captain Wolff stepped from the cover of the stalks, raising her pistol. Firing, she made her way to Griffen. One of the soldiers streaming through the front door of the farmhouse fell. Almost immediately, an answering English shot struck the captain, ripping through her shoulder, her blood coating the sugarcane she landed on.

I rushed to her side, kneeling beside her. All the color had drained from her face. She turned to stare at me, already struggling to reload her weapon and make her way to her feet.

"These are your rescuers, my lady, come to save you." She loaded her pistol, fired hurriedly. Her aim was true; another soldier fell. "Run to the safety of the farmhouse!"

"I cannot!"

Her foot slipped on the uneven ground, causing her to stumble. She caught her balance and righted herself. "You have to go. Now."

"If I leave, they'll cut you down."

"If you stay," she shouted, "you'll die with me."

The decision was mine. If I left, she would be a clear target. If I stayed, I might be shot in the crossfire. My eyes locked with hers, staring, transfixed. Which was louder, the repeated sound of gunfire or the beating of my own heart, I could not say.

With my next breath, I realized there could only be one decision. I reached out, grabbing her sleeve above her wrist, and tugged. I yanked hard, dragging her deeper into the field. The stalks towered above us, camouflaging our movements as we raced back the way we came.

I heard shouting, cursing from a distance, and the ringing of musket balls zipping past. I stumbled often, falling into the mud, tearing my dress. Still, I went on, half-carrying, half-dragging the profusely bleeding Captain Wolff.

Her blood flowed steadily, soaking her shirt and running down her arm, covering her hand and mixing with the mud that covered us both. It freely soaked into the fabric of my dress until I could no longer discern which of us was shot.

I forced my way out of the sugarcane field, struggling up the embankment, sliding in the mud with each step. A mixture of perspiration and rain poured down my face, stinging my eyes. As we crested the hill, I paused and wiped my brow with the sleeve of my dress.

I knelt and peered over the ridge as I had seen Ivan do earlier. The farmhouse was a bustle of activity. Captain Jackson stood in the center of the front yard, shouting orders at his men. Mother stood beside him, looking like a suitably grateful damsel in distress. Captain Jackson's men split into two groups. The first forming a secure perimeter around the farmhouse. The second organized a party, hacking their way through the sugarcane. I pressed myself to continue on. Kris' weight bore down upon me as I helped her to her feet.

We rapidly descended, running down the embankment. Kris grunted, leaning a little harder on me, trying to keep pace. I lost my footing; my left knee hit hard. We stumbled, sliding on wet grass, plummeting all the way down the ridge.

We rolled to a stop at the foot of the grassy knoll. We lay there, panting, Kris pinned beneath me. Normally, she would have used the opportunity to attempt to embarrass me. This time, however, she made no effort. She groaned, and I realized the palm of my hand was pressing against her wound.

I quickly pulled myself off her, painfully dragging myself to my feet. I pulled her by her belt, lifting her off the wet ground. She struggled, attempted to rise. I got her arm draped across my shoulder, distributing her weight.

Breath ragged, coming in short gasps, I inhaled deeply, attempting to return my breathing to normal. I turned my head, looking back. No sign of pursuit. I strained my ears, listening. Nothing save the sounds of birds chirping in the trees ahead.

I stopped, carefully lowering Kris to the ground. I propped her back against a familiar tree stump and collapsed onto the ground beside her. Mud squished beneath me as my posterior hit the ground hard.

"You'll get your dress dirty."

Her voice was low, her words cracked out slowly. Her hair was slicked down from the rain. Her ponytail hung across one shoulder, water pouring from it. Blood seeped from her wound. Her arm hung limply, fingers dangling between her open legs. She stared at me through heavy-lidded eyes.

"We have to be going soon." I reached out one hand, tenderly stroking her cheek. Her head lolled to one side. I cupped her chin, forcing her to look at me. She squinted through bleary eyes.

"You go on ahead," she mumbled. "I want to stay here and rest a bit." Her eyes glazed over.

"No, you're coming with me," I insisted. I pulled on her good arm, attempting to get her to her feet.

"No." She leaned back away from me. Her eyes focused on me, staring. "It hurts."

"I know." She sounded like a child, tired and hurting, and I had no doubt that she was half out of her mind from the pain. I bit my bottom lip, tempted to let her rest.

The fluttering of wings caught my attention. I checked the horizon to see birds breaking cover, flying from the treetops. "Come on," I urged, firmly pulling on her arm. "They'll be here soon."

She didn't resist anymore. Perhaps because she sensed the panic in my voice. Perhaps because she dimly recognized our danger. The English troops were closing on our position. The birds' flight signaled their imminent approach.

I hurried us down the now muddy makeshift road, almost dragging the captain with me. The thought suddenly occurred to me that I was glad she was a woman, for surely, I would have never been able to support her weight had she been the formidable man she appeared to be. Mud caked our shoes, weighing them down. Each step was a struggle, sapping our precious energy. I ushered us to the edge of the road, hoping to move us faster through the slick grass.

The sound of a drum beat a tempo in the recesses of my mind. Our pursuers. I had often witnessed them upon the deck of *The Scorpion*, practicing military maneuvers. Marching to the beat of a solitary drum. Captain Jackson had once told me that the drum served a purpose two-fold. Not only did it keep his men in step during marches, but the incessant pounding also disturbed his enemies, causing them to become preoccupied with the sound, leading them to distraction.

On the deck of *The Scorpion*, the drum hadn't bothered me. But now, it pounded into my skull. It sounded like a loud heartbeat, coming closer and closer. Never relenting. I cast a furtive glance over my shoulder. The soldiers had crested the embankment. They were marching in true English fashion, crisp and efficient. The tempo remained the same, regulating them to a standard march. They appeared to be in no hurry.

Why should they be? Their commander shot my captain. And I was a solitary woman, attempting to drag a half-dead pirate across miles of rough terrain. No doubt, they would overtake us before we could reach the safety of the beach.

I tore my gaze away from our pursuers and focused on Kris. She was going limp now. The weight of her body as she leaned more heavily upon me further slowed my pace. I lifted with my hip, attempting to shift her into a better position. Better, but she was still dead weight upon me. Each step became an ordeal.

Still, I kept on, forcing myself to take each painful step, to increase my pace. Behind me, I heard the sounds of our pursuers closing. That insufferable drum grew louder and louder with each heartbeat. I ran off the path, darting into the underbrush. Branches tore at my dress, scratching my face and hands. Brambles tangled in my hair.

I stopped, leaning against a solid oak tree. The bark scratched at my flesh as I rested my cheek against the tree. Perspiring, panting, I attempted to control my erratic breathing. My whole body leaned into the tree, searching for support.

I opened my eyes, focusing on Kris. She was drenched with sweat, mud, and blood. Her skin was clammy to the touch. She barely responded to my fingers caressing her cheek, stroking

107

through her matted hair. Her body went limp, sliding down, the bark scraping at her back until she came to rest at the base of the tree.

"Kris."

No response.

I frantically stroked my fingers through her hair, pushing the clinging mass from her face. "Kris."

Her eyelids barely fluttered. I gained the briefest glimpse of her eyes. The pupils were dilated, her eyes glazed over. Then I saw nothing but the whites of her eyes as her pupils rolled back. Her eyelids blinked closed.

The blood was still flowing. Her shirt was soaked, clinging to her flesh. The stain ran all the way down her torso, beneath her breast, stretching along her ribcage. The sleeve was soaked as well, the blood running off the cuff. With shaking fingers, I removed her glove. Blood fairly poured forth, soaking my hands up to my wrists.

I leaned across the prone body of the captain, fingers stretching. I tore desperately at the thick patches of moss that had fallen from the oak tree. Shaking the clump I had gathered, knocking as much dirt off as I could, I worked it down to a more manageable size.

Fingers shaking, I fumbled at the top lacings of Kris' shirt. My breath caught, my heart pounded as her flesh was exposed. My eyes glued themselves to her tender skin, refusing to look away.

Trembling worse now, my fingers reached out of their own accord, touching her. Her skin was wet with perspiration, and my fingers easily slid along her flesh. My nails lightly bit into her fevered flesh and she moaned, eyelids fluttering.

Holding the collar of her shirt back with my right hand, my left clutched at the moss. Taking a deep breath, I thrust my hand in all the way past my wrist. My fingers glided across her sticky flesh, searching for the wound.

I patted the moss into place, pressing my hand against her flesh, applying pressure. The moss stuck, Kris' blood holding the makeshift dressing in place. I patted the edges, making sure the moss caught firmly.

I heard shouting, the beating of brush signaling the soldiers' presence entering the woods. I gathered Kris up, draping her across my shoulders, arms and legs dangling. Desperately clutching at Captain Wolff, I hurried deeper into the underbrush.

I stumbled from tree to tree, legs dragging, feet catching on hidden roots. My arms grew weak and my shoulders ached from the captain's weight. My heart pounded rapidly in my eardrums. I forced myself not to look back.

They were closing fast. There were angry curses behind me. Leaves and twigs crunching beneath heavy boots, the rustling of bushes being beaten with muskets. I suddenly felt like a fox being hunted by English noblemen, frightened and wounded, and running out of coverage.

I fell out of the underbrush, landing upon wet sand. The beach. The captain had slipped from my grasp, landing several feet away. She lay face down, making no effort to rise. Summoning the last of my reserve, I found the strength to make it to my feet. Both hands on her waist, clutching at her belt, I struggled to pull her from the sand.

Barely standing, breathing heavily, I stood there on the beach, clinging to my captain. I adjusted her weight, once again carrying most of her upper body across my back and shoulders. Head swimming, I willed myself to take step after painful step across the sand. My grip on her belt tightened, dragging her along. She was almost unconscious, barely helping, her feet dragging long lines in the sand. I watched my own feet as I carried us across the beach.

Around me, I heard more gunfire. A bolt of fear shot through me, shaking me from my stupor. My head jerked up in alarm. Through heavy-lidded eyes, I saw the crew of *The Wolfsbane* mounting a defense, staving off advancing English troops. I struggled on, carrying my burden.

Someone was at my side, taking the captain from me. I felt hands upon me, lifting me. Lids heavy, eyes blurred, I barely realized I was being carried up a gangplank. I breathed a sigh of relief when I was allowed to stand upon the deck.

And promptly fainted.

†

Silk sheets slid against my skin, slipping from my undulating hips. My head was thrown back, eyes closed, mouth open, inarticulate sounds coming from straining throat muscles. A breeze blew across my skin, chilling my fevered flesh. My firm breasts jutted forward, the nipples painfully erect.

A hand cupped my right breast. Teasing fingers flicked at my hardened nipple. My back arched, straining to reach those fingers as they threatened to pull away.

"Kris."

Her name rumbled in my throat. I closed my eyes, straining to reach those fingers. I didn't care if I had to plead. Cry. Beg. I needed the touch of those fingers.

"Please," I attempted to coax her. "Kris, please."

†

Hands gripped my upper arms, gently shaking. A voice was calling my name. I blinked my eyes, shook the cobwebs from my head. I blinked again and focused on Vincent.

He was close. So close I could see every worry line on his face. He was weary, looking every bit his fifty-odd years. I vaguely realized he was calling my name again. I mumbled some sort of reply to his repeated questions. I looked around, taking in my surroundings. The room was not my own. Still it was familiar.

A large oak desk stood near the left wall. Directly across from the desk was an open window. My gaze settled on the hardwood floor, worn from repeated pacing. Three wide steps led to a private bedchamber; a curtain was pulled across, hiding that chamber from view.

"...had to borrow a cot from the crews' quarters to house you both in the captain's cabin."

"The captain's cabin," I numbly repeated, focusing all my

110

attention on Vincent.

"Of course." Vincent nodded. "I could hardly tend to both of you with you housed at one end of the ship and him at the other."

"The captain—"

"Hasn't awoken yet." He nodded toward the drawn curtain. "Would you care to see him?"

I rose from the bed, the room tilting at an odd angle. Vincent's hand clutched at my upper arm. I fought against waves of vertigo. Willing my breathing to slow, I attempted to calm myself. Beads of perspiration broke out on my upper lip. The room finally stopped spinning. I looked down, where Vincent's hand still gripped my bare flesh.

"Vincent," I said, looking down the length of my body. To my embarrassment, I felt his eyes follow mine. "Where are my clothes?" I clutched the sheet to my body, attempting to cover myself.

The quartermaster blushed a deep crimson and looked away. He attempted to hide his embarrassment with a discreet cough. "Your own clothes were ruined. Torn and bloodied. So much so they couldn't be mended."

"You threw them out." My face went pale.

"Had to. Would have been unsanitary to keep them."

My stomach churned. I swallowed quickly. "May I have another dress then?"

"I'm afraid all of your belongings were left at the plantation, Lady DeVale."

"Then perhaps something from the ship's hold?"

He coughed again. "Actually, my lady, Captain Wolff instructed that some of the cargo be put off the ship. He'd planned to have the extra clothing delivered to the plantation after you were settled in." Vincent picked at imaginary lint on the leg of his trousers. "I'm afraid it was all left on Bonaire as we made our escape."

I clutched at the sheet, attempting to cover my exposed backside as I padded across the room to the open window. The air blew a breeze through my uncombed hair and chilled my bare shoulders.

I closed my eyes and forced myself to count to ten. I opened my eyes, turned around. Vincent was now seated upon the bed.

"So now I have no clothes?"

He kept his head bowed and refused to look upon me. "No, my lady."

I let out a deep breath. "What am I supposed to do? Run around ship with nothing more than a sheet to cover myself?"

Vincent barely raised his head and glanced in my general direction. His gentlemanly gaze landed somewhere past my shoulder.

"If I may be so bold, Lady DeVale—"

"You've already been bold enough to remove all my clothing!" I did not intend to raise my voice. But the situation was ludicrous. And he was being so insufferably English about the whole ordeal. "Speak your mind, Vincent."

"Perhaps some of the captain's clothes?"

I raised my eyebrows in utter dismay. "Dress like a man?"

"With a few alterations, of course."

He was already upon me, looking at me from head to toe. I closed my eyes and inhaled deeply, willing myself to remain calm. After all, I really had no choice but to endure this torture.

†

I silently approached the large bed. I need not have moved so stealthily. She had yet to regain consciousness. Still I stole into her private chamber like a thief in the night.

She lay on her back, a sheet that matched my own covering her body. Her breathing was shallow and a sheen of sweat clung to her brow. Her damp ponytail was draped across her shoulder, clinging to her wet skin. Shaking fingers moved to the top of the sheet. My fingertips brushed her fevered flesh at the linen's hem. Trembling, I pulled the fabric away, baring her upper body.

Common decency prevented me from moving the sheet farther down her body. No matter how curious I was to see more. I turned loose the sheet, letting it fall. It landed so that it was covering the uppermost portion of her breasts, hinting at wonders to

112

be found beneath the teasing edges of the fabric.

A bandage was securely fastened around her left shoulder, stretching beneath her armpit, fastened in place by sewing pins. Blood caked the bandage, dried dark upon the white cloth. The flesh surrounding the bandage was mottled, discolored. The bruises were dark, almost black. I'd never seen such ugly bruises. The skin was taut, drawn tight by the bandage.

Mesmerized, my fingers reached out of their own accord. My fingertips grazed her flesh with the lightest of touches. Her lips parted, a raspy groan escaping. Her body twitched beneath my touch.

I jerked my fingers away as if they were scalded. Indeed, her flesh was hot to the touch. No doubt infection had brought on a fever. With the removal of my hand, she seemed to relax again.

"I've applied salve to stave off the infection..." I jumped as Vincent's voice sounded near my right ear. "...but she's such a fitful patient, I fear she keeps reopening the stitches."

My gaze fell once again on the bloodstained bandage. "She's shown no signs of awakening?"

"Only for scant moments at a time. Even then, her gaze is unfocused."

He knelt beside the bed. Reaching out, Vincent brushed her matted hair back from her forehead. "I doubt if she even realizes where she is."

We both sat in morose silence. His fingers continued to stroke through Kris' hair. His other hand had found hers, lying limply on the mattress. He gripped it within his own large calloused hand, dwarfing hers by comparison. He watched her face expectantly, waiting for some encouragement, some small movement.

I was suddenly caught by the memory of my own father kneeling beside my smallest sister's bed when she was struck down by a mysterious malady. I'd never seen a sight so sad as my father kneeling there, waiting for his daughter to die.

I ripped my gaze from the scene and stared at the foot of the bed. A stack of freshly folded clothes lay on the sheet. Wordlessly, I moved away, retrieving the clothing from the end of the bed.

I retreated to the other room, just beyond the drapery separating the captain's quarters. Shedding my sheet, I began to dress. Glancing back, I could see the silhouette of Vincent, still kneeling beside the bed.

"How long have you cared for her?" I asked as I dressed.

"For all her life" was the response from the next room.

My breath caught in my throat. Could he be? I paused, my right arm halfway through the tunic sleeve. I peered around the edge of the drapery. "Vincent?"

He looked up at the sound of his name, his weary eyes meeting mine.

"Are you Kris' father?"

His eyes went wide with shock. Laugh lines appeared at the edges, a twinkling sparked new life in his tired gaze. "Hardly. Though, I've loved her better than her own."

I gave a noncommittal grunt hoping it would be enough to encourage him to continue. It was.

"Her mother was an English woman, born of nobility. She was a rueful, willful woman by nature. Sarah Francis Jean. Too many names for one so young. Too much burden and responsibility placed upon her in her youth.

"I suppose that's why she behaved as reckless as she did. Sneaking into town, hanging about the local tavern. Cavorting with sailors and landowners alike. Carousing unto all hours of the night."

I slipped my legs into the trousers and pulled them up. "Surely, there were consequences when her family discovered her actions?"

"Oh, my, yes." I heard the sound of splashing water.

Vincent's silhouette was dampening a cloth, brushing it across Kris' fevered flesh. He lightly dabbed at her forehead with the cool cloth. "Sarah was never one for discretion. She was caught with the groomer in the stables by her own father."

I gasped at the image. "She must have been humiliated."

"And rightly so."

"What happened to them?"

"The groomer was hanged. Sarah was exiled, sent to live in a small cottage that her family owned upon the coast. I was sent along as her only servant. It was my duty to serve and protect her. And try to redeem her in the eyes of her lord and her kinsmen."

I pulled the tunic over the top of the trousers and secured the belt in place.

"Unbeknownst to her family, Sarah had also been engaged in relations with a rather unsavory seaman. Upon hearing of his lover's plight, he tracked her to the cottage.

"He raided the cottage in the dark of night, laying claim to Sarah and all she owned. Including me as her servant. We were transported upon his ship, where I discovered her latest dalliance was a ruthless pirate captain.

"We were well away to sea and settled into yet another new adventure for young Lady Sarah. That's when her pregnancy became readily apparent. The pirate assumed it was his creation. And Sarah didn't tell him it could be the child of another. Given the pirate's violent temper, I'm pleased she never spoke of the possibility. I'm sure both our lives would be forfeit had he known."

"Surely, when he discovered Sarah's pregnancy, he returned to land."

"In a sense." Vincent's silhouette moved from his kneeling position and sat on the edge of the bed. He appeared to be fidgeting with the captain's bandage. "He took us to a hidden cove where his secret lair was. Don't misunderstand. He took very good care of Sarah. Provided her with whatever she desired. He spent many hours comforting Sarah, seeing to her every need. He often lay upon her bed, holding her, telling her how she would be blessed for providing him with a great heir. A son to his father's pirate kingdom, he would rule like royalty."

My heart fell into my stomach. "But Sarah didn't have a boy."

"No." He fell quiet. For so long that I thought he wouldn't finish the tale.

Though fully dressed, I didn't return to the bedchamber. I waited on the steps, hand paused on the drape, the material crumpled in my grasp. I held my breath and willed him to continue.

115

"Fortunately, he wasn't present when Sarah went into labor. When she realized she'd had a girl, she rightfully feared for the child's life. She devised the plan that Kristen—whom she insisted we call Kris—be raised as a boy. That her true gender be kept secret from her father."

"That must have been quite a formidable task." I finally pulled back the drapery and stepped into the room.

Vincent glanced up, nodded his approval. "Like her mother, Kristen has always been…willful. She was quite a handful to keep out of trouble. And out of her father's watchful sight. The first five years were complicated, even with Sarah's help.

"Then when Sarah fell ill, her pirate captain spent even more time at the cove. Despite his other faults, he did dearly love Sarah. He swore to care for Kris till his dying day. Sarah extracted a similar promise from me upon her deathbed. With the inclusion of protecting Kristen's identity from her father, of course."

"Where is her father?"

"He was lost in a battle at sea. With his dying breath, he willed command of *The Wolfsbane* upon Kris. We've changed crews many times since that time, building a family loyal to their captain. But not one of them has ever been privy to the truth about Captain Wolff."

I looked at Kris—Kristen—lying upon the bed. Here now, she definitely resembled a woman. How much more feminine would she look with her hair loosened, its mass draped across both her shoulders? But I knew from memory that she passed for a very formidable man. More often than not, I had thought she was a virile lad.

"There," he said, "Look at how you've fared."

He grabbed me by the arm, steering me toward a full-length mirror. He stood behind me, hands resting on both shoulders as I studied my reflection.

The boots were standard, soft leather. The leggings, a butter caramel color, were tucked snugly into the cuffs of my boots. The tunic was bright green, almost perfectly matching the color of my eyes. Long, blonde locks draped around the shoulders of my tunic. The front strings at the neck of the tunic were loose, opening the material from the neckline, exposing the thin cleft of flesh between my ample bosom.

"I doubt if I'd been Sarah's offspring, you would have been able to pass me off as her son."

"Hardly." To my delight, his reflection was blushing. I laughed at his obvious discomfort.

"I'm glad you find my predicament amusing."

I wiped tears from the corner of my eyes. "Oh, but I do."

"Good. Because it's your predicament now, too."

My laughter died. My smile fell. "Pardon?"

"You heard me." His face was set in stone, his tone severe. "I can't navigate our course, tend to the captain, and perform her duties, as well."

I cast a wary glance at Vincent. "Meaning?"

"Meaning that since you share in our captain's secret, the responsibility falls to you to help protect that sacred trust."

I couldn't believe my ears. "What do you expect of me?"

"You will assist in the care of the injured captain. Under no circumstances must any member of the crew save ourselves see her in this condition. If they do, they'll instantly know of our deception. And all our lives may very well be forfeit."

I looked at Kris lying on her bed. Helpless against enemy attacks, unable to defend herself. I heard the rustling of the drapery and followed Vincent to the other room.

"So you want me to make sure no one comes in to the captain's cabin." It sounded a fairly simple task.

"In addition to assisting with the navigational duties."

My mouth opened in protest.

He ignored me, trampled right over my attempts at speech. "It seems the English and Spanish have decided to assail us in attempts to rescue you. Enemy ships have been pursuing us ever since leaving the Island of Bonaire. Perhaps you can help to elude our pursuers."

He gathered several logbooks and charts up off the desk and thrust them into my arms. "Study these. Learn them. I'll expect to see you upon the deck tonight."

"Surely, there's someone more suitable to the task—"

"These are bloodthirsty pirates, my lady, not educated school lads. Most of the crew can barely read, let alone guide a

117

ship. The only other two capable of navigational skills are the captain and the second."

"Kris is incapacitated—"

"And Ivan is dead. The tasks fall to you, my lady."

I was still mouthing feeble protests when he crossed the room, gathering his long jacket from a rack near the door. He donned his jacket and gave me a quick nod as he ducked outside.

"Tonight," he repeated, closing the door behind him.

He left me standing open-mouthed in the middle of the cabin, arms laden down with charts and books. One of the books slipped and fell. I shifted my weight, juggling the stack, attempting to catch the volume. It hit the floor. And to my consternation, so did the rest. I dropped to the floor, sitting upon the hard wood, surrounded by a mess of books and charts. Groaning, I lay back on the pile, covering my face with my hands.

†

The ship glided along the surface, slicing the black water beneath us. I pointed the bow straight ahead, guiding us along our northerly course. The helm responded easily to my commands, the wheel spinning smoothly beneath my palms.

To the left of the ship was nothing save open sea. To the right, a wall of coral and barrier reefs. Some sections jutted as high as three feet above the surface. These were magnificent in stature. Algae and kelp grew fast on these formations. Oyster shells embedded in the reefs reflected moonlight in sparkling prisms.

Beautiful.

Devastatingly dangerous.

For just below the surface ran rows of rock and shoal. Like the ones that jutted above the surface, these also grew to staggering proportions. However, they hadn't broken the surface yet, making them next to impossible to discern from the bow of the ship. One wrong calculation and the hull of *The Wolfsbane* could be ripped open from stem to stern by a jagged protrusion.

That was what we were hoping for when Vincent and I

planned this course. If our pursuers were so determined to risk following us in the darkness in unfamiliar waters, perhaps we could use their own eagerness against them. If they anchored or cut speed, they may lose their quarry. If they pursued at full sail, they may err off course. One wrong adjustment and their ships would flounder upon the barrier reefs.

A movement to my left caught my attention. A pewter plate was placed upon a barrel, a bottle beside it. I smiled in the darkness.

"Thank you."

"Ye missed dinner again," Rufus grumbled beside me.

I didn't take my hands from the ship's wheel or my eyes from the sea. "I didn't think you delivered special orders any longer."

"Aye, well." He poured from the bottle into a goblet, passing it to me. "Ye duties keep ye from joining us for sup. The least I can do is bring ye a plate now and then."

Without comment, I took the goblet from Rufus. I brought it to my lips, sipping. Water. Good. I couldn't afford a clouded head for that night's mission.

"Ye've become quite adept at steering."

Was that a compliment? "You sound like Vincent."

"Well, we've been talking."

"About?"

"Ye."

"Oh?"

"Aye." He shrugged. "He seems to think ye show great promise."

I felt a blush growing. "Vincent's a great teacher."

"Still to leave ye to guide the ship by yerself after only four days."

I arched an eyebrow.

"'Tis not natural."

"As you said, I've become very adept." My tone was sharp. "Perhaps I have a natural talent."

He nodded absently and produced a small flask from his apron pocket. "That could be, Lady DeVale." He unscrewed the flask and took a deep swig. "Could be that I was mistaken about

119

ye."

My grip tightened on the wheel. My jaw clenched as I fought the urge to retort.

"I accused ye of being a siren, luring the captain to his doom. Yet when ye had the chance to throw him to the hunters, ye helped The Wolff to escape."

"Perhaps I did not care for the hunt."

"Or mayhaps ye care for the captain more than I've believed."

The barrier reefs now flanked the left and right sides of the ship. I forced myself to concentrate on guiding *The Wolfsbane* through the narrow strait. A slip now could prove fatal.

"Do you have a point to make, Rufus?" My words were clipped, my agitation obvious.

He took another swig from his bottle. The smell of whiskey permeated the air as he spoke again. "I was just noticing that ye had the perfect chance to escape—and for whatever reason, ye failed to take it."

I jerked the wheel sharply to the left, then right. The sudden jostling caught Rufus off-guard, knocking him off-balance. He stumbled and reached out for the rail, fought to keep his footing.

A sly smile stole across my face. "Perhaps you misjudged me, Rufus."

"Mayhaps." His voice was light, but a frown marred his features. His eyes narrowed to tiny slits. "Or mayhaps I was dead on."

I cocked my head. Arched an eyebrow. That was my only response.

"We've lost men since ye've come onboard. Countless. Including Jon, Griffen, Ivan. Our very captain has fallen before yer spell. And now, suddenly Vincent has put trust enough in ye to guide our ship through dangerous waters."

"Are you more afraid of dangerous waters," I asked, "or dangerous me?"

Whiskey spewed from his mouth as he choked on the latest swig. "Ye are but a slip of a girl."

A smile played across my lips. I leaned into the wheel, edging as close to Rufus as possible. "If you believe me a siren, why bring my dinner every night?"

"Mayhaps I've poisoned yer meal."

"You've picked off my plate, just as you have for the past two nights." I shook my head. "You think I've bewitched the entire crew, yet you've made no move to harm me."

"Aye, 'tis true enough." He paced to the bow and leaned over the railing, spitting into the sea. "Curse me for a fool. I've fallen to yer spell, as well. I see ye for what ye are, but I'm still drawn to ye. Like a moth to a flame."

Rufus made the sign of the cross in the air. "Be gone, ye foul temptress."

I couldn't help laughing.

He threw his whiskey flask over the side, swearing off drinking if only the good Lord would save him from my evil clutches. Rufus backed away from me, across the deck, toward his galley, making the sign of the cross all the way.

I chuckled at his superstitious beliefs. To think that I was the source of all evil aboard ship. He was so sure I was one of the legendary Sirens come to life. Yet, he left me alone on deck, a siren to guide *The Wolfsbane* through barrier-laden waters on the most critical leg of our journey.

Chapter Nine

THE CAPTAIN

Darkness covered me like a shroud. Breathing was difficult, as if my chest was being crushed. My arms and legs were like lead, weighing me down. The only sound I heard was roaring thunder.

In my lifetime, I've come close to drowning once. That was the sensation I had then, exactly what I was feeling now—struggling, fighting, even as my strength ebbed away. Not knowing which way was up but still fighting blindly for the surface.

I broke the surface, gasping aloud, taking in huge gulps of air. My eyes opened but the painful searing of sunlight forced them closed again. The cool waves lapped at my neck, my face.

I blinked my eyes open again, slowly this time. A silhouette blurred before me. I squinted. A mass of blonde hair. Deep green eyes. The most beautiful mermaid I'd ever seen.

I reached out, stretching to touch her face with my fingertips. The effort was too much. I fell onto my right side, my arm falling limply at my side. My eyes rolled, barely catching sight of fine, trousered legs.

"Where yer tail?" I slurred.

I passed out.

When next I woke, things were much clearer. I blinked, my surroundings coming into focus. I was in my own cabin, on my own bed. The early morning sun streamed in through an open window.

I moved to sit up. A sudden wave of dizziness overtook me. I lay there on my back, heart beating wildly, drenched in sweat. I struggled to sit upright again.

Hands were on my bare shoulders, pushing me down. "Easy there, lie back."

I relaxed, allowing her to guide me back down.

The sunlight filtering in the window made me squint. The light shone off her blonde locks, forming a halo around her head. Not my mermaid from the night before, but a welcome sight nevertheless.

She gingerly wiped at my brow with a damp cloth. I took a deep breath, forcing myself to relax beneath her ministrations. I smiled wanly.

"Good morning, Alexis." My mouth was dry...and my voice croaked.

"Good afternoon," she corrected.

"Already?"

She nodded. "You've been in and out of consciousness for days now."

My eyes went wide. "Days?"

Again, she nodded. "You were badly injured."

"What happened?"

"You were shot."

"No," I said, memory flashing back in bits and pieces. The image of a musket ball ripping through my flesh shot through my mind. "What happened after? How did I get to the ship?"

"I brought you."

Her words came so rapidly, it took a moment for me to digest them.

"My lady?"

No response.

The damp cloth wiping at my skin increased its tempo.

Her rubbing persisted, threatening to scrape my flesh from the bone. I reached out a shaky hand, caught her fingers within my own.

Her hand stilled beneath mine.

"What have you done?" I asked. "What has it cost you?"

She refused to answer.

My left hand remained closed about hers. My right moved to her face, cupped her chin. My thumb stroked her silky flesh, my fingers tilted her chin up.

123

Her eyes met mine. Tears threatened to spill forth from liquid green pools.

My words came out in a hushed whisper. "What have I cost you?"

"Everything."

I stared at her, my mouth gaping wide open. "I—"

My words were cut off by a sharp rapping.

We both looked up in shock.

The sound came once again. Someone was at the door.

"Lady DeVale!" A booming voice sounded from the other side of the wooden door. "It is Sven!"

I struggled to sit up.

Alexis stopped me by placing both hands on my shoulders.

I resisted.

She persisted, shaking her head, eyes wide. "No."

She turned her head, yelled across the room. "I'll be right there, Sven."

My eyes flashed with sudden anger. "What the hell—"

She placed a finger to my lips, silencing my tirade. "Hush," she said through clenched teeth, her voice a strained whisper. "He cannot see you here like this."

I looked down. I was naked beneath my sheet, except for the dressing that covered my wound. If my crew knew...I nodded numbly.

She climbed off the bed, padded across the room.

I watched her go. Only then did I wonder at her odd choice of clothes.

She paused at the drapery, placed a finger across her lips. "Remember, not a word, my Captain."

And she was gone.

†

She was gone for quite some time. I tried to sit upright. I made it about halfway up, then fell back onto the bed. I lay there panting, fighting to control my breathing. My breathing slowly returned to normal. Had they heard my attempt to get up? I lay very still, listening, cocking my head to one side, straining to hear. I could barely make out their voices coming from the next room.

"...was nothing more that could be done."

"Not even for my brother?"I could hear the anguish in Sven's voice. Ivan had fallen. Before I was shot? The details were fuzzy in my brain.

"Not for any of them."

I couldn't discern what Sven's response was. I heard what I thought was a sob and Alexis making soothing sounds. I imagined her holding him in her arms, comforting him as he mourned.

They were as close as any two brothers could be. They were different as night and day, but they were totally devoted to one another. Ivan was the older of the two, and he constantly kept a watchful eye on his brother, even when Sven didn't want him to. As for Sven, he worshipped the ground his older brother walked on.

"We need to know that our captain is well."

"Your captain is not well," Alexis said. "He was shot. He needs time to heal."

"And we need our captain."

"Not until he's healed."

I felt a knot of apprehension in my gut. Alexis was determined, but Sven was persistent. He would keep pushing until he angered her. I just prayed that she would keep her wits about her and not refer to me as a "she" by mistake.

"I've already lost my brother. I shan't lose my captain, too."

A deep sigh from Alexis. "Your captain will be fine, Sven. But he needs time to recuperate."

Alexis's back was suddenly framed by the drapery. The shadow of her arm pressed against the fabric, her open palm braced against the wall. Her back was taut, rigid. The shadow of Sven loomed on the drapery, as well, no doubt attempting to push past Alexis.

"No. The captain is resting and must not be disturbed."

My eyes locked on the drapery, I inched toward the edge of the bed. Every movement I made begged to be screamed out in

125

anguish. I bit my tongue to keep from crying out. My arm dangled over the side of the bed as stretching fingers searched and walking fingertips groped the carpet.

My hand made its way beneath the edge of the bed. My fingers found metal. My fingertips worked their way up the steel blade, clutching the hilt firmly in my grasp.

I gritted my teeth, steeling myself against the coming pain. In one great effort, I pulled the sword from beneath the bed. It landed across me, its weight upon me. A sharp gasp escaped my lips.

The edge of the curtain moved. Sven's fingers curled about the fabric. Alexis's hand clutched at his, resisting.

Let him come, I thought. I would defend myself upon my own bed. To the death, if need be. But I would never surrender.

"Very well, Lady DeVale." He seemed to be giving up. "But the men will expect to see their captain. Soon."

I heard his retreating footsteps and the slamming of the door.

I breathed a sigh of relief.

The drapery opened and Alexis came into the room. She momentarily hesitated when she saw the sword, then approached the bed. She sat beside me.

"Where did you get this from?" she asked, reaching for the hilt.

I found the strength to lift the sword. The tip pointed at her throat.

"Ivan...dead?"

She nodded.

The others, too, I knew. The memory of their deaths flashed painfully in my mind. "Those were English sailors from *The Scorpion*! You knew." I accused. "You betrayed me."

"No." Her voice was calm, her words sure. She held my gaze steady, unwavering. Even with my blade pressed to her throat.

Of course, I realized, she wasn't that threatened by me. All she would need to do is step back beyond my reach. If she could get up that quickly from the bed, I mused.

"You betrayed me once. And you cost me twenty-six men."
My words were harsh, my voice much stronger than I imagined
was possible. "Now you've done it again. Now I've lost Ivan and
Griffen and Lars. Because of you."

Her eyes narrowed. "No." Her voice was no longer so calm.

"Yes." I insisted. "Yes, you did. You brought *The Scorpion.*"

"No. I would not do that to you."

The tip of my sword pressed the flesh of her neck. A drop of
blood appeared. "Why should I believe you?" I rose halfway up
from the bed, propping myself on my elbow.

"Because I love you!"

My mouth dropped open. The sword tip drooped. Her hands
flew to her mouth as she realized what she'd just said.

"You love me?"

"Yes, damn you." She jumped off the bed, snatching the
sword from my grasp. "I love you!" She pointed the tip at my
heart. I felt the metal bite into my flesh. "And I would never
harm you." She spat the words vehemently, tossed the sword
away.

It hit the dresser, clattered to the floor.

Alexis turned on her heel, stormed out of the room.

Seconds later, the heavy wooden door to my cabin slammed
shut.

†

I reached out, my open palm brushing against the headboard. I struggled to catch my breath. Sweat poured from my
body. Pain spread throughout my shoulder and chest. My pants
were a struggle. I hadn't realized the effort dressing would be.
The real strain was when I stood and the waves of light-
headedness came crashing across me.

Now came the hard part. I took a deep breath, steadied myself. I closed my eyes and braced myself against the pain I knew
was coming. I grabbed the tail of my undershirt, quickly threw it

over my head in one move. I cried out in anguish as searing pain shot through my entire body. Sparks flashed in front of my eyes.

I clutched at the headboard of the bed, gripped the hardwood with my fingers, nails pressing into the oak. I picked up the cloth from the porcelain bowl, swiped at my face and neck. The coolness helped to calm my overwhelming nausea. I steeled myself and reached for my tunic. Taking a deep breath, I prepared to throw it over my head.

A hand reached out, gripping my forearm. I stopped and looked up in shock. I hadn't heard anyone come in. Vincent took the tunic from my grasp.

Words weren't necessary.

Like an impatient child, I watched as he rolled my tunic in his large hands. And just like he'd done so many times during my childhood, he lifted the tunic over my head.

My head popped outside the hole. He took each arm, pushing them through the sleeves. The motion pulled at my wound, but the pain was nowhere near the level it had been. I smiled wanly as he finished dressing me. He pulled my ponytail from the collar of my tunic, returned my smile.

"Where are you bound for?" he asked.

"To the deck. I need to see my crew."

He cast a disapproving glare. "You need your rest."

"I've rested long enough. Now it's time to do my duty."

He tied my belt round my waist, passed my gloves to me.

I tugged them on and made my way to the outer cabin.

Vincent held the drapery open with one hand and latched onto my elbow with the other. He guided me, steering me down each step.

"Really, Vincent," I protested, trying to jerk loose his grasp. "I'm not so decrepit that I can't walk downstairs by myself."

"You couldn't when you were two, young lady. And I doubt if you could now."

"And do you also plan on changing my swaddling cloth in front of my crew?"

"If it pleases the captain," he said in his best snooty English accent.

"My crew needs a strong captain to guide them, not some helpless toddler and her nanny."

"I think you'll find the crew has gotten on quite well in your absence."

"Oh, really?"

We paused at the cabin door. Vincent opened it, guiding me through. The sunlight instantly blinded me, and I had to shield my eyes. It was many long minutes before I could bear to open them. I was sorely tempted to retreat to my darkened cabin until nightfall.

"Indubitably."

I raised an eyebrow.

"Yes," he said. "Brodey and Sven have taken over most of Ivan's duties. When Sven is done grieving his brother, he'll be able to take over Ivan's duties completely."

Members of my crew were about five paces distant, working on hemp. I straightened to my full height, brushing off Vincent's hand. They looked up as we approached, broadly grinning. I nodded my approval. As we passed out of view, Vincent's hand returned to its place at my elbow. I relaxed somewhat, leaning on him for support as we walked. To his credit, he didn't harp on my need for rest.

This became our routine for most of the afternoon. I attempted to make a complete tour of *The Wolfsbane*. Vincent supported me the entire way, by allowing me to strut on my own when we saw crewmembers, but permitting me to lean upon him when we were alone.

By the time we reached the galley, I was exhausted. We stepped inside, Vincent bolting the door behind us. He guided me to the first chair he could find. I was grateful for the cool darkness and rested my head upon the table before me.

I was just drifting off toward sleep when I heard footsteps crunching upon the floor behind me. *Vincent*, I thought vaguely, edging toward sleep once more. I felt a sharp slap on my back and my eyes flew open. My head jerked up and I fought to stifle my scream.

"Up and about, are ye now?"

"Aye, Rufus," I managed to groan out through gritted teeth.

129

Rufus slammed a tankard of ale on the table in front of me, pulled up a chair, and joined us. He leaned back, balancing his chair on two legs.

"'Tis about time." Rufus continued to pat me on the shoulder. I gritted my teeth against the pain. "We were beginning to think of mutiny if ye didn't return to yer duties soon."

He laughed heartily, his belly shaking. I flashed a quick smile, then a scowl. How true were his words? Was my crew ready to desert?

"I'm afraid the captain still needs time to fully recover from his injuries, Rufus. He won't be performing a great deal of his usual tasks for a bit," Vincent said.

I raised my tankard in salute to Vincent. It might be nice to take some time off. Just as the first taste of alcohol touched my lips, Vincent snatched the tankard from my grasp. So suddenly that the metal clanked against my front teeth.

"That includes drinking alcohol." Vincent shook a finger at me, then Rufus. "Water only."

My mouth dropped open. "No alcohol?" Rufus and I spoke at the same time.

"Not a drop." Vincent lifted my mug, drained its contents in one gulp. "You are in dry dock until you're fully recovered. And if you cheat, I'll know."

Rufus chortled.

I narrowed my eyes, fixed him with my most ruthless sneer. "That order could be extended to include the ship's cook, you know."

"Ye do, and ye won't eat for a month."

"If you intend to make threats, do it with something that will matter." A deep baritone voice called from the doorway. "The captain never eats your cooking anyway."

My spine stiffened. I knew that voice. But it couldn't be, he'd been at the plantation with me. I slowly turned around.

"Lars."

"Captain. It's good to see you up."

"I thought you dead."

He laughed. "Lars run like deer. It takes more than panty-waisted Englishmen to kill Lars."

130

"You reached the beach before us?"

"Yes." He thrust out his chest proudly. "I tell you Lars run fast."

A broad grin split his lips. "Your lady run fast, too. Even carrying your ass."

I coughed, tried to disguise my growing blush. "She carried me?"

Lars laughed. "Over her shoulder like a sack of flour."

Rufus chuckled.

Vincent brushed at the edges of his mustache. The corner of his mouth turned up and his shoulders jostled as he fought to suppress his laughter.

I pushed my chair back, staggered to my feet. I held onto the edge of the table until I regained my sea legs. Vincent was already rising from his chair as I turned to leave.

"Where ye goin', Cap'n?" Lars bellowed. "We've just now started drinking."

I brought myself up to my full height, posture straight. I pulled at the hem of my tunic, smoothing it down. "As the captain, I must see to the welfare of my ship." There. I sounded just like a Royal Navy commander, eager to do my duty.

That said, I staggered as proudly as I could to the door. Vincent followed close behind, ready to catch me should I fall. My ears perked up and my face blushed beet red as Lars and Rufus continued to make jibes about how the damsel in distress had saved the fearsome Captain Wolff.

†

My muscles were aching, my shoulder was hurting, and my head was throbbing. Eyes closed, I hung my head over the railing. I prayed for my head to quit spinning, my stomach to stop churning.

Slowly, I opened my eyes. The ocean came into focus. Dark blue waves capped with white peaks. The bow cut through the waves at a brisk clip. I knelt upon the deck, one knee pressed into the hard wood. Sea spray dampened my trousers legs, the

131

wet chilling me all the way to the bone. I ignored the burning sensation in my upper thigh, like a hundred tiny needles pricking at my flesh. I leaned closer and studied the water. It was much darker than the waters I was familiar with. Almost black in color. Barely visible, a line of reefs passed just beneath the hull of the ship.

"How long have they chased us?"

"Since we left Bonaire."

I looked up and frowned. The sails were at full mast. Several were showing signs of tattering and fraying, the wind whipping through the open holes. Brodey and his men worked fifty paces distant, rapidly sewing linens together for replacement sails. The sky above was darkening with gathering storm clouds.

"You take great risks, Vincent, running full speed through unknown waters, with the danger of reefs just below us." A quick glance at the anchor chain curled into a lump confirmed my suspicions. Bone dry, it hadn't been dropped in days. "And at night, too."

"A necessary risk, I assure you." He scratched at his chin. His beard stubble was thicker, longer than I'd ever seen on Vincent. Normally after two days worth of growth, he was taking a straight razor to his whiskers.

My eyes grew wide in realization. "My God, Vincent! How many are there?"

"Four in all. Flying English and Spanish flags."

"An alliance?" I was stunned. The thought of the English and Spanish together had never occurred to me.

"Your abduction of the Lady DeVale seems to have sparked a common interest in our capture."

"Brought on by the duchess, I'm sure." No doubt she'd spent most of her newfound freedom organizing the crowns of England and Spain against me.

"She is a formidable enemy."

"Still, I would have thought the Spanish would be a bit more reluctant. I haven't attacked their ships." I snatched the telescope from Vincent's waistband. Pointed it southward, focusing, I brought the horizon into view.

Nothing but water.

A cough from Vincent.

"Recently," I added.

"Perhaps they took offense to you abducting the betrothed of their royalty. Or perhaps it's because it was their gold coins in the chests we took from Bonaire."

I almost dropped the telescope. I lowered it, turned my head, and stared at Vincent. "Spanish coin?"

Vincent nodded. "Two coffers full. Left at the specified co-ordinates."

I cocked an eyebrow. "Spanish coin is worth far more than English."

"No doubt, the English chose not to pay the ransom. Captain Jackson and the crew of *The Scorpion* tortured Brandy and her father. That's hardly the actions of someone intent on meeting the demands of the abductors."

I rubbed my chin, scratched my head. I was lost. The workings of parliaments never ceased to give me a headache. "So the English don't care if they get Alexis back?"

"Not particularly." Now I was doubly confounded.

Vincent elaborated. "The DeVale's have a second daughter."

"Elizabeth." I nodded.

"Elizabeth. No doubt she's already being groomed to take her sister's place as the bride of the future king."

"King?"

"There is no prince in line for the crown. When Lord Rafael's uncle dies, he becomes the next to rule. The Duke of DeVale would be eager to marry off any of his daughters to the heir to the throne."

"Alexis told me it was her duty as eldest."

I felt a feeling of dread creep over me. Vincent took my hand, squeezed it reassuringly. It was a habit of his when he bore bad news.

I steeled myself for his next words.

"Elizabeth…departed our company fairly quickly. I'm sure the English doctors have determined that her virtue is quite intact. The same cannot be said for Alexis."

"I haven't—"

"It matters not." He cut me off with a flick of his wrist. I scowled. I hated when he did that.

"The lady has spent so many months aboard ship that the English no doubt assume she must be tainted goods."

"But—"

"Keep in mind they have her sister's own testimony as to the happenings aboard ship. If Alexis were to be rescued now, think of the embarrassment it would create for the duke. By law, the eldest must be wed first. And by no means would the queen allow her marriage to proceed given the circumstances. Another maiden would be chosen. And the duke would lose favor with the courts."

"If the English capture us—"

"They may very well have orders to kill the Lady DeVale."

My stomach churned. Bile crept into my throat. I closed my eyes, fighting back waves of nausea. "And the Spanish?" I asked. "Why would they pay the ransom?"

"Customarily, before a marriage arrangement is made, a portrait is sent by the bride's family for approval by the groom's court. Alexis's blonde locks and green eyes would mark her as an exotic beauty among the people of Spain. The man who made her his bride would be held in awe by his people."

"And it matters not to him that she might be…soiled?" I had to force the word through clenched teeth.

"Her….attributes far outweigh the Spaniards' need for virginity. She won't be subject to examination by Spanish doctors. The only ones need ever know are Alexis and her husband."

"But she's been on *The Wolfsbane* for so long."

"His court can keep the matter of her abduction private. Tell his courtesans that her arrival was delayed due to foul weather. Or perhaps a prolonged illness at home. What is widespread news in England is not likely public knowledge in faraway Spain."

I sat upon the deck, my feet dangling over the side. I rested my cheek against the railing, leaned over, and peered at the ocean below. The waves were choppy, beating against the hull. I clenched my fists, weak muscles straining with the effort. I wished I had the strength to lash out in protest like the waves.

"I do wish you'd return to your cabin for a proper rest."

"And I wish you weren't my watchdog." The words were out and said before I could bite them back. I exhaled loudly, shook my head. Cursed. At myself, not him. "I'm sorry," I said, not looking up. I didn't want to see pain reflected in those tired, old eyes. Pain that I had a knack of causing. "I didn't mean to snap at you."

Vincent's hand found my good shoulder, squeezed reassuringly. It was one of the few displays of affection he permitted.

"Does she know?" I asked, my voice a strained whisper.

His hand tightened upon my shoulder.

Of course she knew. She would have realized the minute she saw the Spanish doubloons.

"No doubt, she suspects." Vincent's idea of not delivering bad news was half-truths. He didn't know the answer because they'd never had a conversation about it. "Perhaps that's why she's been so eager to lend a hand."

I nodded. "She carried me back to the ship."

"She's done more than that."

I twisted about and looked up at my mentor.

He looked at me from the corner of his eye. "She helped to nurse you back to health. Watching over you like a mother hen. Forgoing her own meals to look after you."

"For me?" I asked dubiously.

"She slept on a cot in your cabin during the day to guard you from intruding seamen. She bathed you. Fed you. Changed your dressing."

I couldn't fight the growing blush that rose at the thought of Alexis bathing me. Thankfully, Vincent ignored my crimson face.

"At night, she's guided the ship through these treacherous waters."

"Alexis?" I asked. I had taught her how to read the stars, but I never dreamed she could be a navigator.

"She's taken to it quite well. I'm training Sven during the day. And he's a good pupil. But he pales in comparison to the Lady DeVale."

I was stunned. Alexis guiding my ship at night. Sven learning the trade, following in his brother's footsteps. The pursuit by the alliance of England and Spain. I'd been out for a few days, but it seemed like a lifetime. So much had changed, I felt like a stranger on my own ship.

I pulled myself onto shaky feet. Stumbled off toward the stern of the ship.

Vincent grabbed me by the arm, pulling me back.

I spun around, facing him.

"Where are you bound for?" he asked.

"To find Alexis. I need to—"

"Wait."

"Wait?"

"She's returned to her cabin to rest." He started walking, his hand still on my arm. I allowed him to lead me to my own cabin. "You should do the same."

"But...." My protests were feeble. We were already at my door and he was ushering me inside, urging me toward the bed.

I no longer had the strength to resist.

"You can see her tonight." He had my boots off.

I fell back onto the bed. I felt him lift my legs, settle them upon the bed. "On the deck. She guides the ship by night."

I had every intention of feigning sleep till he left. Then I would go to Alexis's cabin. Tell her I knew everything now.

Vincent sat by the edge of the bed, though and before I knew it, sleep did overtake me.

✝

The ship was quiet, the crew turned in for the night. The wind was blowing hard, whipping the sails. Light raindrops pelted the deck. I paused at the rail, leaning over the edge. The water was choppy. The white-capped waves broke hard against the hull of the ship. The deck swayed beneath my feet. Yet there was no doubt that the ship was still making good headway against the turbulent sea.

She was at the wheel, her back to me. Her hands gripped the wheel loosely, guiding *The Wolfsbane* with ease. She, too, seemed at ease with the position. Her blonde hair was loose, whipping in the wind as it cascaded down her back and around her shoulders.

Her tunic was a dusty gold color. The fabric clung to her, showing all her curves. The tail of her tunic ended just below her buttocks, framing those golden globes that begged to be touched. Her leggings were dark in color. Like her tunic, they were also tight fitting. Her dresses were beautiful, but they hid her figure from view. I'd never seen the curve of her leg before. Never seen the muscles flexing in her strong thighs; the tender calf that disappeared into the cuff of her boots.

My breathing came more quickly now, my heart beat faster. I ran my tongue across my parched lips. My feet moved on their own, bringing me to a stop scant inches behind her. We were so close, I'm sure she could feel my breath upon her neck. If I leaned in closer, my body would be rubbing against hers. My shaking hands made their way to her shoulders, gently cupping them.

She jumped, turned around quickly. Her back was pressed against the wheel, the wooden spokes pressing into her flesh. My hands slipped from her shoulders, sliding down her arms and about her waist to hold steady the wheel.

"You frightened me." Her words came rapidly, her breathing faster.

.I couldn't help but notice how her chest heaved with each breath. The falling rain left a moist sheen on her hair. Her skin was damp. Mesmerized, my hand reached up, wiping the moisture from her cheek. Her fingers closed tightly upon my own, removing my hand. I noticed, however, that she didn't just let my hand drop. Rather, she held it clasped within her own.

"Should you even be up and about?" she asked.

"I needed to see you."

She bit her bottom lip, her teeth leaving tiny indentations.

"I know what you did. How you brought me back. You saved me."

She shrugged. "I could not leave you on Bonaire."

"No one would have blamed you, considering the consequences."

She averted her eyes, refusing to meet my gaze.

There was an awkward silence between us. I thought about moving back and giving her space. My feet refused to move.

"Why do you do that?" Her voice was low.

I had to strain to hear her. "Do what?"

"That." She pointed a finger at me. "Why do you have to do that? Say the wrong thing. Do the wrong thing. Make things uncomfortable again."

"Are you uncomfortable now?" I asked, acutely aware of my hand still upon the ship's wheel and the proximity that placed us in.

"Is that what you wish?" She thrust out her hands, pushing me away.

I arched an eyebrow. The lady took liberties that no one else would even think of with me.

"I...I apologize." She ran a hand across her face. Exhaled loudly. She looked at me. "You make me crazy. What you are drives me insane."

"My being a pirate is the problem."

"Piracy is bad enough. Perhaps I thought given time, I could change that about you. But being a woman..."

"You can't change that."

"No matter how much I would like."

"Then don't try to change me. Just accept me for what I am."

She stared up at me with those big green eyes. Bit her bottom lip. She turned from me and wrapped her arms about herself as her hands rubbed her arms briskly.

The wind and the rain had picked up considerably. There was a definite chill in the air. Thunder rumbled overhead.

She spun around quickly. The ship pitched and swayed beneath our feet. She reached out, clutching me for support.

I tried to steady her as best I could.

My world tilted with the kiss. My tongue danced with hers. Her hands were everywhere. Stroking through my hair. She ran them down my back, fingernails biting through material as her hands clutched at my hips.

My hands were firmly locked about the wheel. My knuckles clenched white even as my fingers longed to feel the searing heat from her body. I heard a loud rumbling in my ears. Whether it was the sound of thunder or my own heart beating, I was unsure. But it shook me to my very feet, knocking me off-kilter. We were both gasping for breath as we broke the kiss. I lifted one hand, removed my glove and used my bare index finger to catch her beneath her chin, tilting her face up. Her eyes met mine. I leaned in for another kiss. Her open palm against my lips prevented me. I pulled back in surprise.

"You take liberties that you should not."

"You want me to," I said. "You protest with your words, but your body begs for more."

"No." Her answer came a little too quickly, much too loudly. She lowered her voice demurely. "I mustn't, no matter the temptation."

My fingers stroked her cheek. The rain cascaded off her hair, down the side of her face, across my fingers. My fingers moved to her chin, gently cupping. The green eyes that met mine burned bright with fever. I briefly wondered if my own eyes reflected my lust as readily as hers did.

"Your body aches for me."

"No." Her protest was weak.

"Your heart races for me. Your knees are weak with desire. Your skin is on fire for my touch."

"No." Her protest was now a whisper.

I lowered my voice, intentionally dropping in pitch. Low and gravelly. A soft whisper upon the wind. "You love me."

"I hate you," she whispered.

"You admitted you love me." *Would she now try to say she lied?*

"I love you."

A victorious smile played upon my lips.

"And I hate you."

I felt the scowl slither across my face. "You can't feel both for me."

"I can. And I do."

I arched a brow. The woman talked in riddles.

"I want to pull you close to me, Kris. Then I want to push you away. I long to kiss you yet I feel the urge to slap you." Her fingers found my face, smoothing my wet hair away. "I thank God for you. And I curse the day I met you."

I half-smiled. "So many feelings for one so young."

Her eyes flashed. "You mock me."

"I do nothing of the sort."

I lowered my head, kissing her. Not my usual plundering kisses. But rather a sweet, gentle kiss, my lips brushing against hers with just the lightest of touches. "Do you hate me still?" I whispered, my breath hot upon her lips.

"Yes."

I kissed her again, drew back by a hair's breadth from her succulent lips. "Still?" I whispered into her open mouth.

"Yes."

Again, I kissed her. The way I longed to kiss her, with my tongue thrust deeply into her mouth. My thigh pressed between her legs, my hands cupped her buttocks, carefully pulling her against me. Her back arched, breasts pressed to mine.

Breathless, I leaned back. My hands were still upon her buttocks. Her own hands were upon my shoulders. For once, though, she wasn't pushing me away. Her fevered eyes searched my face, awaiting my question.

"Still?" I asked.

She faltered. "No."

The deck rolled and pitched, nearly hurling me off my feet. I staggered, stumbling into Alexis. She fell with me, both of us crashing into the ship's wheel, tumbling to the deck. We landed hard, her falling on top of me. I brushed her hair out of my eyes as I tried to gain my bearings. I was twisted at an awkward angle, my weight bearing down on my left side.

My head lolled to the side, my face upon the wet deck. Waves were cresting above the side of the ship. Water was running across the deck, rushing toward us. I tried to shove Alexis off my lap, attempted to scramble to my feet. I didn't quite make it. Sea spray splashed my face. I came up fast, spitting salty seawater from my mouth.

The ship's wheel was spinning wildly, *The Wolfsbane* lurching out of control. We were both on our feet, struggling to reach the wheel. The deck was tilted at an odd angle. I fell to my knees, slid across the deck. My upper body hit hard against the wheel. I gripped the wooden spokes, used them to pull myself up. I felt a throbbing sensation rip through my shoulder.

Alexis was beside me, her hands upon the wheel. The deck banked sharply to the right, our lower bodies sliding from beneath us, our legs scraping against the wet wood. We leaned with our upper bodies, pulling, trying to turn the wheel to the left.

I felt a body pressing against my back, leaning into me. Hands braced on the wheel with mine. I looked up, shaking my head rapidly, wet hair flinging away from my face. *The Wolfsbane* was a flurry of activity. Half-dressed crewmen were everywhere, scrambling to their duties. Brodey was scrambling up the mast, attempting to lash the sails that blew wildly. Their ropes and pulleys banged against the masthead, a metallic ringing sound echoing above our heads.

Lars was at the bottom of the mast, holding the rope to the mainsail as steady as he could. Dressed only in his drawers, his flesh trembled beneath the bone-chilling onslaught of rain. He planted his feet firmly upon the deck, his bare feet offering better traction than my own boots.

Vincent barked orders at the mostly naked seamen pouring forth from the crews' quarters. They scrambled across the foredeck, slipping and sliding as they struggled to reach the high side of the ship.

Groaning loudly, I pulled harder, leaning into the wheel. Alexis and Sven struggled beside me, putting all their weight behind it. The pressure eased up. The wheel landed on its center axis.

"I have her!" Sven shouted above the howling wind, centering himself behind the wheel.

With the wheel centered, the ship righted itself. We still rocked violently upon the sea, but we were finally able to stand upright. Waves still towered above *The Wolfsbane*, crashing down on us violently. The force of the water threatened to sweep us off our feet again.

Vincent held onto the railing, inching his way toward us. He grabbed me by the elbow, pulling me toward the bow. Alexis followed close, clutching at my shirtsleeve for support. When we were well out of earshot, he stopped, addressing both of us.

"You're soaking wet." He looked meaningfully at me. "And your...ahem...binding is coming unraveled."

I looked down. My tunic was clinging to my upper body, my attributes quickly becoming visible. I blushed as I met Vincent's gaze again.

He nodded toward Alexis and leaned closer, speaking low. I had to strain to hear him above the howling wind and the crashing waves. "Take the captain back to her quarters. Stay with her. Let no one in. I'll cover your departure with an excuse about your wound reopening."

I followed Alexis's lead. Hunching down, I tried to compact my upper body as much as possible. She grabbed my arm, pulling herself up to whisper in my ear.

"Lean against me," she ordered. "Stagger your walk a bit. Your stride is too strong for nursing an injury."

I did as the lady commanded. I leaned against her, pressed my weight upon her. She staggered beneath me before catching her balance. My left arm draped across her shoulder, my palm resting just above the swell of her breast.

Her hand clutched at mine, attempting to restrain my stretching fingers. Her other hand grasped my belt, holding me firmly at the waist.

Few crewmen paid heed to us. Most were far too busy trying to weather the storm. Those who did notice cast concerned glances in my direction. No doubt worried that their captain was suffering a relapse.

"I believe our ruse worked," she said the moment we reached the safety of my cabin.

As she locked and bolted the door, I brought towels for both of us. I quickly ran mine across my face and through my hair, briskly rubbing. By the time Alexis turned from the door, I was standing there, towel ready. She flashed a smile as she took the cloth from my grasp. Like me, she briskly towel dried her hair, wringing water from her long tresses.

Alexis passed the towel to me. Our hands brushed during the exchange. My fingers somehow found hers and clasped her hand. Our eyes met and I was lost in a sea of deep green, burning brightly as if on fire. I leaned in, my lips brushing lightly across hers. She opened her mouth beneath mine. My tongue darted in, claiming her for my own. My head swam; my heartbeat pounded in my ears.

She pulled away, stepped back. She was already pressing up against the door. Hands on either side of her body, I leaned in, the weight of my palms bearing down upon the doorframe. The floor beneath us shifted as the ship rolled and pitched with the storm. Alexis's fingernails dug into my waist as I increased my pressure upon the doorframe, using the wood's solid strength to brace us both. My mouth searched for another kiss.

Her fingers against my lips stopped me. I opened my eyes, barely able to focus on her through a lust-filled haze.

"Kris, I—"

"No, don't. You can't." I took her hand within my own, kissed her perfect knuckles. "You can't touch me like that. Nor look at me like that, your eyes burning so feverishly, your gaze ravishing me every time you look at me."

Her eyes darted back and forth. An apology was already forming on her lips.

"You can't do that to me, then tell me you don't want me."

Her open palm touched the side of my face. Her fingers tenderly stroked. "Oh, my Captain, if you only knew how much I wanted you."

I kissed her open palm. Caught, held her gaze. "Show me," I whispered.

Her grip moved from the support she'd found upon my waist. Hands planted firmly on my shoulders, her mouth found mine. Her lips were upon mine, barely touching. Her tongue darted out, tracing the outline of my lips. My mouth opened beneath hers. She teased me, the tip of her tongue darting in and out, just barely entering my mouth. My hands clutched at her hips. A groan escaped my lips. Finally, her tongue thrust in all the way.

She broke our kiss off sharply. We were both left panting, gasping for air. She leaned back, her fevered gaze raking across my body. Everywhere she looked, my flesh burned with need. Her mouth closed upon my throat. Her teeth softly bit, nibbling at my flesh. She left a trail of kisses down my neck. I arched, rising up to meet her mouth.

Alexis lifted her head, her eyes meeting mine. I saw her lips moving, barely registered what she was saying. She pulled at the collar of my tunic. My lady wanted it off of me. Her hands ran along my shoulders, down across my chest. Alexis pulled away from me, a look of horror on her face. Eyes wide, she held her hand outstretched. Blood coated the palm of her right hand.

"You're bleeding." She wiped her hand on the towel she was still holding. "Why did you not tell me?"

I shrugged. "It's nothing."

"Nothing? It's soaked clear through your tunic!" She swiped at my shirt with the towel. It came away covered in crimson. "If you weren't wearing black, I might have noticed sooner."

She had the tail of my tunic in her grasp and she firmly yanked it over my head in one fluid motion. My lady grabbed my hand, pulling me along behind her. Unused to the sudden, unpredictable rise and fall of the floor that came with any squall, she moved with an unsteady gait. She took us from the bookcase to the desk, using the furniture to steady our way until we made it up the stairs and into the bedroom. I was settled on the bed, my back pressed against the headboard. She sat beside me, one leg curled beneath her.

She pushed the strap of my undershirt away. When it got in her way again, she yanked my top off, tossing it onto the floor. She roughly jerked my blood-soaked bandage off. It was only when she began to unwrap the binding about my breasts that her shaking hands revealed her unease.

I watched quietly as she made a paste from ingredients Vincent had left out on the dresser. Alexis set the paste to one side to thicken. She reached for a vial of yellow liquid. My eyes widened as she poured the alcohol onto a rag.

"It's fine. I'm fine." I held out my arm, attempted to block her from reaching my wound with the cloth. "It's better. Really."

"Glad to hear it. Let's keep it that way, shall we?" She easily deflected my arm. I flinched as the alcohol-soaked cloth touched my open wound. First, the numbing cold hit me. Then, almost instantly, the burning set in.

"Be still," she scolded.

"It burns." I said, my bottom lip pouting.

"Don't be such a big baby." She lifted the rag, blew cool air across my flesh. "If I don't treat it properly, infection could set in."

I didn't say another word. She slapped the paste onto my wound. It was sore, but I wasn't in much pain otherwise. She wrapped another dressing, securing it beneath my arm. Tenderly, she patted the bandage into place.

"If you wanted my top off," I teased with a smirk, "you could have simply asked."

My lady smiled broadly now, once again bringing her lips to mine. She kissed me deeply, her tongue thrusting into my mouth. Alexis withdrew, dragging her upper teeth across my bottom lip. She caught my lip between her teeth, gently pulled. Her fingers upon my breast found my hardened nipple and she pulled on it.

I was squirming, writhing beneath her. Her mouth left mine, working its way down my neck. To my collarbone. Between my breasts. Leaving tiny bites and kisses as she went. Her mouth settled upon my right breast. I arched beneath her, my fingers tangled in her hair as she sucked. Her teeth closed, gently biting my nipple. I bucked hard beneath her.

Determined in my passion, I staved off the pain, ignoring everything save my need to possess this woman. I rolled her over, pinning Alexis beneath me. I licked, sucked her breast through the wet material of her tunic. My hands were beneath her blouse. Fingers sliding across heated flesh. And then her tunic joined mine on the floor.

My eyes fastened upon her breasts. Young and firm, the nipples dusty rose in color. I bent my head. And my mouth feasted as my eyes had, devouring her softness.

My tongue swirled. Licking. Sucking. Biting. Taking my pleasure from her soft moans of encouragement. Her hips lifted beneath me. Fingers curled into my hair, pulling me to her.

My mouth left her breast, my breath blowing cool air across her damp skin. She shivered beneath me. I extended my tongue, licking just the tip of her hardened nipple. She groaned, writhed beneath me.

Hands dropping lower, I found the waistband of her breeches. With nimble fingers, I undid the tethers. She tensed beneath me.

"Easy." I reassured her with a soothing kiss. "No harm shall befall you."

I tenderly kissed her lips again. She was so eager, so passionate in her determination to bed me that it was easy to forget her inexperience. Now she was as shy as a maiden should be her first time.

She gradually relaxed beneath me. I bent my head, kissing beneath her breasts. I licked my way down her body to her navel and at the downy blonde hairs that ran from her navel to the waistband of her trousers.

I slowly pulled the trousers from her hips. As much for my benefit as hers. No doubt she would appreciate the tender, gentle manner. While I, on the other hand, appreciated the slow, sweet torture of it as her flesh was revealed to my sight inch by tantalizing inch.

I paused only long enough to remove her boots. I worked my way back up her shapely legs. I resumed my quest. For the legendary Golden Fleece, I thought, as her sex came into view. A treasure to behold like no other.

My fingers stroked through her damp curls, seeking that hard little nubbin that I knew was hidden there. She lurched half off the bed when I found it. My mouth found that jewel, closed upon it, even as her legs attempted to close, her thighs tightening about my ears. Her hands clutched wildly at my hair.

I parted her puffy, swollen lips. She was soaked wet with

the evidence of her arousal. The smell of her sex filled the air. I inhaled deeply, drinking in the scent of her. She gasped as my fingers entered her. This time, I didn't hesitate. Tongue working, fingers moving, I took her. With one swift, deliberate thrust, she was mine.

Chapter Ten

THE LADY

When next I opened my eyes, she was gently sucking at my breast. I stretched languorously, enjoying the sensation. She moved easily into my arms. The kiss that claimed my lips was soft and gentle, but no less passionate than before. My mouth responded eagerly to hers.

I pulled back, ending our kiss. My eyes sought hers. The often murky depths of gray were now calm. She had nothing left to hide from my gaze. I reached out, my fingers stroking her cheek. Her face, usually tight with apprehension, was now relaxed beneath my touch. My fingers found the bleached white line above her eye, tracing the scar. She rewarded me with a smile.

Once again, my mouth found hers. My tongue slipped easily between her lips, past her teeth. She sucked greedily at my tongue. I tasted myself on her lips, in her mouth. And the thought made my head swim.

My hands trembled as they journeyed toward the waistband of her breeches. She caught my shaking hands within her own.

"It's fine," she said, tenderly dropping a kiss upon my forehead.

"It hardly seems fair."

"What?"

"You've had me three times now." And each time, she had managed to send me to higher and higher levels of ecstasy. There was no reprieve from those thorough fingers and that talented mouth. "I haven't even gotten your breeches off of you."

With a delighted laugh, she flipped onto her back. Her injured arm was cradled against her chest. Her other hand was above her, gripping the headboard as she stretched out her body, offering it up for my approval.

"Do with me as you will, my lady."

A wicked smile played upon my lips. "Rest assured, I will, my Captain."

I had resigned myself long before to the knowledge that I loved her. I loved a woman. No matter what my family, my country, my church might decree. I had wanted her desperately. Still, though, it took all my courage to give myself to her. It wasn't courage that fueled my actions now. But lust. Love. For I knew I did belong to this woman. I had lied to her—and myself—with every excuse, every denial that sprang forth from my lips. After all the months of temptation and torture, I had finally given in to what I wanted. And desired. And needed.

My eyes drank their fill, my gaze sweeping across her body. Her breasts were small. Smaller than mine. But large enough to fill my hands. I had discovered that repeatedly as I clutched at her in the throes of passion. I blushed at the memory.

Her body was lean, muscular, her stomach flat. A thin scar ran along her side, to the right of her navel, stretching to her hipbone at a smooth angle. Caused by some opponent's lucky sword stroke, I reflected. How different our lives were. There were days that I thought I would surely die of boredom, subjected to the torturous rigors of needlepoint and other such tasks as befell a lady of my standing. While she, my brave pirate captain, faced a far more tangible death on a daily basis. Her many scars attested to the very real truth that she could have been taken from me countless times in the past. I gingerly kissed that scar, my tongue darting out, licking her hot flesh. A low moan escaped her lips.

My gaze continued on, lashes demurely lowering as I realized I was passing her sex. I focused upon her upper legs and thighs. They were long and supple. She flexed beneath my touch. She waited impatiently for my fingers, her eyes clouded with desire. Yet she remained quiet, allowing me to proceed at my own pace.

My hand reached up, stroking through her ebony hair. My fingers pulled the cord loose and her ponytail came undone, her locks falling about her shoulders. My lips found hers. And somehow, my fingers had left her hair, stroking down her body, between her legs, upon her sex. I delighted in the sensation as she arched beneath me, her body responding to my touch. She moaned and gasped, writhing in my arms and calling out my name as waves of pleasure crashed down upon her.

†

The bed moved beneath me. The lantern hanging on the wall swung wildly back and forth, sending light and shadows chasing one another about the room. Rain pelted at the window. Lightning flashed across the sky. A loud crack of thunder followed.

"It's quite a squall out there."

"Yes, it is." My tone was even. I held her gaze steady with my own.

"Vincent and the others will be kept busy."

"For hours, no doubt."

A twitch tugged at the corner of her mouth, one eyebrow arched suggestively. I readily returned her grin. I bent to kiss her lips again.

†

The sun was shining brightly by the time I stepped out on deck. The air still smelled of rain, but the sky was clear. I shielded my eyes from the sun as I picked my way toward the bow.

The Wolfsbane had more or less survived the onslaught of the storm the night before. She sailed on an even keel. No doubt her seams had held against any onrushing water. Vincent had taught me that if she ever listed to one side, that meant we had sprung a leak and were taking on water. The hull had held. The deck had not fared nearly so well. The sails were badly damaged, ripped by the rushing wind. The smaller sails were in fair shape. But the main sail had suffered, barely hanging from its moorings. Part of the railing was missing from the port side. Broken wood-

en planks littered the deck. Already, crews were working at re-
pairing the damage. Bleary-eyed sailors had no doubt worked
throughout the long night to keep *The Wolfsbane* seaworthy.

I found Kris at the ship's wheel with Sven. She was studying a parchment as Sven guided the ship. Her gloved hands idly
stroked up and down the edge of the parchment as she read. I
recalled those hands, those fingers upon my body, stroking in
much the same fashion. I felt the heat rush to my cheeks.

"How do we fare?" I asked, approaching the wheel.

"We weathered the storm well." Sven's grip relaxed on the
wheel somewhat. "Nothing but clear sailing ahead."

"Thanks to Sven." The admiration was evident in Kris'
tone. "He kept us from floundering on the rocks. We cleared the
last of the reefs an hour ago."

I was surprised. "I thought we wouldn't clear the reefs for
another day or so."

"The storm did considerable damage," Sven said, "but the
fierce winds gave us a strong push in the right direction."

"The other ships?" I asked, already grabbing the telescope
from Kris' belt. I eagerly scanned the horizon.

"Gone." Kris took the telescope from my grasp, replacing it
upon her belt. "We found pieces of planks floating upon the sea
this morning. No doubt they anchored during the storm."

"Our ship would surely have been lost if we anchored, too."
Sven looped a rope around one of the wheel spokes and secured
it in place upon a pegged mooring. This way, the ship was held
on a steady course without somebody needing to be upon it at all
times. "That's why Vincent and I decided to ride out the storm."

"You've certainly taken to the job." Kris patted Sven on the
back. "You've filled your brother's shoes..." Her words trailed
off.

An embarrassed silence hung in the air.

"I'm sorry."

Sven shook his head in despair. I reached out, patting his
arm. "He died very heroically," I said.

"Sometimes, he was too much the hero."

"Pardon?" I was perplexed.

Sven caught and held my gaze. He turned from us, pacing upon the deck. "The captain himself ordered Ivan and Vincent to retrieve the ransom." Sven fixed his gaze upon Kris. "I was to accompany you."

Kris shrugged. "When Alexis and I," she paused a half-beat, glanced at me, "fell behind. When we caught up, the others had already left our group. I assumed it was an error in the plan."

"No." Sven shook his head, leaned in closer, his voice low. "My brother pulled me to the side. He ordered me to accompany Vincent because he had an omen something bad would happen."

"And you followed his orders."

"Yes." Sven nodded. "I thought he meant I should go to protect old Vincent. I realize now that he sent me to keep me safe. To take my place." Another awkward silence hung in the air. "I'll be fine. Given enough time."

"Of course." Kris reached out and patted Sven on the back. "Go, rest. The ship is on a secure course. The watch will call if there's sign of danger."

I looked skyward. Lars stood at the top of the mast, perched in the crow's nest. From his position, he could see for great distances in all directions. Seeing me below, he waved. I self-consciously returned the wave.

When I looked back, Sven was already gone. Kris watched me expectantly, reached out to take my hand. I shrank back from her touch. At her puzzled look, I glanced skyward. Her gaze followed mine.

"What troubles you so, my lady?"

"The watch in the crow's nest."

She arched an eyebrow and waited for me to continue.

"How many times have I been on deck with you, Kris? How often have we been spied upon by a bored crewman?"

She shrugged. "There's always a watch during the day, eyeing the seas."

"And us." My voice was louder than I'd intended. I leaned in closer, lowered my voice to a more appropriate level. "What about at night? Are they out then?"

She shook her head. "No, Alexis. Until recently, we've always anchored at night. No reason for a night watch."

I breathed a sigh of relief. Most of our…indiscretions had happened at night. Not to say that we hadn't been carelessly intimate during the day, as well.

She smirked. "Are you afraid that we were seen? That someone else may have seen us together?"

"No." I cringed at the half-lie. "Yes."

Her jaw set.

"Not because I'm ashamed of you. Of us." Her gaze remained wary. "But what if one of your crew happened to see us and realized what I already know? That you couldn't possibly be a man?"

She caught my fingers within her grasp. Her eyes searched mine. "Is that what this is about?"

I nodded. "If they saw us together upon the deck—if they caught us kissing, my hand upon your breast."

"They would realize their captain is a woman. They'd mutiny for sure."

"And what would become of us?"

She ran a hand across her face, exhaled loudly. "You'd be safe. I can trust Vincent. He'd get you safely off the ship."

I shook my head vehemently. "I've given up all I possess for you. My religion. My family. My freedom. I refuse to give you up, as well."

"Your freedom?" She looked stricken. "Your ransom was paid in full. You could have had your freedom long ago. You chose to return to the ship. To me."

"You may have set my body free, but my heart has always been your captive."

She came to me, casting a furtive glance upward. Lars's back was to us. She took me in her arms, hugging me closely. "I'm sorry," she said. "I thought you wanted…that you didn't want to be—"

Did she actually think I did not want to be with her? My fingers stroked her cheek, strayed to her lips, tracing their fullness. "Are you daft?" I asked. "I love you, Kris."

A smile tugged at the edges of her lips. Her eyes crinkled with laughter. Impetuously, she kissed me.

"We must exercise caution." I glanced at the crow's nest again. Lars still faced the opposite direction. "We can ill afford to be caught in a passionate clinch upon the deck."

"Very well," she said and leaned in closer, grinned lewdly. "From now on, I'll only grope you within the privacy of our own quarters."

I slapped at her playfully. "You, my dear Captain, are incorrigible."

I turned to go back the way I'd come. I'd scarcely gone two steps before she was behind me, her hands cupping my derriere. When I turned to protest, she swiftly clasped both hands behind her back, whistling nonchalantly.

I turned away, keeping careful watch out of the corner of my eye. When her hand crept again to my buttock, I quickly turned around. This time, I was fast enough to catch the culprit in the act. I gripped her wrist firmly.

I pulled her close to me, acting as if I meant to kiss her. When she bent to taste my lips, I seized my opportunity and her own bottom. My fingers sharply pinched. When she yelped in pain, I dropped her wrist and ran for all I was worth, with her following close behind, threatening me with all sorts of obscene promises.

†

We somehow managed to tumble from her bed long enough to make it to dinner. The galley was lively that night, celebrating the recovery of their captain. The liquor and the music poured forth freely. Even Sven appeared to be in good spirits. He was in the center of the room, drinking from an uncorked jug, dancing a lively jig. He sauntered to the beat, swaying his way toward our table.

"Dance?" he asked.

I glanced in deference to Kristen. She shrugged. I took it as a sign of approval. Excusing myself, I took Sven's proffered hand. We moved easily along the dance floor. He was a talented dancer, switching easily into a waltz as the music changed.

154

Around us, other sailors hooted and hollered their approval from their tables. Brodey stood atop his table, raising his mug in a drunken toast to us.

By the time Sven had enough, I was exhausted. We settled into our chairs, taking mugs of whiskey from Rufus. Sven immediately gulped his down while I demurely sipped from my tankard. Vincent and Kris were engrossed in conversation, poring over the map I'd seen her consulting that morning. I leaned in close, glancing over Kris' shoulder. I immediately recognized the Island of Bonaire, the course we'd just taken.

"We've just passed this point," Vincent said, marking a narrow channel on his map. "Another day, we'll pass this inlet. Then it's out to the open sea."

"Still no sign of pursuit?" I asked.

Vincent shook his head. "Perhaps they were all lost during the storm."

"We couldn't be that lucky." Kris reached over, leaned past her own mug and reached for mine. She had her fingers clasped around the handle, the mug halfway to her lips when I snatched it from her grasp.

"This one is yours." I nudged her mug toward her. She scowled as she raised it to her lips. She grimaced in disgust as she sipped at the water.

"How much longer must I endure this swill?"

"Until you've completely recovered." Vincent glanced up from the map and looked pointedly across the table at Kris. "And it'll take twice as long to heal if you don't take things easier."

Kris rolled her eyes. "It's a night for celebration," she protested.

"We shouldn't celebrate too quickly." Vincent's face betrayed the seriousness of our situation. "We may not be out of the woods yet."

"There may still be danger about?" I asked.

"Most assuredly, Lady DeVale."

The music still played loudly. Sailors drinking and dancing, the sounds of merriment were all about. Save for our table, where the mood had gone somber.

155

"What danger do you suspect?" I asked, leaning across the table.

Vincent glanced around the room, drew Kris and me in closer. Sven seemed to be oblivious to our conversation.

"Treachery of the utmost kind, I'm afraid." Vincent's face was grave, his voice low. "You and your mother were responsible for our first loss so many months ago."

"That's in the past." Kris' voice broke off, her jaw clenched.

I reached out, patting her wrist, attempting to soothe her.

"Vincent's correct, Kris. I was responsible for betraying you." I admitted my guilt. "That time," I added pointedly.

"The question becomes, who is responsible now?"

Kris fairly slammed her mug down on the table. "Look, Vincent, if you think for one minute that Alexis—"

"Keep your tongue in check for a moment." Vincent's tone was harsh, his features severe. Kris clamped her mouth shut, allowing him to continue. "No one is accusing the Lady DeVale of any wrongdoing."

"Then what is the point of this?" I asked. My own patience was beginning to wane. I was weary of constantly being under suspicion.

"You may not have been your mother's only ally."

I arched an eyebrow.

"Were you aware she offered several crewmembers a reward if they helped her escape? Brodey and Griffen told me about it on separate occasions."

"I knew she made the attempt." I caught Kris' surprised look out of the corner of my eye. I ignored her. "We made no secret of our desire to escape. But as far as I am aware, not a single member of your crew showed the slightest interest in her offer."

"What if someone did take the duchess up on her offer?" Vincent asked.

"You mean…"

Vincent nodded. "We may very well have a traitor in our midst."

156

Kris coughed, sputtered, spewing water halfway across the table. She wiped at her mouth with her sleeve.

Sven brushed water off his face, then returned to his whiskey as if nothing odd had happened.

"A traitor on board?" Kris asked, her tone incredulous.

"We spent too long planning our strategy. The English no doubt learned of our destination from Klaus. But someone had to tell them that the tavern keeper was your contact in Port Royale. And none but a member of your crew would know of your relationship with Brandy."

I bristled at the mention of Brandy's name. I was sympathetic for Kris' loss. But at the same time, I felt a sharp stab of jealousy for this other woman who had obviously meant something to my captain.

Kris voiced my own unspoken fear. "Then our traitor is still on board."

"That's a fair guess," Vincent said. He leaned forward, lowering his voice so Sven wouldn't overhear. "Assuming, of course, he wasn't one of the crewmen lost on the Island of Bonaire."

Kris cocked an eyebrow. "Payoff for a job well done?"

"It wouldn't surprise me a bit," I said, my voice strained to a whisper. "Mother would want to deal with any loose ends as quickly as possible."

Kris nodded. "She was pulled into the farmhouse before the shots turned deadly."

"I think we're in agreement then." Vincent said, glancing around, lowering his voice conspiratorially. "We must be on our guard against a traitor. Everyone is suspect."

"Including us?" I asked warily.

Kris' gaze flicked back and forth between Vincent and me. She seemed reluctant to take sides on this issue. Finally, she voiced her decision. "I trust you. Both of you," she said, her eyes fixed on me.

"If it had been one of us," Vincent added, "we could have turned the vessel around at any moment and delivered the entire crew into the waiting hands of our enemies."

"Aye," Kris said. "As far as I'm concerned, you're both above suspicion."

"Yeth, above suspicion." Sven slurred, raising his mug in salute. He teetered precariously on his chair. He slipped, hitting his chin on the table, spilling his drink. He wiped at the wet wood with his shirtsleeve.

"I think it's time Sven was put to bed." Kris rose from her chair and circled the table to where Sven sat.

Vincent intervened, pulling Sven from his chair. The brunt of his weight was on Vincent as they made their way for the door. He still held his mug in one hand at an odd angle, the whiskey pouring from his cup.

I grabbed the map from the table and rolled it up, sticking it in the waistband of my trousers. I sidled past Rufus and Brodey, seated at the next table over. Pushing past Lars, I rushed after my party.

†

Kris' gloved hand tenderly stroked my cheek, her leather-clad fingers soft against my flesh. She leaned in, her lips barely brushing mine. Still, it was enough to send my heart pounding.

"I'll only be a moment," she promised. "Just long enough to help Vincent put Sven to bed."

My lips curled into a smile. I arched an eyebrow. "Then perhaps you could put me to bed, as well, my captain?"

She exhaled loudly, her breath coming in a short puff upon the chilly night air. "It would be my pleasure." Her grin was broad, her teeth flashing.

She ducked through the doorway leading down to the crews' quarters. I watched her white tunic fade from view as she disappeared below the deck. Even though I could no longer see them, I could hear. Sven was belting out a particularly bawdy ballad. Vincent was doing his best to quiet him.

The cold bit sharply at my cheeks, my nose. I pulled the sleeves of my tunic down to cover my fingers. The farther north we traveled, the colder the nights became. As I waited, I saun-

158

tered to the riggings. I grasped the ropes and leaned over the edge of the ship, studying at the depths below. The sea was calm, waves gently lapping at the hull as we sat anchored upon the sea.

Looking up, I studied the stars. I had learned quite a bit about night navigation and constellations. I thought back to a time when I had tried to convince Elizabeth to join me. But she had no interest of learning the stars, she had said. It would hardly be required of a lady.

Elizabeth. She had surely returned to England by now. I imagined she was recovering from her ordeal at our family estate in the country, where she would no doubt be booked on every social calendar, attending all the masques and balls, relating the terrible story of her horrific ordeal. Every gentleman would be enthralled, every lady green with envy.

And Mother? At first thought, I imagined her well on her way back to England. On further reflection, she had probably sent word to my father that she was staying on a while to tend to my welfare. I could well imagine her advising Captain Jackson on how best to capture The Wolff. Or perhaps she realized what I had done and left me to my fate. No, that would be too kind. If Mother knew of my deeds, she would want to see me punished herself for my sins.

I was still contemplating such things when I heard a rustling sound to my right. I turned suddenly, catching Rufus off-guard. He had crept from the shadows and was now standing no more than two feet away. He grabbed my elbow, pinching, pulling me toward him.

"I see ye've finally completed your spell." Though lowered, his voice carried upon the wind.

"Pardon?" I asked, jerking my elbow roughly from his pinching fingers.

"Ye've cast a hex on the captain."

"I do not know what you mean."

"Don't ye, though?" he said through clenched teeth. "Ye've worked yer magic, haven't ye? And before long, ye'll have his soul, won't ye?"

I inhaled sharply, smelled an odd odor, sniffed again. "What is that God-awful stench?" I leaned toward Rufus, sniffing loudly. "Rufus! Are you wearing garlic?"

"Aye." He proudly pulled a long string of garlic from beneath his shirt. He wore it around his neck like a chain. "'Tis to keep yer sort away."

I could not find the words to respond. All I could do was stare, mouth open, eyes wide in disbelief.

"Demons and vampires and such can't stand the smell of garlic."

"Neither can most humans," I said. I shrank away, covering my nose and mouth with the sleeve of my shirt.

He fumbled in his apron pocket, producing a small wooden cross. He held the base between his fingertips as he attempted to place the surface of the cross to my bare hand. I jerked violently, attempting to escape. The cross went flying, landing several feet away, skittering across the deck. The cross came to rest beside the water barrels some twenty paces distant.

"What is the meaning?" The Wolff's voice boomed, much louder than I had ever heard her before. I jumped, startled by her outburst.

"I—" Rufus pointed a shaking finger at me. "She's a siren, my Captain."

"A siren?" Kris' hands were now placed firmly on her hips. Her fists clenched into tight balls. She stood straight, her full height intimidating.

"Aye, Captain. She's bewitched half the crew." He paused, licking his lips. He looked back and forth from Captain Wolff to me and back again. His eyes flicked to the deck. He pointed at the cross. "And she's bewitched ye, too." His eyes grew wide with fright even as the words escaped his mouth.

Kris took two steps nearer Rufus. She folded her arms across her chest and stared down at the round, little man. Her lips curled into a sneer. "Let me make one thing clear, Rufus." Her words came out slowly, ominously, as if she had to fight to get each syllable out between clenched teeth. "I'd best not ever—and I do mean ever—hear another word about Lady DeVale being a witch or demon or a vampire or a siren or whatever else your superstitious little mind may think she is."

"Aye, Captain." Rufus was visibly shaking in his boots.

"And another thing," she was poking a finger at his barrel chest, "I'd better never learn that you've been casting your *white magic* to rid my ship of what you deem is ill luck."

"Aye, Captain." Rufus's nostrils flared. He shot a scathing look beyond Kris' shoulder, directly at me.

Kris caught Rufus by the collar of his jerkin and forced him to look at her. His eyes were wide with fear. Hers, cold as steel with barely controlled rage and determination.

"Don't force me to choose, Rufus," she said. "I guarantee you won't like my decision."

Kris turned around so suddenly, and I was standing so closely, I was sent stumbling backwards. She reached out, catching me before I fell. Rock-steady arms supported me. Somehow, despite her touch and the reaction it caused in me, I managed to find my footing.

"Come," she said, pulling me by the hand. "Vincent can finish with Sven, and Rufus can return to his galley." She glanced back, staring pointedly at the old Scot.

I offered no resistance and allowed her to lead me away. In fact, I was glad to be as far away from Rufus McGregor as possible. The whole ordeal had struck too close a chord, reminding me of young Jonathan Fitzpatrick. An involuntary shiver ran through me.

"Cold?" Kris asked. She draped an arm about my shoulder and pulled me closer to her.

"No," I said. But as we walked, I snuggled in closer, my head nestling just below her chin.

We walked like that in silence for several more paces. She stopped, turning to face me. Both hands planted firmly on my shoulders, she looked at me, her eyes darting about my face.

"I'm so sorry." Her voice, loud and intimidating only moments before, was now soft and full of concern.

"For what?" I asked, making light of the situation. "Rescuing me?"

The glimmer of a smile flicked across her lips at my poor attempt at humor.

"My apologies, my lady, for the behavior of my crew. Rufus's actions were intolerable."

"He likes you," I said. "I think he genuinely liked me, too, until he realized how you felt about me."

She cocked an eyebrow. "And now, he doesn't like you? Because I do?"

"I think he does." I leaned back against the railing. "In his own way, even though he doesn't want to."

She ran fingers through her hair, exhaling loudly. "I can't believe he thinks those old tales about women on board ship being bad luck are true."

"Rufus is of an Old World lineage, Kris." I couldn't believe I was actually defending his actions. "He puts a lot of importance on ancient superstition."

She rubbed her chin thoughtfully and cocked her head to one side. "Still, how can he think you're a siren come to lure me to my doom?"

"What would be his reaction if he realized his captain was a woman in men's clothing? Who would he call witch then?"

"There's nothing bewitching about that. Joan of Arc passed herself off as man."

A smile formed upon my lips. She obviously idolized Joan of Arc. My heathenistic pirate captain's hero was none other than the Maid of Orleans. "Surely, you don't compare yourself to Savior Joan?"

"Of course not. I'm just pointing out that she wore men's clothes." She held out her arm. I looped mine through hers and fell in step beside her. We strolled along arm in arm, enjoying the brisk night air. "Besides, you English burned her at the stake."

"Hypocrite." I playfully slapped her on the arm.

"What?"

"I'd wager there's more than a pint of English blood running through those veins of yours."

"My lady, I must object." Her face was serious, but there was a laughing lilt in her voice. "It's very common knowledge that is not true."

"Then who were your parents?"

Her face froze. "My—"

"Parents." I arched my brows suggestively.

She squirmed uncomfortably at the question. She was obviously unaware that Vincent had confided in me. I was anxious to know her answer, whether she would admit to being born of noble blood.

She shrugged nonchalantly. "My father was a man of the sea, with no country to call home."

"And your mother?"

"She was—" She paused and watched her boots as she walked. Glancing up, she looked at me out of the corner of her eye.

"Yes?" I prompted.

"A mermaid."

My mouth dropped open. "A mermaid?"

"Yes. Quite."

Her answer was deadly serious. A small twitch tugged at the corner of my mouth. It started as a tiny giggle, and it grew until I was bent double with laughter, tears streaming down my cheeks.

My laughter was contagious. We were both still chortling when we reached my door. I paused with my hand upon the latch. My back was pressed up against the door, the rough wood scratching through my tunic.

I wiped the tears from my eyes and glanced up at Kris. She was staring at me, her gray eyes clouded with longing. My laughter caught and died in my throat. Her lips were parted, begging to be kissed. Sweat trickled off her brow, despite the cold. I swallowed hard. I looked beyond her, glancing up and down the deck. The deck was deserted, the crow's nest empty. A smile curved upon my lips.

I reached out, my hands finding her hair. My fingers stroked through her locks, fumbling with the knotted cord binding her ponytail. It pulled free, her hair falling loosely across her shoulders. I lifted the locks with my fingers, separating, allowing the strands to fall back into place.

She remained rooted to the spot. Unwilling—or unable—to raise a hand to stop me. I was insane. We both were. Me for doing this to her out in the open, where we could be discovered in a compromising position. Her for allowing me.

Her breeches were her customary black leather, tight in all the right places. Unfortunately, most of those places were hidden from view because she wore such a loose-fitting tunic that fell to mid-thigh. My fingers remembered what was beneath that tunic, though.

I knew what lay beneath that silk white shirt. A tight fitting, sleeveless shirt that hid those delicious breasts from view, unless you knew what to look for. And I most certainly knew what I was looking for. My hands reached out, my fingers unerringly finding her nipples.

Her nipples hardened quickly beneath my touch. My nails pinched, biting into the tender buds. I gently pulled. A soft growl escaped her lips. I licked my lips in response. A wicked smile formed as I had a delightedly devilish thought. I leaned forward, licking her lips. My teeth closed on her bottom lip, pulling, biting.

We were both breathless by the time I broke the kiss. Her chest heaved as she took in great gulps of air. Those gray eyes were now burning brightly with fevered lust. My fingers stroked down her cheek and across her neck. Her flesh was incredibly hot beneath my touch. I traced the fabric of her collar and slid my fingers down the middle of her shirt, between her breasts, to the waistband of her pants.

I grabbed her shirt, belt, and breeches all in one greedy handful. My other hand fumbled for the latch. I opened the door and backed inside, pulling her along with me, our mouths locked together.

She kicked the door closed with her boot. Hands on her shoulders, I pressed her up against the doorframe. Still kissing, my fingers fumbled for the latch. A metallic click echoed as it securely fastened in place.

Her own hands were on my waist, backing me, steering me across the room. She was grabbing at the end of my shirt and had it pulled off my body before I knew it. Her hot hands locked on my cool breasts, quickly warming them with her touch.

Something brushed against the back of my legs. Still, Kris continued to kiss me, tongue intertwining with mine as she guided us backwards. I was falling, reaching out for support. The bed gave way beneath my weight, creaking in protest. She was already upon me, a wolf pouncing upon her prey. She had tracked me to my own lair. Now she meant to devour me upon my own bed.

Eyes wild, face feral, she licked her lips as she looked at me, her tongue sliding across her lips in anticipation of the tasty morsel before her. The Wolff grinned at me, her features half-hidden by the shadow created by the lantern light.

I felt her teeth biting, nipping at my neck, my breasts, closing on my nipples. And I welcomed The Wolff with open arms, begging her to devour me.

†

We lay in my bed, arms and legs intertwined. The lantern still illuminated most of the room, though the oil had been burning for hours now. We were bathed in a mixture of light and shadow. I was curled up in her arms, head resting on her shoulder. My hand was on her breast, my fingers idly stroking up and down. Every now and then, my fingertips would stray up to the edge of her bandage.

I had changed the bandage before dinner. To my delight, it was still clean. No new traces of blood were visible. That was my greatest fear of late. That she would constantly keep reopening the wound with her exertions.

Medical resources were limited on board *The Wolfsbane*. Infection could prove deadly if improperly treated. Fortunately, her wound was healing nicely. The flesh surrounding the area was a healthy pink in color, only slightly swollen. But still tender to the touch.

Kris was fast asleep beside me, softly snoring. She was snuggled close, one arm draped possessively across my hipbone. Subtly, I rolled over, careful not to jostle the bed too much. There was a soft moan, the rustling of bed sheets as I gingerly made my way from the bed.

It was well past midnight when I stumbled from my cabin. The deck was dark, the moon hidden behind the clouds. There were no stars to guide ourselves by that night. The deck gently swayed beneath my feet, a sensation I'd grown accustomed to during the months since coming on board. I seriously doubted if I'd be able to keep my balance on level ground now. Steadying myself, I picked my way along the darkened deck.

The Wolfsbane was essentially deserted. Anchored for the night as she was, there would be no need for a navigator at the wheel. Her crew was resting below deck, their captain sleeping peacefully in my quarters.

Passing the main mast and riggings, I suddenly halted. There, upon the rear deck, someone stood with a lantern. Not my captain, I knew; she was securely tucked into my bed. Then who? I could not tell. The height was average. His long hair blew in the breeze. But long hair was common amongst the crew. I ducked into the shadows, watching.

He opened then closed the slits on the lantern casing, flashing beams of light through the slits. Open. Closed again. Another flash of light caught my attention. At our rear, across the sea, in the direction we had just come. I knew we'd passed no land. Therefore, it must be another vessel. I watched from the shadows. The crewman returned the signal.

My heart beat loudly. Perspiration trickled down my brow. I was alone on deck with the traitor. With no weapons. And no sign of help.

I crept along, keeping my body pressed into the shadows. Each footstep was carefully measured, each movement delicately constructed. I sent a silent prayer that I would not be seen. As I took another cautious step, a board creaked beneath my weight. He turned around. I froze. His eyes searched the darkness, his ears alert, listening for the slightest sound. I held my breath. I waited.

166

He turned around again, resumed his signaling with the lantern light. I stretched out my hand, reaching for the rope hanging outside the galley door. I pulled frantically, ringing the bell as hard as I could.

The shrill clanging broke the night's spell. He looked dead at the galley, coming straight toward me. The crew streamed up from down below, flooding the deck in a sea of activity. They were in various forms of readiness, eager to respond to my alarm. When my gaze returned to the railing, he was gone.

"What is it?" Kris asked, appearing at my side. "What's happening?"

"Someone was on deck," I said. Crewmen were beginning to mill around me, eager for my news. "He was using a lantern to signal out to sea."

I pointed at the stern of the ship. Brodey rushed over, searching the deck. He retrieved the dropped lantern, brought it to his captain. Kris stared out to sea. The answering signal had stopped. She held the lantern firmly in her grasp.

"Where is he?" she demanded.

"Gone when I sounded the alarm." I rushed to the rail, looked over the side. "Possibly overboard."

She turned to Sven. "Gather all the men. The one that's either drenched or missing is our traitor."

"Aye, Captain." Sven rushed off with a party of men.

"What the devil is going on?" Vincent asked, just now joining us. Properly English, he had taken the time to fully dress. He was still buttoning his shirtsleeves, though. He looked as if he'd been roused from a deep slumber.

"It appears your ships survived the storm, Vincent." She plucked the telescope from Vincent's belt and pointed it to our aft. "And someone on board has been signaling them, guiding them straight to us."

The deck was a bustle of activity now. Lanterns washed the deck in light as sailors rushed to and fro. The anchor chain was pulled up, the sails unfurled. We caught the wind and were moving in no time. Vincent moved to the ship's wheel. Unlocking the wooden peg holding it in position, he began to steer us straight ahead. There were no stars to guide by; he would just have to hold us on a straight northerly course.

Sven rushed up to us, breathless. Sweat streamed off his bare chest and arms. "Everyone is accounted for, Captain Wolff."

"Did you check everywhere?"

"Aye," he said. "They're all here. No one's been over the side, either."

"Are ye sure the wench saw anything at all?" Rufus asked, appearing at Sven's elbow. He wore a dressing gown atop his kilt and white undershirt and was tying the ends closed.

"We found the lantern," Kris said. "He went over the side when she sounded the alarm."

"Then he's likely drowned," Rufus said. "Pulled down by our undertow."

"Perhaps," Vincent said. "But we thought the ships pursuing us were gone, as well."

His words hung in the air. I shivered against the cold wind that blew across the ship. I pulled Kris' loose tunic tighter about myself. My teeth chattered violently.

"Go back to your cabin and rest," Kris said. "There's nothing more you can do here tonight."

I nervously looked in the direction of my cabin. It wasn't that far off. There were plenty of crewmen on deck. It was childish to be afraid. Still, I didn't want to go alone.

"Will you escort me?"

She glanced at the ship's wheel and her waiting men, then looked longingly at me. I knew what she was going to say. She was the captain. Duty demanded she stay.

"I'll be along shortly," she said. She turned, called to Brodey. "Take her to my cabin," she ordered.

"Aye, sir."

"You'll rest far easier there," she said, clasping my hands. "Rest well, Alexis. You're safe."

I nodded numbly. I felt silly, scared of the boogeyman in the night. She had her ship to see to. She didn't need me underfoot. Still, I thought as I allowed Brodey to lead me away, I would have felt more reassured if she'd gone with me.

✝

It was just after dawn when next I came out on deck. I blinked and shielded my eyes against the harsh sunlight. A yawn escaped my lips. I had slept fitfully. Not wanting to sleep at all until my captain joined me. But fatigue had eventually overcome me. Still I only slept briefly, jerking awake at the slightest noise.

The crew was up and about, as well, rushing to their tasks, except for a half dozen men who were stumbling toward the lower decks. Undoubtedly these men had worked with Captain Wolff throughout the night, ensuring our escape.

The nauseating smell of eggs assaulted me as I passed the galley. Lars came from the open door, passed me a hot plate. I took it, thanking him. He wiped breadcrumbs from his beard and rushed past me to join Brodey and Hughes. They were with another group of men, lining up the ship's cannons. Loading them for battle. Sven led a party of his own, loading muskets beneath the main sail.

I found Kris still at the ship's wheel with Vincent. She smiled gratefully as I handed her the plate with warm bread and eggs. Her smile was weary, just as she was. Her eyes were red-rimmed, dark circles beneath them.

"Want some?" she asked, biting off a piece of bread, chewing voraciously.

"No, thank you." I picked up Vincent's telescope, focusing on the water. "Are they still with us?"

"Aye," Kris said. "Vincent spotted them off our port side with the rising sun. Both bearing English flags."

My heart sank. "How far away?"

"Some leagues distant," Vincent answered. "If we can get past the inlet and reach the open sea, we'll have a chance at outrunning them."

"If?" I asked, lowering the telescope, staring at Vincent and the captain.

"If," Kris said. "Use the telescope. Look to your right."

169

I raised the telescope, focusing. The inlet lay ahead of us. Coral reefs flanked the inlet on both sides, leaving barely enough room for two ships side by side to pass through. The reefs gave way to mighty cliffs overlooking the sea, atop the right cliff, stood a structure. I refocused, bringing the image in clearer. It was a fort, flying a Spanish flag.

"They guard our only escape route. And the English ships are steadily driving us into their waiting hands."

"How long?" I asked.

"If we don't stop," Vincent answered, "we'll reach the castle just before dusk."

"And if we stop?"

Vincent and Kris looked at one another. "We stand no chance against two English Navy vessels."

"But against the Spanish?"

"Their cannons are aimed at the sea. We'll be cut to pieces before we can get close to the inlet."

I frowned, studying the map, looking through the telescope again, at the fortress by the sea. At the enemy ships, their English flags barely visible in the distance. I bit my lip in concentration, trying to decide if there would be time enough for my plan.

Kris was eating heartily, shoveling eggs into her mouth. Now she stopped, fork in midair. She stared at me. "What is it, my lady?" she asked around a mouthful.

"I have a plan." I leaned in closer, motioning them nearer. "We need to anchor just out of reach of the fortress's cannon fire."

"Go on, we're listening." Vincent's voice was barely a hushed whisper.

I glanced up and down the deck, looking for any sign of an eavesdropper. I lowered my voice. It wouldn't do for our plans to be overheard. If nothing else, the night before had proven we weren't alone. "We're going to need all the luck we can get."

Chapter Eleven

THE CAPTAIN

We were anchored in the bay, as per Alexis's orders. The Spanish cannons were fixed on our position, waiting for our attack. The English ships were still far enough off that they posed no immediate threat.

We were safe. For the moment.

Brodey and Lars were loading men and muskets into the longboats. Three boats in all, fully loaded to capacity. Two of the boats were already in the water. I was in the third, readying the signal to lower.

"Hold the boat." Alexis was at the side, reaching out a hand. Sven grabbed on, preparing to help her in.

"You're not going." My voice was firm.

"Yes, I am." She looked as if I'd slapped her. "It's my plan."

I glared at her. "It's far too dangerous."

"I'm going."

Hughes was climbing out of the longboat. Alexis was already going in, Sven helping her. Hands folded across my chest, I refused to budge.

Vincent appeared at my elbow, whispering into my ear. His hot breath tickled my flesh. "We're wasting time. Permit her to go with you."

I looked at the horizon. The sun was lower in the sky and setting lower by the minute. Its orange rays were casting long shadows across the water. It would be dark within the hour. There was no time to force her to remain.

171

Without further delay, I stepped into the boat, gave the signal. Hughes and Watkins lowered the boat into the water. Brodey's longboat was already halfway to shore. Lars's party was just behind him. Our boat was barely pulling away from the ship.

"Light the torches," Alexis said.

"It's barely dark," I protested. "It's still light enough to see."

She flicked her hair back, looking pointedly at me. "We have to make a good showing of it."

"Light the torches," I snapped.

Long slats were pulled from broken boards upon *The Wolfsbane*. Rags tied to the ends, soaked in oil. Flint struck together, sparking, set the rags on fire. Torches aboard the longboat ahead of us were lit. Brodey's boat was quickly approaching shore, their torches unlit. One crewman jumped from the longboat, landing in shallow water. He splashed as he ran, catching onto the ropes at the bow of the boat, pulling it to shore.

I looked back. *The Wolfsbane* was barely visible by now, the setting sun casting long shadows about her. No light was coming from anywhere upon the ship. There was no movement above deck. She looked to be deserted.

Sven jumped from our longboat, grabbing the rope at our bow. He wrapped the rope round his forearm. He pulled, dragging us ashore. Several of the men helped him embed the bow firmly into the muddy bank.

Torches held high, we disembarked, making for shore. Those who didn't have torches carried packs of bedrolls underneath their arms. I climbed the muddy embankment, wiping my boots upon the wild grass that grew near the water's edge. I reached out a gloved hand, helping Alexis up the steep rise.

"Which way?" Lars asked, his party of men joining us.

"This way." Alexis pointed to her left, starting off in the direction of the fortress.

The men flanked her, following her directions. I allowed her the lead, deferring to her orders. We caught up with Brodey's men some twenty paces distant. They were hunkered low in a throng of reeds, watching the fortress.

"What's the word?" I asked, kneeling beside Brodey.

He pointed at the stone structure in the distance. "There are troops upon the battlements. Cannons at the ready, pointed out to sea." He crouched low, inching forward. "I don't think they've spotted us yet."

"Light your torches then," Alexis said.

"My lady!"

"Do it, Brodey," I said.

"Captain Wolff," he protested, "we stand a chance of taking them by land."

"Do it, Brodey!" I snapped. "We have neither the time nor the means to wage a land war on a Spanish fortress."

"Aye, sir." He snapped back, his lip curled in open disdain. He nodded at his party. "You heard the captain. Torches high."

Despite a sea of mumbling protests, they obeyed orders. Flint struck together in the darkness; torches were lit. The silhouette of the cannons on the turrets slowly shifted, aiming toward us.

✝

This part of Alexis's plan caused me the most unease. Even though it was our intent all along to bring as much notice to ourselves as possible. We were to be the decoy, drawing all attention away from the channel. And *The Wolfsbane*.

Out of my entire crew, it was the Lady DeVale who first rose from her position, making her way through the reeds, directly toward the fortress.

Was it her courage or her innocence that made me follow her? I picked my way through the waist-high reeds. The three parties from the boats were directly behind us, torches held high, announcing our approach.

Moving as we were, it took us another half hour to find a small clearing. We wanted to attract attention, but I didn't want my men running pell-mell through darkened woods. I signaled for a halt, crouched down, watching the clearing and the trees just beyond.

"Anything?" Alexis asked, kneeling beside me.

She was so close I could feel her hot breath upon my cold neck. Her right hand rested upon my upper thigh for support. She bit her bottom lip as she surveyed the clearing.

"Nothing," I said, my voice a hoarse whisper.

"Even if they sent troops, they couldn't reach here till dawn," Brodey said, kneeling in the bushes beside us.

"Unless they had scouting parties out closer."

I continued to watch the trees just beyond the clearing. My left eye twitched. I didn't much care for this business of sneaking around in the dark, torches fully lit, announcing to our enemy our precise location.

I pulled my pistol from my belt, checked to see that it was loaded. Of course it was. I was merely stalling, thinking out our options. I signaled for Lars to move up from his position some fifteen paces back.

"Lars, I want you to take a man with you. Circle the clearing this way," I instructed, making a sweeping motion with my arm to the left. "Brodey and I will go that way." I pointed in the opposite direction. "We'll meet straight across from where we are now. If you encounter anyone, fire a single shot."

Alexis stood, readying the pistol I had given her. She started off with Lars. I grabbed her by the tunic sleeve, spinning her around.

"Where do you think you're off to?"

"Scouting for the enemy."

"No."

"No?"

The torchlight cut an eerie glow upon the area, illuminating bits and pieces in a flickering light, chasing shadows back. Only half her profile was illuminated by the firelight. The other half was hidden in shadow. Still, the half that I saw was enough to let me know she was vexed. Her mouth was set in a hard, thin line. Her brows were narrowed. She stared unblinking at me.

I held my ground, folding my arms across my chest, coolly appraising the situation. I heard snickers coming from the darkness. My crew was no doubt amused by the obvious standoff.

For someone who swore to protect my secret, she was doing a splendid job of undermining my authority at every turn.

"You're going to stay with Sven," I said. "When we reach the far side, I'll signal that the area is safe. Then you'll proceed with the men into the clearing. We'll continue to watch the perimeter until you're set."

I turned to go with Brodey, sneaking through the underbrush, watching our surroundings for enemy movement. I'd barely gone twenty paces when I heard a twig snap behind me. I paused, listening. Brodey was at least another fifteen paces ahead of me, easily picking his way along. A quick glance back confirmed that my crew waited in the woods, burning torches marking their position.

Another twig snapped. I knelt down. My tunic and breeches were both black. I was positive I couldn't be seen in the darkened woods. I crouched, holding my position, waiting. The sound of rustling leaves broke the silence. Stealthily, I pulled my knife from its hiding place inside my boot. I flipped the blade with a flick of my wrist, catching the hilt in my open palm. I balanced its weight in my hand, anticipating my prey.

Footsteps approached. A pair of long legs covered by tan breeches came into view. I scarcely breathed as kneecaps went right past my nose. Every muscle in my body tensed. I counted the seconds till those breeches walked past.

I pounced from the underbrush. I grabbed him around the waist, knocking him to his knees. We scuffled until I managed to land him on his back, straddling him. I leaned in, my blade pressed to his throat.

I recognized the mass of blonde hair. The tight jaw, clenched teeth, and furious green eyes.

"Get...off...me," she demanded, fists flailing.

I dropped my blade, grabbed her wrists in one hand, squeezing. "Hold," I demanded. Still, she bucked beneath me. It took all my strength to keep her from tossing me off. I used my free hand to pin her shoulders to the hard ground. "Alexis, stop." She continued to thrash about beneath me. "It's me, Kris."

Her struggles abruptly ceased. Her body slowly relaxed. Her eyes focused on me.

175

"What do you think you're doing?"

"I might ask you the same thing."

Her eyes flashed with anger. "Get off."

I remained firmly planted atop her, my powerful thighs holding her in place. The weight of my upper body pinned her beneath me.

"First, tell me what you're doing out here."

"Fine." She exhaled loudly. "I followed you. It's my plan and you're excluding me."

"Yes, it is your plan," I said. "That's why I ordered you to stay behind. To implement your plan as we protected you."

"You ordered me—"

That was the wrong thing to say. And I knew it. Still I couldn't let it be. She had to realize she was wrong. "Yes, my lady. I'm your captain," I said through clenched teeth. "And I ordered you to stay behind."

Her struggles increased once again. "Let me up!" she yelled. "Get off, you bastard."

She bucked wildly beneath me, nearly throwing me. I slipped, braced myself, landed on my outstretched forearm. She tried to squirm from beneath me. I raised my head suddenly, straining to hear. She continued to hit me with her fists, belting out a litany of curses. I scrambled back on top of her.

"Quiet." My mouth was at her ear.

"Why, you son of a—"

My hand clamped down over her mouth. I pressed down with all my weight. "Hush," I ordered, my voice a strained whisper. "Someone's coming."

Alexis's struggles abruptly ceased. Her body remained tensed beneath me. She looked back and forth.

There was the crunching of leaves, the rustling of bushes. My left hand remained clamped on Alexis's mouth. My right reached out, searching blindly. Sweat rolled off my brow, stinging my eyes.

Black leather boots walked past. Stopped, came back. The point of a musket repeatedly thrust into the brush. My fingers found and closed upon the hilt of my knife. I strained my neck and looked up. Through the foliage, I could see a pair of white-trousered legs.

Gathering all my energy into one movement, I lunged forward, slashing with my knife, severing tendons behind his knees, bringing him down. My knife flashed again, slicing his throat open. He fell to the ground, blood gurgling as he tried to choke out a scream. I clamped my hand over his mouth, held it firmly in place until his body stopped twitching.

Alexis was at my side, her eyes riveted to the soldier's still body. "Is he—"

"Dead." I wiped my blade on the soldier's pants leg. I grabbed the Spaniard by one boot, tugging. "Help me drag him into the bushes."

She hesitated only momentarily before grabbing his other boot. Together, we tugged, dragging him into the underbrush. I kicked loose dirt onto his body, attempting to hide his bright white trousers. Picking up my musket, I passed it to Alexis. She stared at me, mouth open, eyes wide.

"From the stripes on his coat sleeves," I said, "he's a sergeant. Part of a scouting party."

"How many?" she asked, eyes nervously scanning the woods.

"Usually, a platoon of five travel together." I searched the woods as I spoke. Not seeing any immediate danger, I looked at Alexis. For the first time since I'd known her, she looked every bit like a scared little girl. "Go back the way you came. Tell Sven what's happened."

I turned to go, took two steps before she grabbed me by the arm, pulling me back.

"Where are you going?" she asked.

"To take care of the rest of the platoon. They're sure to miss him soon," I said, nodding at the dead soldier.

Alexis's eyes were panic-stricken. "You're going to leave me? Just like that?" Her lips visibly trembled. "What if I encounter one of them before I reach Sven? What will I do?"

"Do what you must," I said. I leaned in, kissed her cold lips tenderly. "Work quickly."

I darted back into the underbrush before she could stop me again. For if she did, if she dared to plead with me, I wouldn't have the strength to go. I glanced back. My breath caught at the sight of her blonde hair through the overgrowth. I felt the urge to go to her.

I pushed Alexis to the back of my mind, and concentrated on my task ahead. I had to stop them. All of them. Before they could learn of our plan and report back to their commander at the fortress. Not a single one could be allowed to escape. Clutching my knife in my hand, I ducked low, pushing through the thick woods.

†

I leaned against the south side of the tree, pressing my back against the trunk. The rough bark bit into the thin fabric of my shirt. My breathing was labored. And despite the chill in the air, sweat poured off my body.

Involuntarily, my mind drifted back to the last time I was upon dry land. I had been gravely injured. Only Alexis's quick wits saved me. She alone guided me through the sugarcane crop and into the woods. Woods very much like these. I was in and out of consciousness, but I recalled vivid patches of clarity during which she tended me, nursing my wound as we took shelter. She had placed her hand beneath my tunic, pressing against my wound. Shaking my head vigorously, I banished the memory.

Casting a furtive glance back, I focused on the bodies of the two soldiers on the ground nearby. Their backs had been to me, watching the activity at the clearing, readying their muskets. I had worked quickly, subduing them, efficiently hiding their bodies in the underbrush. The first one died quickly. The second one only wished he had.

I stood at the edge of the wood, camouflaged by underbrush and darkness. I studied the clearing, the woods surrounding the open field. I felt a hand upon my shoulder and nearly jumped out of my skin from fright.

"How many more?" Brodey asked, kneeling beside me in the brush. He wiped his knife blade upon his shirtsleeve, threw a Spanish musket over his back and adjusted the shoulder strap.

178

"Only one."

"You sure?" He looked wildly across the terrain.

"Aye," I said. "Pedro over there doesn't speak much English." I nodded at where the soldier lay upon the ground, bound and gagged. He was stripped stark naked, his clothes in a bundle beneath my arm. "But he understands enough to tell me there's only five of them."

Keeping low, Brodey darted back to where our prisoner lay balled up on the ground. He drew his knife, pressing the tip to the Spaniard's throat. A trickle of blood ran down his neck. "How do you know he's not lying?" Brodey pressed the knife in deeper. The Spaniard made muffled protests against his gag, struggled to squirm away from Brodey's knife.

"He was at first," I said, my voice remarkably calm. "Until I told him I would strip his clothes off of him and skin him alive until he spoke the truth." I sauntered over, knelt beside the soldier. I reached out, easily taking Brodey's knife from his grasp. I flashed my most menacing grin and the soldier's eyes went wide with fright. "Barely got to prick the skin," I said, a twinge of disappointment edging my voice.

I flipped the knife in my hand, catching the blade in my open palm. I offered the weapon to Brodey, hilt first. Chuckling, he slipped the long-handled knife back onto his belt. Retracing my steps, I paused at the edge of the thick wood. Brodey joined me, peering over me. We remained hidden in the thick foliage, cloaked by darkness.

A roaring fire was in the middle of the field. My crew rushed about, hurrying to complete their tasks. Several of the men were building fires of twigs and grass, striking pieces of flint together to spark the dry leaves.

I could have spotted Alexis a mile away. She was standing near the center of the clearing, the large bonfire silhouetted behind her. The light from the fire cast a glow about her, emphasizing every delectable curve. Her long hair was loose, falling about her shoulders, the glow from the fire creating a halo around her blonde tresses. She was giving directions, instructing the crew to place the bedrolls upon the ground. I watched as she directed them to fill the bedrolls with leaves and twigs. She herself placed clumps of moss at the head of each of the bedrolls.

A flicker of movement beyond Alexis's left shoulder caught my attention. It was a tiny glow, too far away from the clearing to be from one of our campfires. I elbowed Brodey in the ribs, nodded in the general direction. He nodded in agreement.

"If nothing else, the Spanish will smoke us to death."

Sighing, I started to my right through the underbrush. The soldier was almost directly straight across the clearing from my position. It would take precious time to work my way around the clearing through the dense woods, but it couldn't be helped. We dare not risk anyone witnessing our ruse. I picked my way through the underbrush with as much haste as I could. I'd scarcely gone ten yards when I heard the loud rustling of leaves, the crashing of twigs. My head snapped up, looking to the clearing.

Brodey was racing across the open field, powerful legs and arms pumping, carrying him in great strides. He was already halfway through the field before I could react. The glowing ebb from the cigarette disappeared, thrown upon the ground. I caught sight of a white shirt running deeper into the wood.

"Damn." I cursed, breaking cover. I made a mad dash after him, running across the field, stumbling across uneven ground. Shouting at Brodey, yelling for my men to help. "Stop him! Don't let him get away!"

Alexis and Sven were near the largest campfire. Both stared open-mouthed at me as I darted past, chasing Brodey at a pell-mell pace. I heard the shouts behind me, knew that they were organizing a group to help with the pursuit. Brodey was several yards ahead of me by now and gaining ground with every long stride. I struggled to close the gap. My heart was pounding wildly in my chest. My lungs burned with each breath. Sweat poured off me, stinging my eyes. I blinked rapidly, swiped at my face with my sleeve.

I leapt over a small thicket as the open field gave way to thick woods. I crashed through the underbrush. Dodging branches and trees alike. I worked my way deeper into the wood. Legs aching, heart pounding, I finally caught sight of Brodey. He was standing between two trees, frantically turning this way and that, hands thrown up in frustration. Breathing heavily, I came to a halt beside him.

"It's no use, Captain," he said. "We've lost him."

My face contorted with rage. "What the hell were you thinking?"

He ran his hand through his long curly hair. "That it's well past dark and we don't have time to sneak around, playing cat and mouse."

"So you decided to charge across a wide open field?"

He shrugged. "I thought I could catch him."

"You thought you could catch him? It never crossed your mind that he would bolt like a deer as soon as he saw you?"

My crew had caught up. They stood by, watching the confrontation between Brodey and me.

I folded my arms across my chest, staring him down. "Because of you," I pointed an accusing finger at Brodey, "he's on his way back to the fortress to tell his commander what he's seen."

"It'll be dawn before he can reach the fortress by foot," Brodey said.

I ran a hand across my weary face. "What if he has a horse?" I yelled.

A hand tugged at my arm. I turned, came face to face with Alexis.

"What's done is done. Arguing will not change anything," she said. "We must hurry. Time is of the essence."

I nodded. "You heard her," I bellowed at my crew. "Move it. Now!"

They ran from the woods, a sea of sailors breaking across an open field. They ran headlong across the field, making for the ocean of reeds that lay somewhere beyond the darkness. They disappeared into the darkness as one by one they doused their torches in buckets of water waiting beside the campfires.

My legs were aching, muscles burning by the time I reached the edge of the camp. I slowed to a jog, then stopped, looking back at Alexis's handiwork. Frantically, I looked for sight of her. She had created the campsite. From this distance, it looked real.

Complete with pirates sleeping in their bedrolls around the small fires, resting before a full-scale attack by land.

It would look equally realistic from the Spanish fortress. Even with the use of telescopes, the Spanish wouldn't be able to see much more than the glow of enemy campfires. To learn more, they would have to send scouting parties across marshes and woods in the dark.

Lars rushed by, pulling me by the arm. I turned, stumbling upon uneven ground. I fell to my knees, hitting hard. I came up almost immediately, desperately looking around. It was difficult going in the darkness, but I raced on as fast as I could. I caught sight of two heads of long blonde hair, running side by side. Relieved, I breathed easier. It could only be Sven and Alexis.

The reeds slapped hard against my thighs, making a wet smacking sound with each step. Mud sucked at the soles of my boots, weighing me down. My legs were like lead by the time I reached open ground. I stumbled upon the soft ground, jumped from the embankment without hesitation. Water splashed my face as I hit the ocean floor hard, landing feet first.

The final longboat was rowing from shore. Water thigh high, I splashed through the surf, running toward the boat. The water slowed me down, my recovering body already tired from the night's activities.

The water was chest high. I reached out, catching the rope that ran the length of the boat. Hands were on me, grabbing at my shirt, hoisting me into the longboat. I fell into the bottom of the vessel. I lay there, breathing hard, chest heaving, lungs burning. Weary, I stayed in the bottom of the boat, awaiting our return to *The Wolfsbane*.

†

The Wolfsbane was a ghost ship floating upon the sea. No light, no sign of life. A large black vessel upon a sea of black water, framed by a black, starless night. The short sails were unfurled. The main sail was left rolled, so as not to be seen from the shore. The anchor chain made a ghostly moaning sound as it was pulled up, metal clanging against metal.

Vincent was at the wheel, strong hands smoothly gliding across the rough wood. Arms flexed as he steered us straight toward the fortress. He barely moved as I reached around him, snatching the telescope from his belt.

"Well?" he asked.

I pointed the telescope at the fortress, bringing it into focus. I trained my sight upon the walls, following the battlements.

"The cannons are pointed inland," I said, smiling broadly.

"Keep watch," he said. "The closer we are, the more vulnerable we become."

I watched, praying that the Spanish would not notice the ship moving closer. I glanced at the sky. It was late. Dawn was only hours away. We needed to reach the inlet before sunlight. We'd be obvious during the day, sitting ducks upon the water.

Our short sails caught the wind, moving us steadily. I watched through the telescope, focusing as we approached the rocky shores.

"The coast is clear," I said. "No guards to be seen." I swiveled, moving the telescope across the walls again. "No movement upon the battlements."

I wiped my sweaty palms upon my breeches, fought to slow my breathing. This waiting was more excruciating than facing a dozen enemy ships. Striding to the aft deck, I trained the telescope upon the open sea. I turned, ran back to the ship's wheel.

"The English are coming," I said between clenched teeth.

He nodded. "While you were upon the shoreline, they made good use of the time. They've been steadily closing upon us for hours now."

We were sailing into the passageway. My crew fell silent, watching. Several of them manned the cannons in case we needed to make a fight of it. Walls of rocks crested both sides of *The Wolfsbane*. Vincent took us straight down the middle of the passage, hoping to dodge any hidden sandbars.

"We've been spotted!" I shouted. The men ducked, crouched low upon the deck, diving for cover.

The wall nearest the passage was a sudden flurry of activity. The sound of stone scraping upon stone filling the night as the Spaniards moved to reposition their cannons. Dozens of musket barrels appeared, raining a barrage of lead upon us.

"Get the mainsail up!" Sven yelled, the crew rushing to the mast.

Our own cannons erupted, smoke coming from their barrels. The balls found their targets, smacking into the fortress walls. The south turret was brought down by a well-placed shot, bricks falling, rolling, careening off the cliff, splashing into the water. There was no answering cannon fire, only the volley of lead from their muskets. Their shots were harmless. Not powerful enough to reach our ship, the shots fell short, landing in the sea.

I ran to the aft deck. The two ships were coming, mainsails billowing. English flags crested each mast, swelling as the wind caught them, the colors displayed proudly. Their decks were brightly lit. I could see their long-nines being loaded, their barrels turned toward us.

I seethed, knowing Jackson would not rest until he caught us. And I was powerless to do anything but run. "They're bearing down upon us. They'll be within range soon."

"They'll have to slow when they reach the passage," Vincent said. "Or risk being shattered upon the rocks."

The Wolfsbane continued upon her steady course. Nervously, I paced the deck, watching the English ships drawing nearer. The soldiers on the battlements worked rapidly, repositioning their cannons for a clear shot.

We were out of the passage and well on our way before the first cannonball was fired at us. It fell short, slamming into the water just off our port side. It hit with such force that water spewed up over the deck, drenching us. I shook the saltwater from my hair, wiped my face upon my wet sleeve.

"They're in the bay, near the passage! They're firing cannons!"

Vincent turned the wheel sharply, steering us up the coastline. With luck, the slower-moving English vessels would have a rough time maneuvering to follow us up the shoreline. I ran for the mainmast. I tucked the telescope into my belt, hurried up the pole. When I reached the top, I scrambled into the crow's nest. I yanked the telescope from my belt.

"They've slowed!" I yelled, leaning over the edge, shouting down at my men.

Cannon fire erupted from the decks of both ships. The cannons were no longer aimed at *The Wolfsbane*, however. Rather, they'd been turned toward the coastline. More cannon fire erupted from the fortress. Cannonballs whistled through the air, hitting the foresails on one of the ships. The mast cracked, crashed upon the deck.

"They think the English are with us!" I yelled. "They've turned their cannons upon the ships in the bay."

Cries of joy rang out from my crew. Rufus pulled a flask from his apron, hoisted it in the air. The crew fell silent as he spoke.

"May they sink the both of them before the dawn comes," he toasted, raising his flask, drinking heartily.

The crew danced and laughed merrily upon the deck. I remained in the crow's nest, watching the action unfold. I cast a glance at the horizon. It was lighter already, dawn wouldn't be far off. And with the coming daylight, the Spaniards would cease fire, realizing they'd been attacking their allies.

Still, it was a small victory, giving us maneuvering room, a chance to rest. I leaned back, watching the battle, enjoying the smoke and fireworks.

✝

Much later, I shimmied down the mainmast. My leather boots echoed loudly upon the wooden deck as I jumped the final few feet. The deck was deserted, my crew having retreated below for a well-deserved rest. Each and every one of them had been up throughout the night, implementing Alexis's plan. Now with the coming dawn, they were finally able to sleep.

A sudden wind came up. I huddled deeper into the warmth of my tunic. My fingers curled up, my hands becoming tight little balls firmly tucked into the sleeves. A yawn escaped my lips.

185

Hunkered down for warmth, I shuffled off toward my cabin. Head bowed, I watched my feet upon the uneven planks as I hurried along.

I reached the doorway to my cabin. Hand grasping the handle, I paused, staring at the latch. The door was ajar. With a determined shove, I jerked the door open, rushed inside, and ran right into Alexis. The impact jostled both of us, and she was sent stumbling backwards. Her boots caught upon the edge of the rug and she fell, landing on her ass.

I was at her side instantly, kneeling upon the rug, helping her to a sitting position, one hand about her waist. The other at her face, fingers stroking hair back from her reddened cheeks.

"My apologies, Alexis," I said, my hand absently stroked down her thighs, down her legs, across her ankles, checking for injuries. "I didn't expect you. Have I hurt anything?"

Her eyes coolly appraised me. "Only my pride."

"You come to celebrate?" I said, winking at her.

"My plan worked well then, did it?"

"Very well, my lady," I said. "Your camp made the Spaniards believe we were attacking by land. All their cannons were turned inland. They didn't expect us to sneak through the passage under their very noses."

Alexis pushed away from me, stood on shaking legs. She crossed to the open window. With her arms wrapped about her waist, she stared out to sea.

"But the English ships—"

"An hour ago, I watched the Spanish fortress open fire upon the English vessels. In the dark, they thought the ships were our allies. With luck, they'll sink both ships before the dawn comes and they realize their mistake."

Alexis turned from the window, looking at me sharply. Her eyes were clouded, her face stricken. "Well, that's something, at least."

I barely caught her words before she turned back to the window. I came to stand behind her, hands upon her waist. I had expected her to melt into my arms. Instead, she jumped at the contact. My lips came to her ear.

Fingers brushed blonde locks from her neck. My lips found her flesh, softly kissing, teeth gently biting, mouth suckling. She stiffened. My hands moved on her body, about her waist. I pressed into her from behind. My hands closed about both breasts. I felt her tense beneath me. My right hand continued to fondle her breasts, fingers flicking her hardening nipples. My left moved down to cup her center. She went rigid beneath my touch. I let loose her breast, blindly groped for the telescope upon my belt. Bringing it around, I made certain she saw it in my grasp. My hand dropped lower. I pressed deeper into her. A gasp escaped her lips. She squirmed. My left hand held her firmly in place.

"Shall I do you with this, Alexis?" I used the narrow end of the telescope to trace the outline of her lips through her breeches. "Shall we see how deep it can go?"

"If it pleases the captain to take me that way." Her tone was dry, her anger simmering.

I gripped her by the shoulders and roughly spun her around. Her eyes were closed, lips parted. My mouth closed upon hers. My tongue roughly pushed between her lips. Seeking, taking what I pleased. I jerked back, abruptly ending our kiss.

"You're here for no mere dalliance," I said. "You're angry." My tone was flat, my voice cold.

Her eyes opened, flickered briefly upon me before looking away again. "Do I have cause to be?"

"No," I said. "But you are." My left hand thrust between Alexis's legs, cupping, roughly rubbing. "You stiffen at my touch." I looked at her accusingly, my jaw set firmly. "You didn't come for my caresses. Why are you here?"

Caught as she was, her defiant chin didn't jut forward quite so proudly. Her cheeks flushed a deep crimson. She looked furtively about, refusing to meet my gaze. She attempted to step back but was already firmly against the wall. She was cornered, with nowhere to run. My fingers continued their assault, eliciting responses from Alexis's body that I was certain she wasn't quite prepared to give.

Her nostrils flared, eyes narrowing to tiny slits. "Fine," she spat out vehemently, crossing her arms over her chest. "I came for answers."

I bowed my head. Rubbed the back of my neck and exhaled loudly, looking at her from the corner of my eye. "What do you seek answers for?" I asked warily.

"Was the plan not successful? Was it not mine?" She glared at me. "How dare you attempt to exclude me, then order me as if I were one of your crew!"

I gave a loud snort and my eyebrows shot up in dismay. "You believe this of me?"

She nodded stonily.

"Those soldiers would have killed you as soon as looked at you. I was merely acting to protect you, my lady."

"Exactly." She tapped her foot impatiently. "You pretend to have my best interests at heart, placing my welfare above your own. Yet you are the very one who endangered me to begin with."

This game of hers was growing tiresome. I exhaled loudly. "The way you yourself pretended to have my interests at heart?" I accused, turning her own words back upon her.

Her eyes flickered with annoyance, the green deepening to a dark emerald.

"I've known of your plan right from the start."

"My plan?" She rolled her eyes. "Exactly what is my plan, pray tell?"

I cocked my head in her direction, snickered beneath my breath. Did she really think I hadn't guessed? "To make your way upon *The Wolfsbane*. To worm your way into my confidence. Then when the time was right, your ships would attack, capturing *The Wolfsbane* and her entire crew. With your Crown's new laws against piracy, the hanging of The Wolff would be quite a demonstration of your queen's iron will. It would make anyone take pause before daring to confront her. On any issue."

"Beg pardon. I never stood on deck, shouting out, pleading for the fearsome Captain Wolff to come ravage me." Her voice fairly dripped with sarcasm. "If you will recall, you flew false colors in a trading route, luring my vessel closer until you could attack, seizing the treasures she carried without mercy."

I opened my mouth to protest but was quickly cut off by her continuing tirade. "Furthermore, the queen of England does not need to hang you to prove that she is a formidable monarch. The kings of France and Scotland fear her power. She doesn't need your reputation to build upon." Her lip curled in disgust. "And if I was a pirate hunter out to capture you..." Breath hissed, teeth flashed. "...I could have had you in chains long before I had you in bed."

That hit as hard as any slap I'd ever received. "Fine." I tried to recover as best I could from that blow. I hadn't intended to dredge up her past transgressions. True, when she first came aboard, her mother had openly encouraged her defiance of me, prompting Alexis to pursue me in an attempt to lull me until she could lodge a knife in my back. But I'd not suspected Alexis capable of such treachery for quite some time. I merely hated being on unlevel footing and sought to even the odds somewhat by my accusations.

Fists clenched, she stomped her foot angrily. "Oh! You are a fool if you think this is about my turning on you to save myself."

"What is it about then?"

"The very fact that you need ask..." Her sentence trailed off. I caught something flicker in her eyes. Wordlessly, she turned her back to me. I reached for her, my hand closing upon her elbow. She easily shook me off, rushing for the cabin door. Helpless, I allowed her to go.

†

SHIP'S LOG – NOVEMBER 20, 1703

Luck is with us this day. Not only did we outwit the English and Spanish, but we also stumbled upon a treasure of sorts. A Spanish galleon beached upon a sandbar. Her hull split open at the side when she struck. The crew, fearing she would no doubt sink, abandoned ship.

But with the receding tide, she wasn't a loss yet. We were able to send crews in to salvage most of her cargo before the tide rose again. When it did, the inrushing water filled her hold, leveling her. We watched as the tide lifted her off the sandbar. She floated free for several moments before she started to sink from the water rushing into her open hull.

It was an easy haul, gaining us gold and jewels. As well as logbooks, chests, and military papers. Sven's group raided the crews' quarters, gathering clothing and blankets. Rufus's group raided the galley and storerooms, collecting enough food to feed my crew for months.

The crew is pleased, reveling in our good fortune. As their captain, I cannot afford to become lost in celebration. I cannot rest, knowing that as long as Captain Jackson breathes, he will continue in his pursuit. Jackson's spirit is not all that dampens my taste for festivity. Alexis DeVale continues to haunt me, our past encounter preoccupying my thoughts.

†

I found Alexis upon the open deck near the galley. She was sitting upon a crate, peeling a potato. A large barrel full of potatoes was beside her. She held her knife with her left hand, slicing away from her. The peelings flew wildly upon the deck.

"Rufus put you to work?" I asked, pulling up a crate, sitting near her. She shrugged. Her knife bit sharply into the potato she was carving. I picked one of her peelings up off the deck, used my own knife to peel the excess potato from the skin. "Do I need to peel your peelings?" I asked playfully.

A sidelong glance was her only reply.

I frowned, picked up a potato from the barrel, and began peeling it. We worked in silence. She dropped her finished potato into a large pot, reached for another. "I waited for you in my cabin." I cocked my head in her direction, arched a suggestive eyebrow. "I thought by now you would come to me."

190

"Did you think no woman could resist the charms of the dashing Captain Wolff?"

"You believe me dashing?" Her knife bit sharply into her potato. My eyebrows arched suggestively. "Perhaps when we're done here?" My hand shot out, landing upon her upper thigh.

"No." She jerked back and her head shot up. Her bright eyes glared at me. "You insult me, offer up no apology, yet you have the audacity to think that I would succumb to you after a mere touch?"

I exhaled loudly. "You're mad at me about something."

"Half right." She stabbed a potato out of the barrel, cut deeply into the skin. "I'm still mad at you."

"Still?" I frowned, looked at her sharply, felt the color drain from my cheeks. My mouth fell open.

Her eyes gleamed. "Oh, yes." Her words were bitten out between clenched teeth. "Yet again, you've accused me of betrayal. I've saved your crew, your ship, you. Time and time again. I've proven myself again and again, yet you still do not trust me."

"I'm sorry. I didn't think—"

"No, you didn't. You just did it. And then you did what you always do. Pretend the situation doesn't exist and trust everything to work out fine on its own."

Arms folded across my chest, I glared at her. "Since when?"

"Since forever. Your whole life is make-believe, Kris. Starting with you pretending to be a man, pretending to care for me."

I felt as if she'd kicked me in the gut. "I have never pretended about us."

Her face was splotched red with anger. "We can't go on like this, pretending we belong together. That nothing is wrong."

I jumped to my feet, grabbing her by her upper arms. The blade of her knife pressed against my breast.

"I thought we had settled this," I said. "Despite our differences, we belong together. You and me." I leaned in closer, lowered my voice to a soothing hum. "You love me."

"Yes, I do, damn you." She brought the knife up, pricking my nose with the tip of the blade.

Not the reaction I was hoping for. I lifted my hands from her, held them in the air. Palms up, non-threatening. But I didn't retreat. We were so close I could feel her hot breath upon my cheek.

"And I tell you all the time," she said, "but you never do."

"Do what?"

"Tell me that you love me!" she fairly shouted, waving the knife wildly.

I stepped forward, cautiously taking the knife from her grasp. She let me take it easily. I balanced the hilt, threw it. It landed in the side of the barrel, deeply embedded in the wood.

"I do, you know."

"Do what?" she asked flippantly, throwing my own words back at me.

"I—" I faltered, trying to get the words out.

"You cannot even say it," she spat out, turning away from me.

She retreated to the railing, back to me, staring out at the rocky coastline. I came up behind her, placing a hand upon her shoulder, gently squeezing. She shrugged me off.

"Just because I can't say it doesn't mean I don't feel it." It sounded weak, even to my ears.

"And why can you not say it?"

My mouth went dry. My throat muscles tightened. I suddenly couldn't speak. "Why is it not enough to simply know that I feel it?"

"Because you do not. You do not trust me. Why should I believe you love me?"

She turned around, facing me. The anger had drained from her face. Her eyes stared at me somewhat less accusingly. "Again, you have no answer."

She advanced upon me, stopping a hair's breadth in front of me. "It would be wise to figure out why you cannot say those words to me." She pushed past me. "Or you might find that by the time you are able to say the words, I may no longer be willing to hear them."

✝

I sat in a corner of the galley, quietly eating my stew. The men were still in high spirits. Laughing. Drinking. And dancing. At least they were enjoying our fortune, I thought miserably. It was a day since I'd spoken to Alexis. Or even seen her. She hadn't come for dinner the night before. *Or to my cabin for dessert*, I added bitterly.

I wondered how much longer she would make me endure this torment. Surely, her body ached for me as much as mine ached for hers. I had thought once I'd bedded her, my feelings of lust would diminish. If anything, they had increased tenfold, fueled by her hot passions. And it wasn't only in the bedroom that I missed her. I missed her smile, her laughter, our conversations. The things she tried to teach me about her homeland.

A bowl hit the tabletop in front of me. Sven sat down, swinging his legs over the low bench. He picked up his wooden spoon, slurping his stew eagerly. "Have you seen Alexis?"

I shook my head, tearing off a piece of bread.

"She was supposed to relieve me hours ago," he groused, reaching across the table for the loaf. He bit into the end, tearing the bread with his teeth. "I thought I'd starve."

"She's probably been in the hold, inspecting dresses we got from the galleon yesterday," Brodey said, sauntering over. He tore the bread loaf in half, dunking the end into his mug of ale. "You know how women are. Especially the rich wenches."

My jaw clenched. Eyes narrowed.

"Alexis isn't like that," Sven said.

"Sure she is. All women are." Brodey laughed. He flipped his long dark mane back, curtsied low, with his fingers delicately picking up an imaginary dress line. "I'm the Duchess DeVale, heiress to all things good and decent." His voice was high-pitched in an ill attempt at mocking my lady.

A low growl crept up my throat. "You've had too much to drink."

"And you," he said, laughing, turning to face me, swaying on his feet. "The woman is destined to marry royalty. How soon before she grows weary of the heathens? Especially their captain? You're nothing more than a rich girl's dalliance."

I sprang from my seat, knocking my chair backwards. I slammed my fist down on the table and reached for my knife. "Do not speak of things that do not concern you," I warned.

"Enjoy it while you can, Captain Wolff." He leaned across the table, staring pointedly at me. "She'll not be yours for long. Soon, she'll be where she belongs, in the bed of royalty."

I lunged, leaping across the table. Sven grabbed me, restraining me. Still, I fought to reach Brodey. Vincent appeared at my side, gripping my arms. I fought to break their hold on me. Brodey staggered off into the crowd, drinking heartily from his mug.

"Let him go, Captain," Sven said. "He's drunk."

I finally relented, fell back into my chair. "Bastard." I slammed my fist upon the table.

"He's drunk," Sven repeated, picking his spilled bowl up. Stew was spread across the table. Sven held his bowl at the edge, scraped the meat and potatoes back in. "He doesn't know what he's saying." He shrugged and popped a spoonful of the rescued stew into his mouth.

"I wouldn't be too certain of that," Vincent said, pulling up another chair. "This may all be part of a carefully constructed plan of our friend Brodey's."

"You still mad because he overreacted?" Sven asked. "I might have done the same thing, gambled that I could break cover and catch the Spanish soldier before you could sneak all the way around the field."

"He may have purposely done it so the trooper could escape," I said, my voice hushed. "We still have a traitor on board."

"And you suspect Brodey because he didn't reach the soldier in time?" Sven asked around another mouthful.

"And because of what he said regarding the Lady DeVale." Vincent pulled a parchment from his breast pocket, spread it out upon the table. "And because of this."

I reached out, snatching at the parchment on the wet table. I leaned close, reading the words in Alexis's own handwriting.

I shan't stay with you under these circumstances. Nor as nothing more than a member of your crew. I've left to seek what-

ever sanctuary I may find with the Spanish. Good fortune and may God have mercy upon your soul.

I snatched the parchment off the table, staring at it. My lip curled. Jaw twitched. Nostrils flared.

"She's gone to the Spanish fortress," Vincent said. "The dinghy is gone."

Sven's spoon disappeared into his bowl. He stared at me. "What are you going to do?"

I silently cursed my own stupidity. At what point had I taken complete leave of my senses, giving her free reign of my ship, to go where she pleased without escort? Truth be told, from nearly the first moment she stepped foot upon my ship. Even though I knew she was unhappy on board, I never once thought she would steal our sole dinghy, take to the open sea in search of her freedom. After the incident with Brandy, the ordeal on Bonaire, her recent foray into navigation, I had not expected this sort of behavior.

The revelation of Alexis's flight unsettled me. A sturdy, one-seated craft, the dinghy could easily be rowed by a single person. And by bracing the gunter against the keel of the boat, the lone sail would give her added speed. Coupled with her new-found knowledge of the stars, I had little doubt Alexis would reach shore long before we could catch her.

"We," I said, crumpling the parchment in my balled fist, "are going to get her back."

I threw the parchment across the table. It landed in Sven's bowl, quickly soaking up the juices from his stew.

195

Chapter Twelve

THE LADY

The roses were in full bloom. I leaned over, plucking a red rose. Holding its stem, I turned the rose this way and that, examining it. The petals were bright red near the center, fading to a dusty rose at the tips. I brought the flower to my nose, inhaling deeply.

A cool breeze blew through my hair, shattering the illusion, reality once again intruding upon my solace. The garden was gorgeous. Or I imagined it would be if winter were not upon us. But alas, the beautiful roses lay dormant, and there was a definite chill in the air. I shivered, wrapping my arms about my waist. This act took me to another place, another time. Upon the deck of *The Wolfsbane*, when it was a pirate captain's arms that held me.

The sound of approaching footfalls drew me from the memory. My eyes focused on a pair of white trousers. My gaze followed those pants legs up, past a wide black belt with a military insignia engraved on the buckle. He wore a bright blue overcoat atop a white shirt, bars across both shoulders. His dark brown eyes were set deep in a tanned face. He wore his beard neatly trimmed. His brown hair, graying around the temples and thinning on top, was cut short.

"May I?" he asked, gesturing toward the stone bench.

"Of course." I shifted over, giving him room.

Commander Fernandez sat down, staring unabashedly at me. A soft smile played upon his lips.

"Beautiful," he said. His eyes met mine. "Simply beautiful."

I blushed beneath the compliment. He was a sweet man with a good heart, reminding me so much of my own father. "Thank you," I said. "You have been most kind."

"It is nothing."

"It's more than nothing," I said. "The food and shelter." I placed a hand upon my skirt, smoothing it down. "The lovely dresses."

"Merely dresses borrowed from some of the soldiers' wives."

"They are most generous."

He shrugged. "The families will be compensated for the gifts. The Spanish Empire's wealth is vast."

I nodded. I'd certainly seen proof of that. At first glance, I thought this structure merely to be an outpost for soldiers guarding passage to the northern sea. Now I realized it was much more than that. It was a formidable structure, larger than it appeared from the bay outside. Almost as large as any estate in England, with enough room to house a full complement of soldiers and their families.

"Now that you've had time to recover from your ordeal," the commander said, "I must ask you again—how did you arrive upon our shores?"

I appraised him coolly. We had talked about this time and again. "I escaped from the pirates' vessel during the night. They had drunk too much in celebration, and most were passed out upon the deck. It was a simple matter to avoid detection and leave in their dinghy."

"But still to set upon the waters at midnight. To row in the darkness—"

"My faith and determination guided me to your magnificent castle."

"Ah, you flatter me, Señorita DeVale. My fortress is great, but she is by no means a castle."

I smiled sweetly. Commander Fernandez was easy. A well-placed compliment here and there, and he forgot his line of questioning. I had been eluding him like this for days.

"When did you say the vessel from your empire will arrive?"

197

His face lit up. "The day after today, and I have a very special surprise for you." He dotingly pinched my cheek.

"What, pray tell, is the surprise, my dear Commander?"

"Your betrothed, Prince Rafael, will be arriving upon his personal ship to escort his lovely bride so that no future harm may befall her."

My smile fell. My stomach did somersaults.

"What is wrong, Señorita DeVale? You look suddenly ill."

"I am fine," I managed to squeak out, waving off the commander's concerned hand. "However, I thought...my betrothed...was a lord."

"Ah, yes." The commander's face fairly beamed. The way it did each time he had something juicy to share with me. "Of course, you wouldn't know, being away for so long." He leaned closer, dropping his voice conspiratorially, casting a furtive glance at the women who had just entered the garden. "With the recent untimely death of his cousin, Lord Rafael has suddenly been elevated to the position of prince."

"Next in line for the crown." I realized.

"Precisely. As such, part of his responsibilities includes evaluating the kingdom's military preparedness. He's made it his mission to inspect every garrison personally. It is most fortuitous that your arrival has coincided so closely with his scheduled itinerary."

I silently absorbed this information. While it was my intent to honor the agreement, I had erroneously believed I would still be afforded several more months of freedom before I would be required to fulfill my courtly obligations.

I glanced at the two women. They had purposely circled around us on another path. But they continued to watch us, eyes sparkling. Hands discreetly covering their mouths, they talked in hushed whispers, giggling.

"His uncle is in ill health," Commander Fernandez said. "The prince will be crowned king within the year."

I gasped aloud. I'd had no idea. The giggling persisted. I frowned and turned my head, staring disdainfully. The ladies' smug looks were my only response. *Of course. The commander*

198

and I are seated so closely upon the bench. And our voices are so low.

Damn, I was out of practice with the ways of courtesan life. The improprieties and gossip were a mainstay no matter what position was held. I cast them both a glare that almost dared them to begin a rumor that the commander and I were swooning over one another in the garden like lovesick fools.

"We hold the banquet in the great hall," the commander continued. "Complete with dinner and formal dance."

"It sounds..." I swallowed. "...delightful."

"Excuse me." The commander rose from his seat, bowed low, kissing my hand. "But I must see to last-minute details before the prince arrives."

"Of course." I bowed my head.

I watched the Spanish officer leave the garden, exiting through a side gate. I rose from my perch upon the stone bench.

As I idly walked down the path, I came upon the large fountain in the center of the garden. Made of stone, a large swan grew up from the center of the structure. Clear water rose from its opened mouth and ran in rivulets off its outstretched wings, falling into the pool below. Presumably, the pool represented the lake that the swan swam upon.

My eyes stared at the running water, my gaze focusing on the pool. Several gold coins rested in the bottom of the fountain. The coins reminded me of the ransom The Wolff had received for my return. A king's ransom.

†

The banquet was elegant. More so than I had expected from a mere commander of a fortress outpost at the far reaches of the Spanish Empire. The dinner fare looked exquisite, fit for the royal family. Which in a sense was who was being honored this night. The future king of the Spanish Empire. And his future queen. The thought made me nauseated.

I fought down my waves of vertigo, forcing myself to remain calm. The prince hadn't yet arrived. Perhaps he had

199

changed his mind. I would be spared this dreadful marriage and safely released to my own beloved English shores.

Unrealistic, I knew. The hairs on the back of my neck stood up. A shiver ran along my spine. I turned my head. Captain Jackson was in the center of a group of officers, drinking and conversing, staring dead on at me.

He excused himself, deliberately making a line straight toward me, sipping from his champagne glass as he crossed the room. He bowed low before me. "My Lady DeVale." A smile played upon his lips.

"Captain Jackson." I curtsied on shaking legs.

He passed his empty glass to a passing servant. "Would you honor me with a dance?"

No. "Of course."

He led me to the center of the floor. A waltz was being played. He was a fair dancer, easily gliding us around the hall.

"I understand you escaped from The Wolff on your own, without assistance."

"I managed."

"The Wolff is very dangerous."

"I agree," I said. Her all-too dangerous kisses upon my lips played through my mind repeatedly at night.

"He's plagued us for years. He's cost the Crown dozens of ships, a fortune in gold and jewels, eluded hundreds of trained men." He paused, looking at me deliberately. "Yet you managed to escape his clutches all on your own."

"It was all a matter of timing. Waiting for the best opportunity to make my move."

"And Bonaire wasn't the best opportunity for you?" He cocked his head to one side.

I didn't answer.

"It was for me," he said, dropping his voice lower. "I had The Wolff. On his knees in the mud. He would have died right then and there. But you rescued him."

I arched an eyebrow. "He threatened to kill me if I didn't help him escape."

"You couldn't elude one half-dead pirate on Bonaire." His eyes narrowed. "Yet you managed to escape from an entire ship of bloodthirsty heathens."

"As I said, merely a matter of timing."

"Indeed." A smirk played across his lips. "You have excellent timing." He reached out, fingers stroking my cheek. I stiffened beneath his touch. "I was set to leave port, ready to resume my hunt for *The Wolfsbane*. If you had arrived but an hour later..." His grin widened. "I would have been well underway. And we may have missed one another."

We glided past a group of Spanish soldiers. "That would have been a shame." I attempted to approach the group. Captain Jackson caught me by the wrist, pulling me back toward the center of the dance floor.

"Quite. Imagine my horror if I'd skinned the hide of all on board *The Wolfsbane* from head to toe." His eyes fairly gleamed. "Only to discover that perhaps all aboard was not as it seems."

The waltz ended. Still Captain Jackson didn't release me. His hand was at my side, firmly gripping my wrist. His attempt to discern my complicity where Captain Wolff was concerned was painfully obvious. No doubt, he was measuring my responses, eager to catch any little indiscretion that might confirm his suspicions of Kris' identity. I was careful with each answer, unwilling to betray her with a slip of the tongue.

"What do you wish?"

"Only that which is rightfully mine." Captain Jackson tilted his head, hissed between clenched teeth. "Vengeance."

"The same vengeance you extracted in Port Royale?" I arched an eyebrow. My voice was calm, despite my anxiety. "I doubt Commander Fernandez would condone such behavior in his territory."

"So The Wolff received my gift. In all honesty, I wasn't certain. I waited as long as I could before resuming my search elsewhere. I'd thought perhaps the tavern keeper had lied."

"I imagine he would have said or done anything to keep you from harming his daughter." *Including betraying his friend.*

"Cross me, Lady DeVale," he leaned in, dropping his voice lower. He pressed his lips to my ear so that only I might hear.

"And I promise you a fate much worse than that of The Wolff's barmaid whore."

I attempted to wrest myself free from his grip. He held me tight. I frantically searched the room. Surely, my discomfort was clearly written on my face. Perhaps if Commander Fernandez saw.

A set of white-gloved fingers tapped Captain Jackson on the shoulder.

Furious at the interruption, he spun around, his face contorted with rage. His sneer suddenly fell, quickly replaced by a falsely sincere smile. With a flourish, he bowed low.

He was tall. A head taller than my captain, I thought. His hair was ebony black, neatly cut, trimmed in a typical military hairstyle. His mustache was thin. Given the youthfulness of his face, I guessed that he had difficulty growing that little bit of facial hair.

"Y-your Highness." Captain Jackson uncharacteristically stumbled on his own tongue. "It is an honor."

My breath caught. This was Prince Rafael. Come all the way from his homeland to rescue me. I smiled demurely. He returned my smile, ignoring the efforts of Captain Jackson.

He attempted to step around the captain.

The Englishman refused to yield, still tossing flowery praises upon the prince.

Prince Rafael cast a sidelong look at Captain Jackson, scowling. "If you'll pardon me," he addressed Jackson, his voice scathing, "I would enjoy dancing with my betrothed."

"O-of course," Captain Jackson stammered, retreating into the crowd of dancers. I caught sight of him as he made his way to the edge of the dance floor. He stood near the band, drink in hand, eagle eyes watching my every move.

†

We danced for hours, gliding around the floor. Waltz after waltz played, and we continued to dance. I became lost in the music, distracted in his arms. It was easy to pretend the strong arms that held me belonged to another. Memories of a dance long before with The Wolff brought an unbidden smile to my face.

"Do you enjoy the dance?" His lips were so near mine, he could have kissed me if he wished.

"Yes," I said, never losing a step. "But the band," I paused and, leaning closer, whispered, "they play only waltzes?"

He laughed. "I'm afraid the prince knows only waltzes."

"What do you do when they play something other than a waltz?"

He shrugged. "My courtesans play nothing but waltzes. Tell me, Lady DeVale, do you dance much?"

Memories of the intimate dance with Kris once again flashed in my mind. The way she held me tightly against her body, pressing into me. I felt an involuntary tug at my nether regions in response. "Not as much as I'd like," I said. "I find the exercise of the dance to be most stimulating."

"You will have as many dances as you like at my court."

"You've decided to fulfill the terms of the marriage arrangement?" I wondered if Commander Fernandez had glossed over the details of my arrival in his report to the prince. With Captain Jackson's appearance, the prince may have been led to believe that the English were responsible for my presence. I knew the elderly commander was a kind, benevolent man, but I could not have him taint his honor with deception for my sake. "Are you aware that during my delay to your shores, I've spent considerable time in the company of pirates?"

"My court is not as dimwitted and ill-informed as the English may care to believe." He leaned in closer, lowering his voice. "It was not merely fortuitous timing that I was out touring the farthest reaches of my empire, you know. I've been cognizant of your heading for quite some time now." A smile flitted across his face. "Just as I am fully aware that, by their standards, you are considered tainted goods and your queen is holding her breath in anticipation of what I shall do. Fortunately, for them," a slight pause as he leveled his stare at me, "I have a need for this treaty."

"If you are aware of my plight," my words involuntarily caught at the description of my situation, "surely others in your kingdom are also knowledgeable. Do you not fear that your enemies may use this against you?"

"Another reason for conducting my business on the outskirts of my kingdom."

"No matter the distance," I said, "news of this proportion shall surely make its way back to your throne."

He shrugged. "It matters not. No one at court will ever speak of such things."

"All courtesans gossip," I said. "They will laugh behind your back."

"Then they will lose their tongues."

"Prince Rafael, I have something I must tell you." I hesitated. Bit my bottom lip.

"Do not be afraid. You may speak to me of anything. As your husband, your prince, your future king, there should be no secrets between us." He seemed so young. Yet he was confident and sure. His words were strong and full of conviction.

Still—

He was not my captain.

"I…" *How could I tell him?* "This has been a most magnificent welcome to your empire." I smiled demurely.

"You do not regret your voyage?"

"No, your highness." For how could I regret a journey that had brought me Kris? Fraught as it was with difficulties, filled with deceit and lies. Mine, as well as hers. Once I stopped looking with my eyes and saw instead with my heart, I was able to look past the masquerade, to see Kris for the real woman she was, not the persona she portrayed. And even though I knew I could not have stayed, my memories would always hold her close. And in time, I told myself, the very thought of her would no longer make my heart ache with bittersweet longing.

The dance ended. He bowed low in formal fashion. Before the band could begin again, he took me by the hand, pulling me to the center of the room. Waving his hand high, he commanded the attention of all.

"I have an announcement," he said, his voice echoing throughout the room.

I smiled demurely, expecting him to announce our engagement.

"My betrothed and I set sail from your delightful port tomorrow eve."

My smile fell with his next words.

"After our nuptials."

My mouth dropped open in shock. I quickly covered it with a wide smile that caused my entire face to ache from the effort. Nuptials. The prince planned to wed me before our long voyage. The consummation of our vows would take place upon the high seas. My stomach churned at the thought.

†

I sat at the dresser, studying my reflection in the mirror. Under the physician's care, I had recovered quite nicely from my ordeal. He had prescribed plenty of rest and fruits to counteract the effects of a vitamin deficiency I'd suffered from. Now my cheeks fairly glowed with good health.

"You make the most beautiful bride."

The excited voice came from one of the servants assigned to help me dress. I caught her reflection in the mirror as she fixed my headdress, pinning the delicate fabric to my hair. She was an older woman, gray streaked through her brown hair. Short and plump, much like the other women I'd seen at Fortress Monsarrent.

"Thank you, Luisa."

"You don't seem excited, señorita."

"It is difficult to be excited this late at night." I stifled a yawn. "Must we do this now?"

"Your prince wishes to wed tomorrow. That doesn't give me much time to finish your dress."

"But it's well past midnight."

Luisa pulled away, studying my face in the mirror. "You don't like the prince?"

205

"No, he's very nice,"

"You do not want a prince then?" she guessed.

She urged me to stand so she could fasten the back of my gown. It was lovely. The loveliest I'd ever seen. White with pale blue trim, matching the colors of the prince's regime, sparkling with lace and jewels.

"Perhaps I have difficulty understanding why your prince would want me."

"Because you are very beautiful, with your pale skin and blonde hair." She sat back on her heels, appraising me coolly, pins dangling from her mouth as she paused from her work. "You will give the prince very strong sons. Perhaps with light eyes like your own."

"Sons." The word filled my mouth with disgust as I thought of the prospect of motherhood.

"You certainly don't seem too eager a bride," Luisa continued. She paused at my hemline, looked up at me. "Is it another fellow that has your heart?"

My breath caught. My heart pounded. "No, not another fellow," I managed to choke out.

Luisa's eyes met mine. And for a moment, I thought of confiding in the matronly woman of how I struggled between what I wanted and what I was meant to be.

A sharp rap came at the door. The pounding persisted until Luisa rose from the floor and made her way to the door. She opened it barely an inch. I saw the Spanish uniforms, heard Luisa speaking with the soldiers. As if sensing my prying eyes, she stepped into the hall, closing the door behind her.

One was probably her own prince, I thought bitterly, turning back to the mirror. I slumped down in my chair and stared miserably at my reflection. I heard the click of the knob as the door closed, the sliding of the lock. Luisa returned to finish her duty, no doubt. I steeled myself, rose from my chair to allow her to finish pinning my hemline.

Cold, gray eyes stared at me, her mouth opening in shock at my attire. She stood before me, fidgeting, suddenly unsure of her actions. She wore a Spanish uniform. It was her in the hall with Luisa.

"Why are you here, Captain Wolff?" I asked, my voice hushed so that no one passing by the door might overhear.

"I might ask the same of you."

"I have come to honor my obligations."

She raised an eyebrow and cocked her head to the side. "And what of your honor to me?"

I bristled. "You take a great risk coming here. If they discover you, they'll hang you."

She shrugged. "Sven's guarding the door. He'll signal at the first sign of danger."

She answered my unasked question. "We put pitch in his hair. No one will look too closely beneath a soldier's hat." She nodded toward the entrance. "Are you ready to leave?"

"I cannot." I couldn't believe her. "I told you, I must honor my obligation."

"By simply giving yourself to another as part of a prearranged marriage?"

"I must. Lest you forget, my betrothal was designed as part of a pact to seal a treaty between England and Spain. By fulfilling my duty, I am ensuring a lasting legacy for the Crown." Against my better judgment, I added, "And in the process, I am protecting you from Captain Jackson."

"Hang the blasted treaty!" She scowled. "And forget Jackson and return to *The Wolfsbane* with me."

I shook my head. "Jackson won't rest until he's seen you dead."

She paced the floor, moved around me, sat upon the edge of the dresser. Arms folded across her chest, she glared at me. "I got your note."

"Typically dismissive, as always," I said. "I wish to discuss Captain Jackson's obsessive need to kill you, yet you're more concerned with other matters."

"Such as you leaving because you're angry with me?"

"At you. At me." Her expression was blank.

I came to her, cupping her face in my hands, searching her eyes. "You don't understand, do you?"

She shook her head.

"I love you," I whispered, "so very much."

207

She moved toward me, lips pursed for a kiss, arms ready to encircle me. My hands upon her forearms, nails digging in, prevented her.

"But I cannot stay with you."

She cocked her head to the side, brows knitted in confusion.

"Not like this," I said. "Sailing upon the high seas as a member of your crew, pillaging and plundering, dodging Captain Jackson all the way to Trepassi Beach and back."

"We need not go to Trepassi. I'll take you wherever you wish to go."

"Do you not see?" I asked, my fingers stroking her cheek. "It's not where we are that matters. What matters is that I want to be with you—the real you. Not the ruthless, manly pirate. Not the captain. Just you. And I can't have that if I don't own your heart."

She exhaled loudly and ran a hand through her unkempt hair. A tiny twitch tugged at the corner of her left eye. She bowed her head. When she raised it again, her eyes were clouded over. "You would sooner marry than be with me?" Her words were spoken softly, her voice low and gravelly.

"Yes," I said, my own voice barely a whisper. "If I cannot have all of you."

She pushed herself off the dresser and strode across the room, boots clicking on the stone floor. Her back was straight, her posture rigid.

"Why can you not say it?" *If you did, I would go with you.*

She turned to face me, her eyes bright. Her face was a tortured mask. I had to clutch at my gown to keep from reaching for her.

"I—"

"Because it's not true," I finished for her. I turned my back on her, to prevent her seeing my own tears. They threatened to come in rivers. I stayed like that, not daring to look back at her.

I heard the footsteps behind me. Boots upon stone, coming near. I could feel her behind me, her hand hovering above my shoulder, scant inches from touching me. Her breath whispered upon the nape of my neck.

"I'll await your arrival in the garden an hour before dawn," she whispered in my ear. "Come to me."

I heard the sounds of retreating footsteps, the latch sliding upon the lock, the click of the knob, the slam of the door. Then the sound of my own sobs filled the empty room.

†

A strong gust of wind blew up, sending rustling leaves hurtling across the garden. I shivered, drawing my cloak tighter about myself. Nervously, I paced back and forth in front of the fountain. The rivulets of water streaming off the swan's wings fell slowly into the water below. Slivers of ice hung off the tips of the swan's wings.

Mesmerized, I reached out, fingers dipping into the concrete basin. A mixture of ice and water washed across my hand. My flesh tingled, then burned at the sensation.

"Careful, your hand may freeze like that."

I jerked my hand back, spun around sharply. A set of gloved hands closed about my fingers, quickly rubbing, warming my flesh.

She was still wearing a Spanish uniform, sword dangling at her side. No doubt this was still a covert endeavor. She was brazen, but even Captain Wolff was not brash enough to infiltrate a fortress with a full complement of men. I glanced about, furtively looking for Sven. I knew he must be in the garden somewhere; she would not have come alone.

"He's guarding our perimeter. Do not be concerned, my lady, he will not disturb us." Kris gave voice to my own concerns.

She took great risks coming to the garden like this, even disguised as a soldier. Just as I, too, risked everything by coming to her as she requested. I had waited until the final moment, agonizing about my decision in my room, struggling with the need to stay and the desire to go.

"I couldn't leave without you," she said.

"And I cannot go with you."

"You came to tell me that?" She pulled insistently at my hand. "Come with me."

I shook my head. "I cannot." The words wrenched out painfully. "I must do this, Kris."

"What? Throw your life away?"

"We've talked about this before. It's for the best." *Were those really my words?* "I don't believe that you can't see that."

Her eyes narrowed to tiny slits. "What I don't believe…is that you would want to marry another."

I started to protest.

She cut me off with a withering glare. "I can't believe you would rather be with…that…than with me."

"Kris—"

She reached up, yanked the ribbon from her ponytail, and shook her hair loose. It fell softly about her shoulders. She reached out, roughly took my hand, and brought it to her face, forced me to stroke my fingers through her hair.

My heart leapt into my throat. *She risked all, taking down her hair, showing her true self. What if someone were to come upon us like this? What if someone were to see her for who she really was?* "What are you doing?"

She grabbed me by my upper arms and pulled me to her roughly. Her mouth pressed down upon mine. Her tongue savagely forced its way between my lips.

She broke off the kiss just as quickly. Breathing heavy, she panted, "Tell me you don't want this."

"It's true," I lied. I deliberately wiped at my mouth.

Her hands dropped from my arms and just as quickly found the collar of her shirt. Fingers deftly worked at the buttons, opening her shirt all the way to her sword belt. My breath caught, heart pounded in my ears. She yanked open her shirt. My eyes were riveted to her bare breasts. The nipples were instantly stiffened from the cold. My mouth went dry.

"Tell me you don't need this." Her hands clasped mine, brought them to her breasts. "Tell me you can live without the touch of another woman."

Her words came out huskier, her voice much thicker.

"I—"

Her hands went around my body, down my back, both hands clutching at my hips. I fought to keep my body from arching into her grasp.

"Tell me," she whispered. "Tell me now and I'll leave."

My mouth refused to work, my mind refused to function. My hands gave me away, cupping her breasts, shielding her flesh from the cold breeze. Fingers instinctively closing upon her hardened nipples, I placed a lingering kiss upon the flesh between her breasts.

Her mouth came down upon mine again, her wet tongue easily sliding into my hot mouth. This was not as rough as her first kiss, but no less demanding. Gently, she ended our kiss. She held me tightly in her arms, face scant inches from mine, lips so close they nearly touched. I rested my head upon her shoulder, buried my face in her collarbone.

"I'll go with you," I whispered, planting kisses in the hollow of her throat.

My fingers worked, slowly beginning to button Kris' shirt. I had barely fastened her buttons when I felt something cold bite into the back of my neck, followed by a sharp pain. I slowly raised my head, turned to stare down the blade of a sword.

"Don't—" Jackson used the tip of his sword to lift my neck higher. "I'll cut her."

Kris' arm stilled, her sword jangled as it fell back into the hilt.

"Take your belt off." The sword and belt clattered to the stone floor. "Step back."

Subtly, I felt Kris stiffen beside me. Standing pressed against me as she was, I was acutely aware of every coiled muscle, every knot of tension coursing through her taut body. I envisioned her lashing out, wresting the blade away from Captain Jackson. Jackson sensed her intent, as well, pressing the sword tip deeper. I felt warm blood flow from the tiny prick, saw Kris' eyes narrow. Arms up, palms raised, Kris took a deliberate step away. Jackson nodded twice. Her heels scraped on stone as she backed farther away, out of reach.

"Halt," Jackson commanded. "One false step, and the Lady DeVale will regret it."

"This is between me and you." Kris took a reflexive step forward. "Leave her out of this."

I felt Captain Jackson's grip upon me tighten, the blade press imperceptibly deeper. "Not a step closer," Jackson said. My eyes sought and found Kris', pleading silently with her to control her temper. To my relief, she made no further move against Jackson.

"Let her go," Kris said.

"Shut your mouth!" Jackson shouted. He swung the sword wildly, jerking it clean away from my throat. He roughly pushed me behind him, effectively capturing my wrists in the vise-like grip of one of his hands. The other held the sword pointed directly at Kris, the tip menacingly close to her flesh. "You're not aboard *The Wolfsbane* now, pirate. I'm in command here."

Jackson prodded Kris with the tip of his sword, jabbing repeatedly at her shoulders, her collarbone.

Kris stood her ground and held her tongue in check, jaw clenched, teeth grinding in frustration. Fists curled and uncurled at her sides, arms flexing with pent-up rage. Eyes narrowed, the normally cloudy gray depths becoming focused in fury, constricting to tiny balls of steel.

I met her gaze above Captain Jackson's shoulder, the barely controlled rage emanating from her eyes sending a cold shiver down my spine.

"Let him be!" I shouted, struggling, attempting to wrench myself loose from Jackson's grasp.

"Him?" I heard the incredulity of his tone. Captain Jackson's sword tip flashed, moving to the top of Kris' shirt. "This is twice now that you've attempted to protect The Wolff."

He tightened his grip, attempting to abate my struggles.

"Examine your enemies closely, Lady DeVale." The tip of his sword blazed, the thin blade slipping beneath the fabric, flicking the top button open. "And you will discover all sorts of...." Another button was discarded. "...revealing things."

A sharp gasp escaped my throat, my struggles suddenly ceased. Helpless, I stared at Kris, held at bay by Captain Jackson's sword, tormented by his cruel acts of self-amusement. With every button displaced, his sneer grew. I longed to go to

212

her, to aid her, protect her. Powerless to save her, all I could do was convey my intent with my eyes, pleading for her to find the strength she needed to survive this humiliation. Her eyes sought, connected with mine, unwavering as she took refuge in their depths.

Jackson noticed. "Now I see."

He looked back and forth between Kris and me. "Now I understand your need to protect The Wolff." He blatantly stared at the open material of Kris' shirt and the flesh beneath. "Not only do you know his secret, but you share in this abomination."

"Lady DeVale has no knowledge of which you speak," Kris said.

"Do not attempt to protect her virtue," Jackson said. "For it is painfully obvious that you've already taken that from her. Surely, you do not think me dimwitted enough to believe she has spent so many months on your vessel and not come to know that you are no captain, but rather, a wench masquerading in men's clothing."

Inflamed, Kris charged forward.

Jackson's sword lunged into the opening of her shirt. The blade bit sharply, nicking the area just below her throat.

I shouted as crimson danced to the surface, marring her flesh.

"That's it, Wolff, throw yourself on my sword in one final valiant attempt to protect her honor." Captain Jackson laughed brusquely. "For as formidable an opponent as I thought you to be, it is distressing to see you undone by a woman. Everything you've worked so hard for, all your conquests, all your plunder, all for naught. The pirate king's reign felled by a mere woman's touch."

Captain Jackson laughed raucously, yanking roughly on my arms. In one swift motion, I was hurled about and sent flying, landing hard upon the stone floor at his feet.

"Do with me as you will." Kris rushed to kneel at my side. "But do not harm Lady DeVale."

"Rest assured, it has never been my intent to harm the lady." Jackson glanced down at me, still kneeling upon the stone at his feet, as if I were a common servant to be held in disdain. A malicious smile flittered across his face. "I'm a gentleman. I would never dream of harming a lady."

His repeated use of the word *lady* caused my heart to clench. Of course, he referred to Brandy, who in his eyes was a common barmaid, a plaything to be used, then discarded, nothing more. And he delighted in torturing Kris with that knowledge.

Her body responded to the threat. Eyes burning in intensity, nostrils flaring with each breath, her jaw clenched in rage. "Do with me as you will."

She moved so that she was in front of me, shielding me with her body, placing herself between Jackson's sword and me.

I leaned into her, pressing against her back, my hands clutching at the sleeves of her shirt, feeling her muscles flexing, the tension in her body building.

Captain Jackson's wild-eyed stare focused on me, and I feared he intended to harm me in an attempt at hurting Kris further. I realized Kris must have feared the same as she spoke again, coaxing his attention away from me. "What do you wish of me?"

"What do I wish of you?" he asked. "I wish to know how you would dare attack my ship. My ship, the pride of Her Queen's Navy, upon the open seas." He glared at Kris, advancing on her. "And not just attack her. But decimate her and my crew by posing as an allied ship, flying under false colors, luring me in like a fool, damaging my command, my honor. Then," he sputtered wildly, "then, to track you to a pirate's port, to discover your secret from some barmaid trollop. And realizing that if your true identity was ever discovered, if anyone but me were to kill you, it would damage my honor beyond repair."

He raised his sword above his head, preparing to strike. "What I desire from you is nothing short of your life."

There was the sound of razor-sharp steel as a flash of silver went by. Jackson's sword clattered to the ground. Sven hit Captain Jackson in the stomach, pressed the blade of his sword to Jackson's heart.

Kris retrieved her sword from the ground, returned to my side. "We must hurry," she ordered, giving a furtive glance at the coming dawn.

"Halt!" A shout came from the other side of the fountain. Prince Rafael and a squad of soldiers rushed us.

In the confusion, Jackson lunged, grabbed me, pulled me to him. Sven and Kris moved toward him. The soldiers ran across the garden, down the stone path circling the fountain.

"Go!" I shouted. "There's a side gate not far from here."

Sven ran. Kris hesitated. Sven returned, pulling Kris along by the arm. Jackson kept a tight grip on my arm, scrambled for his sword. Hordes of Spanish soldiers rushed past us.

Jackson's grip on my arm tightened. "Speak the truth and we all die." His hot breath hissed in my ear.

Prince Rafael stopped before us, knelt on the ground in front of me. "Go, stop the pirates!"

Jackson hesitated. "Go, Captain."

The prince looked pointedly at me. "I will see to my bride."

I watched Jackson run off after the soldiers. I prayed they would not catch my captain. If they did....

"Are you well?" The prince's fingers stroked along my neck.

"It is nothing."

He pulled his hand away. Blood spotted his white glove. "It is hardly nothing. I'll have the physicians sent to your room."

"That is not important," I said. "What matters is that you saw Captain Jackson unmasked."

"What I saw were two ruthless pirates holding you at sword point as Captain Jackson attempted to protect you."

I gasped. "No, that's not—"

"Enough!" the prince commanded. "An entire squadron saw my bride in a compromising position with pirates in the garden. As far as I'm concerned, the English captain saved her before any more harm could befall her."

"But—"

"Perhaps I did not make clear my earlier meaning when I spoke of my need for this treaty, Lady DeVale."

He glanced furtively about, pulled me out of the garden, along a corridor, and into my chambers. "My uncle will not survive to see my return. There are those in my kingdom who will be suitably unnerved by both the sudden passing of my cousin

215

and my uncle. It is imperative that I hasten my return with a new bride and a new treaty to secure my place upon the vacant throne before my enemies can rally a coup against me."

"Then this is the true reason you are not concerned that I may have been soiled by a pirate's touch?"

"Do not think yourself indispensable, Lady DeVale," he warned through a tight smile. "With the exchanging of our vows, the treaty is sealed. And although your presence at my side would no doubt please my loyal subjects, it certainly is not a requirement for my taking the throne." He reached out, stroking the backs of his fingers across my cheek. "It would be a tragedy if my bride were to be lost at sea on our return voyage."

I arched a brow at his veiled threat. "Do you believe I would support your contention that Captain Jackson saved me?"

"It is the duty of a good queen to support her husband in all he does. I trust I will have your support." He grabbed my upper arm, applying pressure until I bit my lip to keep from crying out. "I urge you to respond carefully, lest you find yourself without my protection."

I stared, not responding.

"Very well." He exhaled loudly and released my arm. "It is clear that you do not respond to threats upon your own life."

Hands clasped behind his back, he paced the length of the room. He paused near the door and turned, eyeing me askew.

"Perhaps if you do not value your own life, you will value that of another. If you wish me to overlook the possible romantic involvement you are rumored to have with The Wolff..." He paused and stared at me pointedly. "...and not have him tortured and hanged..."

My breath caught.

"...I do have your support, don't I, my Queen?"

"Yes, my Liege."

"Finally, the answer I was seeking." The prince reached back, his hand finding the door latch. "I trust when next we meet, your behavior will be in accordance with this conversation." He smiled, bowed low, and made his retreat.

On trembling legs, I made my way to the bed. Had my life really come to this? *No, not come. I have been groomed for this all my life, to fulfill the duties of wife and mother, as seen fit by my husband, with no ideas, no desires of my own.*

I half-smiled at the irony. Only as a prisoner upon a pirate vessel had I been allowed to pursue what I wanted. Even as I rankled at every turn and constantly demanded my freedom. Now to discover that only aboard *The Wolfsbane* was I ever truly free.

I listened as the door was securely closed, a key turned in the lock.

I sat upon my bed. Alone. Awaiting my fate.

†

Commander Fernandez came to visit. At Luisa's insistence, I'm sure. She was concerned by my listlessness since her arrival. She'd already dressed me by herself, with little or no help from me.

My soon-to-be marriage was a farce. Prince Rafael had made that clear that morning. I was to be nothing more than a figurehead at his side upon the throne. Another jewel to dangle from his majesty's arm.

"I understand you had quite an adventure last night," Luisa said.

"Pardon?"

"Pirates inside my fortress." Commander Fernandez scowled. "Running around like they own the place."

Luisa laughed. "You're just upset because they escaped."

My head snapped up. "Escaped?"

"My apologies, Lady DeVale. I'm afraid they eluded my best trained men."

Luisa paused from applying my makeup. "I hear it was none other than The Wolff."

"Of course it was, Luisa," Commander Fernandez said. "Who else could have pulled off so daring a scheme?"

My heart leapt. My captain had escaped alive. My heart sank with my very next thought. She had escaped to the safety of her ship and left me here alone.

217

Between the two of them, Luisa and Commander Fernandez managed to compose me enough to proceed.

"The ceremony is scheduled in the chapel. It is only a small wedding. There will be a larger ceremony at the palace upon your return to the prince's court." Commander Fernandez cupped my chin and smiled tenderly at me. "You are a gorgeous bride. Be happy."

I made an attempt at a smile. My eyes were bloodshot, my nose red, my cheeks tear-stained. How could he think I was beautiful?

"I go now to tell him the bride is coming." He backed toward the door, never taking his eyes from me. "Don't keep your prince waiting."

He left the room, and my tears started flowing again. Luisa hovered above me, attempting to calm me. She murmured to me, her voice meant to be low and soothing.

Why did Kris have to come? I was managing quite well. I had resigned myself to being able to live without her. To never see her anymore. To never know her touch upon me again. That had all changed in the garden. I never dreamt she would dress as a Spanish soldier, risk capture by sneaking into the fortress to see me. Her words. Her touch.

Just like before, she had intruded upon my life, disrupted my carefully laid plans, and turned my whole world upon its ear. This time, I didn't know if I had the strength to restore my life.

"Hurry, we must go now." Luisa handed me my handbag and ushered me out of the room.

Numbly, I allowed her to lead me into the hall. She led me toward the chapel, heels clicking upon the stone floor. We walked in silence. The only sound was the echo of our shoes. My own shallow breaths and the pounding of my heart.

The chapel bells chimed. I jumped, a sharp cry escaping my lips. I leaned against the wall.

Luisa was instantly at my side, hands soothing upon my shoulders, my arms.

"Are you ill?" she asked, concern showing upon her face.

"I'm fine. Please, give me a moment."

She drew back, eyeing me suspiciously. Apparently deciding it was safe, she nodded.

"I'll be up the hall when you're ready. Don't linger long."

I thanked her and watched her continue up the hall and around the next bend. I knew she wouldn't go far. Still I sorely needed the solitude, even if it was only for a few precious moments. I continued to lean against the wall. The cool stone pressed against my cheek. I closed my eyes, relaxing.

I felt a hand upon my back, caressing my neck. I jumped at the sensation.

"Kris," I whispered, turning around.

"No, not Kris," the voice said, teeth flashed. "Not your precious Captain Wolff."

Captain Jackson's hand tightened about my neck. His other gripped my wrist, forcing my arm behind my back. He shoved hard, pushing me against the wall.

"Where's The Wolff?" He slammed me into the wall.

I cried out, and a sharp pain shot through my chest as he slammed me into the stone wall again. His fingers pressed deeper into my neck.

"The Wolff," he repeated. He hissed in my ear, his hot breath burning. "Or I tell your groom's courtesans what The Wolff really is and what the two of you were doing in the garden together. I wonder what torture the Spanish priests use to purify the souls of the perverse."

"You would not dare tell. For to tell would impugn your own honor." I gasped as his hand tightened upon my neck, fingers digging into my flesh. "I shan't ever tell you where The Wolff is."

"It matters not." He yanked me away from the wall, pushed me down the corridor. "For where you go, The Wolff will follow."

"You cannot intend to kidnap me from the prince's own fortress." I said. "The entire Spanish Armada will be upon you before sunset."

"And why should your prince have strife with me?" He feigned innocence. "He himself saw the notorious pirate Captain

219

Wolff make a brazen attempt at kidnapping you from the gardens this very morning."

He shoved, pushing me down the hall, back the way we'd come. "No, my lady, all the pieces are falling together in my favor. I have you, and The Wolff falls into my clutches. And if anything unfortunate should happen to you, the prince will hold The Wolff responsible."

To punctuate his threat, he pushed me harder, nearly shoving me to the ground. We hurried along the corridors, toward my quarters. Turning sharply, he took me down unknown passageways, through a labyrinth.

Chapter Thirteen

THE CAPTAIN

I sat upon the rocks lining the coastline. Shucking off my jacket, I tossed it, watching it hit the water. The tide took it, carrying it away. Glad to be rid of the uniform jacket, I watched it float off. I would be happy to burn the rest of the uniform once I got back to *The Wolfsbane*.

I should have left long before. My crew would be worried. Vincent was concerned that I risked being captured. He had urged me to use caution, not do anything foolhardy. I kicked at the bow of the longboat, launching it. I scrambled across the rocky shoals, splashing water as I went. Catching onto the side, I pulled myself from the waist-high water, landing in the bottom. I scrambled to a sitting position.

I sat still, resting the oars across my thighs. Idly drifting upon the choppy waves, I watched the silhouette of the Spanish fortress as the boat floated along. The ringing of bells echoed throughout the structure, signaling the start of the wedding, no doubt. Her wedding. To some noble-born prince.

"You want to storm the castle and take her back?"

I rolled my eyes, cocked my head toward the stern of the boat, stared pointedly at Sven. He remained seated, oars relaxed across his lap, casually awaiting my orders.

"No." I shook my head. "I've intruded upon her life enough already."

He stared at me blankly. "What?"

"This is what she wants."

"No."

"Yes." I nodded vehemently.

"Hah. In the garden, she was ready to leave with you."

"Only because I attacked her weaknesses. I know how she reacts, how her body responds to my touch."

My jaw tightened with a bout of self-loathing. "It was wrong of me to attempt to sway her with kisses. She deserves better than to be treated as such by the likes of me."

"Aye," he agreed. "Fix it, Captain. Do what needs to be done to return our lady to us."

I exhaled loudly, rubbed a hand across my tired face. I stared blankly at the waves lapping against the sidewalls of the longboat. Get her back; he made it seem so simple... maybe for him, it was. I was the one who had made things complicated.

It was my fault. I'd driven her to it because I'd relegated her to a role as a member of my crew. Because I couldn't tell her how I felt. I couldn't say the words she so needed to hear.

I tried. Desperately. I had left *The Wolfsbane* anchored five miles up the shoreline. Taken a longboat and rowed it all the long way back, with only Sven along to help me sneak into the fortress to tell her how I felt about her. I froze. The words wouldn't come. And when I realized that she was going to marry....

The boat came to a halt, sending me flying, landing face first in the bottom. A groan escaped my lips as I placed both hands on the sidewalls. Muscles screaming in protest, I pulled myself up.

I hadn't been paying attention. The longboat had drifted back toward shore. She'd lodged against a shallow sandbar.

I climbed aross my oars and jumped from the bow. My boots sank in the muddy sandbar. I leaned in, putting my shoulder to the bow, and pushing hard. Sven stood in the stern. Leaning over, he firmly planted his oar handle in the mud. He strained, attempting to slide us off the sandbar. I grunted, pushing hard, straining. I lost my balance, fell over, landed in the water face first. Hands groping for the bow, I pulled myself to my knees.

My gaze fell across the rocky shoreline. I must have hit my head too hard. I was obviously seeing things—a vision in white upon the coast, descending the cliffs to the beaches. I scooped water in my hands and swiped at my face, washing the mud off. I squinted at the shoreline.

"Lady DeVale." Sven gasped.

This was no illusion. It was Alexis. She was leading the way down the cliffside, an English officer accompanying her. Captain Jackson. My jaw clenched. I instinctively started up the cliff to intercept them. I took three long strides before I halted in my tracks. I couldn't risk facing him headlong on the path for fear that he would endanger Alexis.

I signaled for Sven to join me. We knelt on the sandbar, hidden from view by the bow of the boat. I counted the minutes till they would pass. Muscles tensed. I waited. I heard their shoes upon the shoal, looked up just as they were going by.

Alexis led the way, walking just in front of Jackson. Her step was off, though. Uneven. I looked closer. Jackson followed her closely. Too closely. He held one hand at her neck. The other had her left arm twisted behind her. He pushed her roughly. She stumbled upon the rocks, landing awkwardly.

Sven was upon him instantly, hands on his jacket, pulling him away from her. Jackson turned around, fists swinging. Sven ducked, coming up with a closed fist of his own, catching Jackson beneath the chin. He fell hard.

I pulled Alexis to her feet. She reached out, clutching at me. I pushed her hair back from her face. Her cheeks were wet, tear stains making tracks through the dirt upon her face. Her lip was split and blood trickled down her chin.

Jackson scrambled to his feet, the soles of his boots sliding upon the loose shoal.

I pulled my sword and turned.

He barely raised his in time, deflecting my blow. He thrust.

I parried.

Alexis and Sven were behind me.

He tried to get past me.

I dodged, blocked his wild thrust. Our blades struck, locked. Muscles clenching, we fought for control.

"Run for the longboat," I commanded.

223

Out of the corner of my eye, I saw Sven and Alexis take off running, heard the splashing of water as they jumped into the boat.

Jackson lunged wildly, sliding past me.

I grabbed for him, catching the back of his trousers. A ripping sound and scraps of material came away in my grasp as his under breeches were exposed.

He halted in his tracks and his hand sought to cover his exposed backside.

I leaped, hitting him in the small of the back. We both landed in the surf. My sword went flying, splashing as it hit the water. The shoal cut at my hands, tearing my gloves, my knees. I scrambled for my sword.

Jackson was upon me, his knee pressing into the small of my back. One hand clutched at my hair, pulling my head up, back. His blade pressed against my throat, the cold metal biting into my flesh.

"Die, you cur..." Jackson's foul breath was hot upon my flesh.

"Go...to...hell." I strained to form each word, throat muscles stretching, tightening.

Jackson pulled back with such force that my upper body was dragged up from the surf. My arms hung limply; my knees ached from the tiny bits of shoal.

"You've cost me far too many men and ships you foul demon. You've embarrassed me far too much." His voice was colder than the steel biting at my throat. "I'll take great pleasure in sending you back to the demons that spawned you."

Sharp steel sliced my flesh as he drew his sword a finger's breadth across my neck. Warm blood trickled down my throat. Jackson laughed and I knew he was enjoying himself, intentionally dragging out the moment of my impending death.

Above the pounding in my ears, I heard a single shot from a musket, smelled the gunpowder in the air. Jackson was sent flying backwards from the force of the shot. I was instantly on my feet, running through the surf. Sven was standing in the bow of the longboat, reloading his musket. Alexis was seated, already struggling with the oars.

I heard shouting behind me, boots crunching upon the shoal. I glanced back. Spanish soldiers were streaming from the fortress, running down the cliffside, Prince Rafael leading the charge. Jackson knelt in the surf, cursing, clutching his wounded arm.

"Hurry!" Alexis shouted. "They're closing!"

The sound of musket fire filled the air. Musket balls whipped past, plowing into the water. I fought the waves, leapt into the bottom of the boat. The sound of woodchips flying with the impact of musket balls rang in my ears. Alexis was straining, rowing for all she was worth. Beside her, Sven aimed, returning shot for shot.

I crouched low in the boat, watching the soldiers, praying we would get well underway before musket fire picked our boat apart.

Spanish soldiers chased us into the surf, some of them venturing as deep as waist high before taking their shot.

Prince Rafael and Captain Jackson huddled together in the surf, cursing, throwing threats at our fading longboat.

†

I watched the horizon. The mainsails were still visible in the distance. One English. One Spanish. Both pursuing us for days now.

"Still they pursue us," Sven said.

"They're very persistent," Vincent kept a firm grip on the wheel.

"I would be too if someone stole my bride from the altar," Brodey said.

"That's not what happened." Sven stared pointedly at me.

My breath caught and a lump formed in my throat. I looked to Sven's face. He had been behaving oddly ever since our daring escape upon the beach. No, since before that. My mind recalled vividly the events in the garden, Sven's arrival at the crucial juncture, just before Jackson attempted to lop off my head.

225

My eyes narrowed with suspicion. How long had Sven truly been in the garden before rushing to save us?

"Captain Wolff stole her away long before she made it to the altar."

I continued to regard Sven with suspicion. Did he really have impeccable timing in the garden—or was he truly biding his time now? "I didn't steal her from anywhere," I said. "Jackson was kidnapping her."

"Well, I don't think that's what Jackson relayed to the prince."

"No doubt," Vincent said. "Otherwise, they wouldn't still be allied in their pursuit of us."

Sven was studying the charts we had lifted from the Spanish galleon. Lips pursed, he stared at a line in the far right corner. His fingers traced the outline of a small land mass. I leaned across, curious. Vincent kept his hands on the wheel, but he kept looking to the map.

"Brodey," I snapped. "Relieve Watkins from the crow's nest. I want to know if those ships gain ground on us."

"Aye, Captain."

I waited as he scrambled up the mainmast. "What is it?" I asked when I thought he was out of earshot.

Sven's finger pointed to a spot on the map, tapping. "We're here," he said. "This is a coastline." He pointed to the land mass. "It isn't on any of our maps, mind you." His fingertip traced a small stream of water running through the center of the island. "By the measurements on the chart, this channel runs deep enough for a vessel."

I leaned in closer. "And it runs all the way, clean through."

Vincent rubbed his chin thoughtfully. "The galleon we secured this from was out on an expedition. It hadn't reached port yet."

"Meaning the vessels chasing us may not know of this passage."

"They would lose precious days traveling around the island," Vincent added. "We'd be able to escape free and clear."

I thumped Sven loudly on the back. I grabbed the astrolabe and took a reading and helped Vincent and Sven plot our course to freedom.

✝

I peered in through the open galley window. They were at the counter, chopping carrots together. Rufus gathered them up on the cutting board, poured them into a large pot. Alexis reached for another bunch. Her knife flashed, briskly chopping. She'd grown quite adept at wielding a knife, I noted.

She'd been spending more and more time in Rufus's galley. He had actually seemed to miss her when she was gone. Now he welcomed her into his galley with open arms. Or perhaps he was merely taking advantage of the help.

Rufus turned from his pot, glanced at the open window.

"How long have ye been out here?" The second he emerged from the galley a wave of hot steam followed him out the door.

"Not long," I lied.

He snorted. "Any longer and ye would have been frozen solid." He patted my shoulder, jerked his head toward the door. "Go on, lad. I have to get something from the hold anyway."

"You're a lousy liar, Rufus." I said. "But thank you."

He raised his hand as if he meant to slap me. "Ah, get yer arse in there, ye scamp."

I opened the door, rushed inside. A blast of hot air hit me. I closed the door and slowly turned around. She was staring at me, knife frozen in midair. With deliberate steps, I slowly stalked across the room and stood beside her at the counter.

Eyes still on her, I snatched the carrot she was chopping. I took a bite, offered the rest to her.

She timidly bit the end I held between my fingers. She chewed, her delicate mouth working the carrot. Still, her eyes never left me. They raked across my face, studying me. She bit her bottom lip. "Your nose is red." Her voice was little more than a whisper.

"A northerly wind is blowing hard today." My upper body leaned toward her of its own accord. "It's cold out."

Her face came closer. Instead of kissing my lips, though, she planted a kiss upon my nose. She stepped back, smiling broadly. "All the more reason to stay inside where it's warm."

"I have other places that are cold."

"Such as?"

I swallowed hard. "My lips."

She slid into my arms. Her lips brushed mine.

So lightly that I wasn't certain she had kissed me, save for the burning sensation passing across my numb lips.

She leaned back, holding me at arm's length. "Better?" she asked.

I shook my head.

"No?" Her smile lit up her face, her teeth sparkling.

"I have several other places that have suffered terribly, my lady."

"Well, that could prove most dangerous." Her hands fidgeted at my collar, fingernails scraping along the flesh at my neck.

I shivered beneath her touch.

"We'd best warm you before we're forced to amputate anything."

Our lips met, her tongue plowing into my mouth, her hands on me. She backed me up, roughly pushing me against the countertop. I moaned as the edge of the counter hit me in the small of the back.

Her fingers worked deftly at my buckle. My belt fell to the floor, my sword clattering upon the hardwood. Her hands went beneath my tunic, her warm fingers scrambling across my cold flesh. Her tongue savagely raped my mouth, thrusting deep inside. Her palms ran briskly across my stomach, my ribcage, her touch sure and uninhibited.

My hands gripped her hips, pulling her in closer.

Her mouth left mine and she buried her face in my neck. Her tongue glided across my cold flesh

I flinched as her tongue connected with the scratch left by Jackson's sword.

228

She suddenly stiffened, turned her face into my collarbone. Her roaming hands stilled, dropped away all together.

My hands came up to stroke through her hair. "What is it, my lady?" I breathed into her ear.

With a tortured cry, she tore herself from my embrace, ran to the opposite side of the room. Head bowed, she stared at the countertop, arms firmly clutched about herself.

I bent, picking my belt up off the floor. Straightening my tunic, I slowly crossed the room. I stood behind her and placed my hands upon her shoulders. To my relief, she didn't shrink away from my touch. But her shoulders heaved.

Slowly, I turned her round. My fingers cupped her chin, lifting her face. Her eyes met mine, tears threatening to well in those verdant pools. She bowed her head, her arms remained firmly folded around her waist. Her lips trembled as she spoke. "I was so determined that I was going to make everything right. I was going to walk away from you and not look back." Her words caught. "But then you came after me. Twice. And your actions in the garden…"

My face flushed at the memory of what I'd done.

"I promised myself I'd be strong enough."

"For what, my lady?"

"To not give in. To return with no expectations, be content to stay upon your vessel as just another member of your crew. To resist your touch." She looked up, her eyes searching my face. "But one look at you and I lose all control."

My fingers reached out, stroking her cheek.

She wrenched away from my touch as if it had burned.

My hands fell to her shoulders.

"I cannot!" she cried out. "Can you not see it's tearing me apart, feeling the way I do for you?" Her eyes met mine. "Knowing you don't feel the same for me?"

I bowed my head, deliberately looking at my boots. I knew she desperately needed to hear the words. But if I told her now, would she believe me, or would she think I said it out of pity? My gaze traveled along the floor, settling on her familiar tan boots. My eyes ran up her tight-fitting breeches and over the curves straining at the material of her burgundy tunic.

229

She looked like no other member of my crew, I thought rue-fully. Only days before, I had seen her decked out in a gorgeous gown, the most beautiful bride I'd ever seen. Even now, the memory took my breath away. My gaze moved higher still. Her lips trembled beneath my gaze. They were swollen from our kisses. I longed to kiss them again.

I longed to speak the truth, yearned to tell her what she needed to hear. But I couldn't. Not here. Not now.

"Meet me on deck tonight." My voice came out a strangled whisper. "After everyone's asleep."

✝

It was well past midnight. The moon was high in the night sky, full, with a bright white glow. The stars were equally bright, with not a cloud in sight to diminish their light. The cold wind cut through me and I pulled my cloak tighter.

I rounded the corner just the other side of the galley and came to a halt, frozen in my tracks. My mouth hung open as I stared in awe. She looked like one of the fabled sea Sirens perched upon the railing, ankles interlocked for support. Her eyes were closed, back arched, breasts jutting forward proudly, and her long blonde hair was whipping wildly in the wind.

Mesmerized, I slowly approached. The wooden boards creaked beneath my boots.

She turned toward the sound. My lady pushed her hair back with one hand and her eyes opened, focusing on me.

My gaze fell to settle on her lap. She held her wedding gown crumpled in one hand. She held her hand extended over the edge of the ship. With my approach, she opened her fist, dropping the gown into the sea.

I came to her, peering over the side, watching as the gown momentarily floated, a white shroud upon the sea. All too soon, the weight of the fabric worked against itself, dragging the gown under bit by bit until it disappeared into the depths below.

"Should I offer my apologies, my lady?"

"No, that is hardly necessary." She shook her head. "After

the garden and what transpired there, I have come to accept that I shall never wed."

Her words, her expression, cut me to the quick. It was one thing for her not to marry the prince, yet it was another matter entirely to think of her giving up her future happiness. Surely, every lady dreamed of her wedding day. I stepped closer, fingers cupping her chin, my eyes searching hers for the truth. "Once again, am I to blame?"

"Yes, you are." Tears welled in her eyes, threatening to spill. She swallowed quickly, biting her bottom lip. She struggled with her next words. "My heart belongs to you. Because of you, I shall have no other."

My arms went about her, hugging her tightly, pressing my face into her shoulder, burying my nose in her hair. I squeezed my eyes shut. My hands clenched into balled fists behind her back. I was afraid if I told her, I might lose her. I was terrified if I didn't, she would leave me again.

"I..." My words caught in my throat. "I love you, Alexis."

Fingers clutched my hair and she lifted my head away. Her eyes darted about my face. The pad of her thumb stroked my cheek. She clasped my hands in hers and I aided her down from the rail. She pulled me away from the edge of the deck. She led...I willingly followed.

In silence, I followed her all the way to my cabin. We were barely inside the door before she pulled me in for another kiss. Her touch was so remarkably tender, so feathery light that if my shirt hadn't fallen off me, I'd never have known she'd touched me.

A light sheen of sweat sparkled on her body as she stripped off her shirt, throwing it to the floor. I reached out instantly, taking her full breasts in my hands.

She brought her mouth to mine, her tongue licking my lips. Her eyes were wild with a barely controlled lust. She pressed down on my shoulders and pushed me back on the small cot near the door.

I fell back, resting on my elbows. I stared, fascinated, as she stripped off the last of her clothing and came into my waiting arms. She straddled me upon the small cot, gliding her body across mine, echoing my profession of love.

†

"Land ho!"

I grabbed Alexis by the hand, urging her along. We'd slept in late. It was my fault. I was enjoying myself too much. Wrapped in her silken arms the whole night through, we made love, held one another, and talked about nothing and everything. We napped then made love again.

She ran along the deck beside me, her hair blowing wildly in the breeze, her delighted laughter strong upon the wind. We didn't stop until we reached the bow. "Is that the channel?" she asked.

I nodded. "That little shortcut will take five days off our voyage time. We'll be at Trepassi Beach before you know it."

She looked up at me, eyes beaming, and her lips curled into a smile. Her fingers reached out and she stroked through my hair. "Kiss me."

"What?" I asked, glancing around the deck. With the cry of *land ho* almost every hand was on deck. Given her prior insistence that we control our passions whilst in the presence of my crew, I was somewhat taken aback. "Are you certain?"

"Kiss me," she repeated. "We've sailed beyond the realm of the Spanish Empire. We've long since left English territories. As such, my obligations to both Crowns are at an end. My only allegiance now lies in pleasing my captain." Her fingertip traced my jaw line. "And you are my captain."

I grinned and playfully bit at her finger. "When we reach Trepassi Beach," I said, "it'll be my duty to repeatedly test the strength of your allegiance."

"I believe you'll find it to be steadfast and most determined." She turned within my embrace.

I kissed her. She had asked and it seemed I could deny my lady nothing. As our kiss deepened, I realized that I had no desire even to try. I held Alexis tight in my arms as *The Wolfsbane* glided into the narrow channel. Jungle sprouted up on both sides

232

of the ship. Lush greenery ran down the banks, into the water. Alexis relaxed contentedly in my arms.

I was aware of footsteps behind me and turned to find Vincent and Sven rapidly approaching. Their expressions were troubled.

"We have a situation, Captain."

"I'm sorry, Captain," Sven added.

I looked from Sven to Vincent. I felt a growing knot of apprehension building in my gut. "What's happened?"

"Sven fell asleep at the wheel last night."

A group of men working with the hemp nearby paused from their work to look at us.

Vincent glanced back at them and leaned toward us lowering his voice. "As he slept, someone lowered the anchor."

My mouth dropped open. "Are you certain?"

"Quite." Vincent's voice was grave. "I discovered the deed myself when I came upon deck this morning."

"We could have been anchored for hours," Alexis said.

"Most assuredly," Vincent said. "Certainly long enough for our pursuers to gain ground."

"Any lead we had hoped to gain has surely been lost!"

The group of men looked up sharply at my outburst.

Alexis tugged at my shirtsleeve.

I dropped my voice again. "How could you, Sven? Your negligence has led to this treachery."

A voice behind me said, "Yer a fine one to speak of treachery, aren't ye now?"

I quickly spun around.

Rufus had come up behind us, a pistol pointed at our backs. With him was Brodey and several other crewmen, all armed to the teeth. I tucked Alexis behind me, shielding her.

"What the hell is going on here?"

"We're taking the ship."

"Aye!" A chorus of shouts rose up from the group of armed men.

By now, it seemed as if the entire ship's complement had closed on us. I scanned their faces furtively, attempting to discern friend from foe. My gaze fell upon Sven, and his face paled.

"That's right," Brodey spoke up, flicking his blade at me. I felt the tip cut across my cheek. "Your boy Sven told us all about what happened at the Spanish fortress."

"Captain—" Sven reached for me.

I slapped his hand away.

Raucous laughter rose up from the crew.

"Seems the poor lad was distraught when he returned from your mission, and being good friends of his, we cheered him up with a few drinks. Loosened his tongue right up."

"Aye. Imagine our shock when he told us that our captain is no man at all, but rather a wench."

Vincent stepped closer to my side.

"Is it not true that I've been a good and just captain?"

A murmur of 'ayes' rose up throughout the band of cut-throats.

"And haven't I proved time and again that I'm worthy of your trust?"

"Ye've lied to us and deceived us," Rufus said.

"Aye!" came similar shouts.

"I've also led you to more treasure than any captain you've ever had."

"Aye!" came a few more grumbled agreements.

I stepped backward, attempting to edge us toward the side of the ship. If things turned worse, perhaps we could go over the edge and escape through the channel and into the jungle.

"We shan't have a female for a captain," Brodey said.

Brodey and Watkins stepped forward, swords drawn. They roughly yanked me away from the railing, toward the center of the ship.

Alexis reached for me.

Rufus shoved her back.

Two more sailors approached with chains.

"Man or woman," I snarled, "I'm still Captain Wolff. Scourge of the Seven Seas. The deadliest of all pirates. And still capable of leading the best pirate crew the world has ever feared."

"Wolff! Wolff! Wolff!" arose a chorus of shouts.

"Kill The Wolff!" Brodey shouted. A chorus took up that

cry, as well.

A sword was shoved into my grasp and I soon found myself squared off upon the deck. Alexis and Vincent stood beside me, along with a small band of men urged on by Lars.

Rufus, Brodey, and their mutineers stood several feet away, pistols and swords at the ready.

Sven was somewhere in between. Gradually, he inched toward our side.

A shot was fired. A musket ball grazed Sven's leg. All hell broke loose. Swords clashed, shots were randomly fired. My deck was awash in a sea of blood and falling bodies. Another shot echoed in my ears, this one so much louder than those around me. I looked up just as a tree off our starboard side fell. The deck of *The Wolfsbane* fell ominously silent.

"The pirate hunters are upon us!" The shout came from the crow's nest. Another cannonball whizzed overhead. At least they were far enough back that they weren't able to judge shot accurately.

"How far?" I asked, sword still crossed with Brodey's.

We continued our stare down; neither of us moved a muscle. A loud boom echoed, one of our own cannons responding in kind.

"Both ships have entered the channel behind us," was the answer from the crow's nest. "They'll be upon us soon!"

"Vincent, to the wheel. Sven, mount a defense. Brodey—"

"I'm killing you and taking the ship!" He leaned in, his sword pressing harder against mine.

"You do, and we all die." Muscles straining, I pushed back with an equal amount of force. "It'll take all of us to escape the English and Spanish combined. We have to call a truce and work together."

Brodey squinted, eyeing me appraisingly. For long moments, neither of us gave in. At last, with a grunt, he relaxed his grip. "Aye, truce." He lowered his sword. "I'll kill you later."

†

235

We'd been fleeing for hours now in the channel, the enemy ships still pursuing us. Unlike the narrow passageway we'd last gone through, this one was wide enough for several ships to fit at once. That at least gave us more maneuvering room. Vincent worked the wheel expertly, creating a moving target.

The cannonballs had done serious damage, taking out our mainsail. We were limping, with only our short sails for speed. The enemy ships were close now. We wouldn't be able to elude them much longer.

Sven led a group of five. They were pouring buckets of water upon the small fires that were still burning where the mainmast had once stood. Now it was nothing more than a smoldering block of wood. The mainsail had fallen, landing across the channel some yards back.

Brodey led the counterattack. His men fired well, cannonballs crippling the mainsail of the Spanish galleon. That would slow her some. The English still sailed full speed ahead, nearly unscathed.

"Aim for *The Scorpion*," I ordered. "I want that English flag at the bottom of the ocean."

"Captain Wolff." Vincent maintained his grip upon the wheel.

I ran for the bow, dodging splintered wood where enemy fire had torn up my deck. "What is it?" I came to a halt beside Vincent.

He pointed dead ahead. "The channel doesn't go all the way through."

"You're wrong." I shouted above the gunfire. "It's clearly marked on the map. That's just jungle growth stretching across the channel."

"That's land," he protested. "We'll run aground."

I grabbed a long pole and ran to the bow of the ship. I kicked off my boots and scrambled across the rail, up on the bowsprit, and climbed onto the wolf's neck. I stood on his head and grabbed at an ear. Holding tightly, I swung around beneath his neck. I used my other arm to thrust the pole into the water.

It went in deep, struck bottom, jarring me. I let loose the pole; it stuck firmly in the mud. I clutched at the wolf's neck with both hands. With a firm overhand grip, I pulled myself back to the deck.

Grabbing my boots, I ran back to Vincent. "It's shallow. We're trapped."

Vincent jammed the wooden cog into the ship's wheel. He grabbed his knife and cut the rope holding our short sail. The sail crumpled in a heap upon the deck. We gradually slowed.

"Prepare to be boarded!" I shouted.

Those men who weren't manning the cannons scrambled behind barrels and crates. They loaded their muskets, drew their swords, and waited as the English ship drew near.

"Alexis?" I frantically searched the deck. "Where's Alexis?"

"I sent her to your cabin." Vincent yelled, readying his own weapons.

"I'll return soon," I was already off and running for my quarters. "Hold them off as best you can."

✝

I burst into the cabin, out of breath.

Alexis was there, my spare revolver on the desk. She was frantically attempting to load it.

I raced to her, kneeling on the floor in front of her. I gripped her by the shoulders. She looked at me, my own fear reflected in her eyes.

"The map was wrong," I said breathlessly. "The channel doesn't run all the way through."

She clutched me to her desperately. I hugged her tightly and drew back. She offered me a weak, courageous smile.

"The English are boarding. Bar the door behind me when I leave," I said. "Should the English win, they won't be able to break this door before the Spanish arrive. The Spanish will protect you."

"Can you really hope to defeat them?"

"Of course," I lied. "I am the notorious Captain Wolff, after all." I growled low.

237

A weak laugh escaped her lips.

I turned to go.

She reached out, catching my arm.

I turned to look at her one final time. All the color had drained from her face.

"Come back to me, my Captain."

"I shall always return to you, my lady."

My lips met hers. Soft, bittersweet kisses begged me to stay. Kisses that brought whispers of a promised future if only I would not leave.

✝

The deck was awash in flames. English troops swept across the ship. Most of my crew lay dead or dying. Cannons were useless now. *The Scorpion* had grappled onto the side of *The Wolfsbane* with irons. We couldn't sink *The Scorpion* now without dragging ourselves under.

Sven was backed into a corner, along with a company of men, Rufus included. Their weapons were on the deck, the English soldiers placing them in chains. I lost sight of Vincent. Watkins was lying across the ship's wheel, a knife in his back. I was afraid the same fate may have befallen my quartermaster. I blocked the thought out of my mind and swung my sword wildly.

I felt someone at my back, bracing himself. I turned my head, glancing over my shoulder.

Lars moved beside me, blocking with his sword.

He had a head wound, blood streaming down across one eye. Gunpowder clung to the side of his face, embedded in his skin. My guess was his musket had blown up in his face. That he was still standing was a miracle.

Lars flicked his long mane across his shoulder, nodded at Sven's group. His lip was curled into a sneer. "Better to die fighting than to rot in a hold all the long way back to England."

With a wild yell, he charged into a pack of English soldiers. His sword flashed. He managed to cut down a half dozen before a shot hit him in the back. He fell to the deck, sword clattering from his fingers.

"Lars." I blocked a clumsy thrust, plunging my sword into an Englishman's gut.

The coward that backshot Lars stepped out, revolver still smoking. Jackson. His lip curled into a feral sneer. He spotted me, yelled wildly, pulling his sword from its sheath, charging across the deck.

I barely had a chance to raise my own sword before he was upon me, swinging savagely. Gone was the refined grace of fencing he had learned as a gentleman in the Queen's Navy, replaced by a severe slash-and-hatchet style. I was familiar with the technique. Most of my men preferred this method of attack when we boarded our prey. It didn't require finesse, only brute strength and stamina. And there was little defense against it.

I dodged, blocking as best I could, I found myself losing ground. As a spoiled officer, I had hoped that Jackson would tire quickly. His anger, however, fueled his relentless attack. Slowly, inexplicably, I was forced from the ship's wheel to the rail. Back pinned, one hand braced against the railing, I had no avenue of retreat left.

Sweat was running down his brow and with a glint in his eye, he lifted his sword for the final blow. Quickly, I raised my sword, feeling the jolt all the way to my boots as his sword crashed down upon mine. Muscles straining, arm aching, I held my position, our swords interlocked above my head.

He leaned in, so close I could smell his foul breath. "Today," he snarled, "I kill The Wolff."

He reached for his waistband, grabbing at his revolver. He caught the barrel and deliberately swung the butt at my head, striking me on the temple. The force of the blow knocked me backwards, sending me tumbling flipside over the railing, and into the waters below.

239

Chapter Fourteen

THE LADY

SHIP'S LOG – DECEMBER 9, 1703

Dawn has come. And with it, my nightmare continues. The battle is lost.

My precious captain has been killed in battle by a cowardly attack from Captain Jackson. Most of the crew have been put in irons, taken to the hold, prisoners to be executed upon their return to English soil.

With my captain gone, I would gladly share their fate. I have learned, though, that I am indeed under the protection of the Spanish.

I will travel aboard The Wolfsbane *only as far as Fortress Monsarrent. There, Prince Rafael is awaiting the return of his betrothed. We will be married before returning to the prince's homeland. Where, no doubt, the prince will be eager to begin adding to his royal bloodline.*

How I wish I could join Sven and the others. Their deaths will come soon enough. My fate is far worse. I fear I shall linger in misery for years and years before sweet death will come to release me.

The Wolfsbane *is little more than a ghost ship. The captain dead, her crew locked in the hold. Only a minimal crew of English and Spanish soldiers is left on board to man her. Ropes securely fastened upon her bow, being towed like an obscene trophy behind* The Scorpion.

†

I heard footsteps approaching, voices drawing near. I dropped the quill I'd been using. Opening the drawer, I hid the logbook beneath a false bottom. The cabin door creaked open. I slammed the desk drawer shut, leaned back in my chair. The lock was useless, having been broken when the soldiers had burst into the room, splintering the thick wood.

"Where is the logbook?" Jackson demanded.

"I'm sure I do not know."

"Unlikely." His hand shot out, catching my wrist and squeezing brutally. "No matter. I'll destroy this cabin inch by inch if I must. Believe me, any documents, any witness to The Wolff's true identity will lie on the ocean's floor with her long before this voyage is done."

He clasped his hands behind his back and idly paced about the room.

"I understood I was to rendezvous with Prince Rafael at Fortress Monsarrent." I swiveled upon my chair watching him pace. "More than a dozen Spanish sailors have seen me. How do you expect to explain my sudden death to His Highness?"

He stopped in the center of the room and stared dead on at me. "Unfortunately, all the Spanish sailors died in battle." A smile slowly spread over his features. "We've already cleared the channel. As soon as we've reached open sea, we'll attack *The Rapier*. She's weak; she won't survive an attack from *The Scorpion* and *The Wolfsbane* combined."

"Why wait?" I asked. "Why not attack now?"

"Patience, my sweet. We're still near the island. I don't want to risk any survivors reaching shore. I'd just as soon all witnesses drowned at sea."

I sat quietly watching. There was no reasoning with him. He already had his own agenda.

"I'll be hailed as a hero for defeating *The Wolfsbane* and killing her captain. Unfortunately, the Lady DeVale perished, her body thrown overboard by the dastardly Wolff."

He came to stand before me. He placed both hands on the chair's armrests and leaned in.

241

The overwhelming stench of his breath almost made me gag. I leaned as far back in my chair as possible. The wooden back creaked ominously beneath my weight.

"Rest assured, after I've taken care of *The Rapier*..."

His breath was hot upon me,

"...I'll return to take care of you."

I gave into my rage and spit on him.

He laughed, wiping my saliva from his face. "Bloody wench." He reached out, catching my chin. He squeezed roughly, his fingers gripping my cheeks, tightening upon my jawbone. "Don't pretend false outrage, Lady DeVale." He leaned forward, his tongue flicking out.

I attempted to retreat. There was nowhere left to go.

His tongue snaked along my cheek. "Knowing how you gave it to The Wolff—and those things you let that foul demon do to you..." His free hand dipped lower, between my legs, grabbing my inner thigh. "Surely, you won't object to spreading your legs for a captain of Her Majesty's Royal Navy."

The door creaked open. I looked past Jackson, wondering at this latest intrusion. Brodey loomed in the open doorway, sword hanging at his side. Captain Jackson's back remained to the open door, no doubt expecting it was one of his men. I felt a surge of hope as Brodey came up behind him.

"Guard her well," Jackson ordered, "while I attend to the destruction of *The Rapier*."

"No fear, I will," Brodey answered, blocking the doorway with his massive bulk. Arms folded across his chest, he stared down at me with a broad smirk on his face.

†

Another logbook was yanked from the bookcase and rifled through, pages tearing, then indiscriminately thrown against the wall to land in a heap with the others. Brodey reached for yet another book.

I rolled my eyes. "Wouldn't you think that after twelve volumes, it's not likely that Kris wrote anything revealing in any of her books?"

He paused in mid-reach and watched me out of the corner of his eye. His finger tapped along the spine of the next logbook. In a rage, he savagely ripped it from the shelf, rifled it, and threw it hard against the wall.

"You heard Jackson. He wants any proof destroyed."

I smirked. "And you always do what Captain Jackson wants, do you?"

He glared at me. "I do what I want."

I nodded. "Of course you do."

With one swipe, he cleared the shelf. Muscles flexing, he ripped the bookcase from the wall.

I involuntarily jumped as he knocked it over.

He noticed. His eyes glinted with a feral appetite at the scent of my fear. "You're afraid."

"Of you? Hardly." *Desperately so.*

"Yeah." He stalked to the desk. "Yeah, you are."

He leaned across me.

I shrank as far back in my chair as I could. Sucked in, held my breath.

He yanked open a drawer, pulled it all the way out, and dumped its contents on the floor. "Admit it. You don't like the idea of me rifling your captain's quarters." He grunted as he pulled out another drawer.

I slipped out of the chair and slowly backed away. "I don't appreciate the need for senseless destruction."

Another drawer hit the floor. "I'll wreck this whole cabin until I'm certain there's nothing left that reveals that banshee for what she really was."

"That banshee was your captain," I said through clenched teeth. I slowly inched my way up the stairs, felt the curtain at my back and clutched the material in my grasp.

His hand shot out and cleared the desktop in one sweep. Kris' quill and inkbottle went flying, landing some fifteen feet away, the ink spilling freely onto the floor.

"Is this where The Wolff had you?" he taunted. "On your back, legs spread wide?"

He opened the center drawer, rifled through the papers inside. I caught, held my breath. If he dumped that drawer, he'd discover the false bottom. "I know there's one logbook unaccounted for. Tell me its location or I'll destroy your love nest."

He wasn't watching me. Perhaps I could slip away. My fingers worked the curtain behind my back, inching the drape open.

Brodey's head jerked up. "Speaking of love nests..." He bounded up the steps, grabbed me by the wrist, and roughly yanked my arm behind my back. He jerked the curtain back and threw me across the room.

I stumbled, landing on the bed. My cheekbone hit hard against the headboard. I yelped in pain.

"I'll wager that's not the first time you've gotten banged on that headboard."

My hand reflexively went to my face, fingers gliding above tender flesh. White-hot sparks of pain shot through my cheekbone. I sensed Brodey moving behind me to the right. I heard the dresser drawer nearest Kris' side of the bed being opened and dumped on the floor, Brodey kicked through the contents with his boots.

As inconspicuously as possible, I squirmed about on the bed, freeing my pinned arm from beneath my body. I inched toward the edge, allowing my arm to fall limply off the bed. I strained, my fingertips barely reaching the floor.

My fingers walked along the carpeting, beneath the bed frame. Slowly, as not to attract attention. I strained, struggling to reach with my searching fingers. The bed rustled with my efforts. I froze, held my breath and prayed Brodey hadn't noticed. Heart pounding in my ears, I listened for his movements.

His footsteps came closer.

The mattress bowed beneath his weight. He was so close, I could smell his body odor, feel his foul, hot breath in ragged gasps upon my flesh. I leaned farther over the edge of the bed. He pinned me beneath his body. Despite my struggles, I couldn't budge him.

Bloodshot eyes stared into mine, nostrils heaved. His hot breath hit me full in the face. I shrank back from the odor. He kissed me, his tongue attempting to force its way into my mouth. I resisted, determined not to give an inch. My fists pounded upon his chest and shoulders. He ended the kiss, openly laughing at me as he grabbed my wrists in one hand and pinned my arms above my head.

I briefly considered screaming. But to what end? I was alone with no one left to answer my cries for help. Besides, Brodey would no doubt become even more incensed by my screams.

His large hand landed on my breast, squeezing hard, mauling my flesh. I tried heaving him off with my leg muscles. He refused to budge. He seemed delighted by my struggles. His fingers worked at the tethers of my trousers.

"Stop it!" I demanded.

His grip between my legs tightened.

"Stop it." I warned through clenched teeth.

"Did you let her lick you?" He laughed, waggling his tongue. "Did you like it?"

"Go...to...hell." I strained with each word, attempting to move his weight off me.

His cupped hand, pressed in harder. "No matter what else The Wolff may have done for you in bed..."

I fought to keep from crying out.

"...there's one thing she couldn't have given you."

He let loose my wrists long enough to sit up. Still straddling my lower body, he cupped his crotch, blatantly rubbing his swelling member.

I punched him squarely in the chest with closed fists.

He only laughed at my attempts. He began working loose the tethers on his breeches.

"What about Jackson?"

Brodey cocked his head to one side. "Sounds like Jackson's busy."

I quieted and listened. The sounds of cannonballs being fired echoed in the distance. Jackson's attack on *The Rapier* under way, no doubt. Brodey licked his lips and resumed his untethering with one hand, as the other buried itself beneath my tunic.

I felt it before I heard it. A loud bang, the splintering of wood. The ship violently jerked to the side, sending Brodey tumbling off the bed, throwing him against the wall.

"What the hell?" Brodey was up like a shot, running for the window.

Another shot rocked *The Wolfsbane*. I rolled with it, ending up on the opposite side of the bed. Brodey stumbled back from the window on shaky legs. "*The Rapier* is firing on *The Scorpion*. We're caught in the line of fire."

"Seems the crew of *The Rapier* could smell a rat even from the distance of their vessel," I said. "I guess they weren't as taken with Captain Jackson as you were."

He bristled, his back stiffened.

I reached beneath the edge of the bed.

He slowly turned around.

"The only one being taken is you." His eyes gleamed. His fury took hold and he charged me.

I remained rooted to the spot. My hand closed beneath the bed. My muscles tightened in anticipation.

He launched himself from the floor, his bulk leaping at me. I brought my arm up, gripped and thrust. His own momentum carried him down upon the blade.

It was instantaneous. His facial features went from rage to shock and pain all in the blink of an eye. Blood poured forth from his mouth, drenching the bed sheets. His eyes glazed over. His entire body went limp.

I closed my eyes and gritted my teeth. His weight was unbearable. I had attempted to brace for the impact. Still his weight was crushing the breath from me. I gripped the sword pommel with both hands and strained. The blood pounded in my head, every cord in my neck bulged. My muscles screamed in protest. Still I pushed.

As soon as his body was off of me, I fell back upon the bed, exhausted, heart pounding. The cool breeze upon my perspiration-soaked hair and skin chilled me to the bone. I breathed in deeply, taking in large gulps of sweet, fresh air.

✝

I peered over the edge of the bed. Brodey lay on the floor, sword still firmly embedded in his chest, the pommel firmly lodged in his breastbone. The blade protruded from between his shoulder blades, and his blood soaked into the carpet in thick, red pools.

Another shot pounded *The Wolfsbane*. I was thrown from the bed, landing against the dresser. The sharp corner caught me in the upper arm. As I knelt upon the carpet, I clutched my arm tightly, rocking with the pain. I gritted my teeth, ready to let fly a litany of curses.

Footsteps resounded on the stairs. The curtain was slowly drawn back.

I scrambled for the sword, gripped the pommel with both hands, pulling hard.

"When you bury a sword that deeply into a body, it's murder trying to retrieve it again."

A sword tip pressed into my neck, catching me just below the chin. I let loose the sword, sank back on my heels and looked up at Jackson. His uniform was disheveled. His military coat torn at the shoulders, dust coated his brass buttons. His face was smudged with dirt, his hair dusted with soot.

"*The Rapier* has turned on us. *The Scorpion* is floundering. She won't survive much longer."

I half-smiled. "Pity."

His sword tip dropped. "You don't understand. *The Wolfsbane* is still fastened to *The Scorpion*. We'll all perish."

I said nothing.

"Come with me now. We can escape in a longboat before *The Scorpion* and *The Wolfsbane* go under."

"Do you think me a fool?" I shook my head. "No doubt you intend to ransom me to the Spanish in exchange for your own safe passage. Do you imagine they'll hesitate to open fire upon their prince's betrothed?"

He exhaled loudly, sheathed his sword. "Come with me now and I'll deliver you to any shore you wish unharmed. I give you my word."

"Is it my neck you seek to save or your own?" I arched a bemused eyebrow.

247

A loud crack echoed throughout the cabin. I put out both hands to steady myself. Captain Jackson nearly lost his balance and braced himself. The floor tilted at a slight angle.

"We're almost out of time," he urged. "Come with me now."

"No."

"Lady DeVale, you have nothing left. All of your causes are gone. There is no reason left to resist me."

I nodded in agreement. "You're correct, Captain Jackson. All my reasons are lost to me now." Rage exploded inside of me. I charged, catching Jackson in the midsection. He stumbled backwards, hitting the opposite wall.

He thrust me away. I fell, landing at the foot of the bed. I scrambled to rise. I was to my knees before he had his sword drawn.

He flicked his wrist subtly. The blade tore open my tunic, slicing a thin line along my right side, just above my breast. Again, I flinched as the razor-edge bit into my flesh, leaving a scratch almost identical to the last. This one along my left side, above my heart.

"Scream if you wish, my lady."

"I shan't scream." My words were level, my speech normal. There was nothing more that Jackson could do to me. "My fear left me long ago."

"I gave you every chance to save yourself." He raised his arm above his head, his sword flashed above me. The blade came down, biting into the footboard post. A sliver of wood flew off with the impact.

"Do reconsider." Jackson pulled his blade back again. "It would be a pity to remove your beautiful head from the rest of your body."

"I prefer her intact."

That voice. My head jerked toward the sound of that voice. That distinctive, unmistakable voice that I thought I would never hear again. For a fleeting moment, our eyes met and my heart stopped. "Kris." Her name tumbled from my mouth.

She rushed past me, engaging Captain Jackson, drawing him away. She quickly gained the advantage, forcing him into a steady retreat.

Like me, Captain Jackson had obviously been caught off-guard by Kris' return.

"Lower your weapon," Kris ordered. "Help us free *The Wolfsbane* before we all die."

"You're already dead!" Jackson shouted, thrusting wildly. "I saw you go overboard."

Kris blocked his desperate thrust. "Not quite. I managed to swim back to *The Wolfsbane*. In the confusion, no one saw me secure a place on the scraper's board."

Jackson's eyes narrowed. "Demon."

"True." Kris blocked another thrust, countered with one of her own. "The demon came back to send you to hell."

Kris pressed her attack. Jackson stumbled backwards beneath her onslaught.

"Yield now," Kris demanded. "Most of your crew has been killed."

"Then you've freed your crew," Jackson said.

"They've retaken most of *The Wolfsbane* by now, including the cannons. A few well-placed shots convinced the Spanish galleon that you had turned on them. *The Wolfsbane* will be mine again soon."

"You'll command your ship in hell!" Jackson charged, swinging wildly.

Kris' blade flashed, catching him square in the chest. She pushed, flinging him backward, off her blade.

He clutched at his wound and came at her again.

Kris' blade buried itself in Jackson's midsection.

I was in Kris' arms instantly. She clutched me to her fiercely and buried her face in my hair, inhaling deeply. I felt the wet clothing, smelled the damp leather as I buried my face in her collarbone. I clung to her, afraid if I let go, she would vanish like a ghost.

"I didn't know if I'd be in time," she breathed into my ear. "I thought I'd lost you."

"They told me you were dead." My fingers ran through her hair, down her back, across her arms.

"It would take far more than that to keep me from you." She

stepped away from me. "We must hurry. *The Scorpion* is going under. And she means to take *The Wolfsbane* with her." She pulled me by the hand, rushing us toward the door.

†

We raced upon the deck, Kris pulling me along behind her, heading for the bow. She paused long enough to kick a burning timber from our path. It skidded off the deck, landing in the waters below with a sizzling splash. The deck was strewn with corpses, pirates and sailors alike. Never had I seen such destruction.

The Rapier fared no better. She was awash in flames, her mainmast engulfed by the fire. The ship seemed to tremble violently. Her mast collapsed, crashing to the deck, sending the bow plummeting into the ocean.

Vincent was unharmed. He led a handful of men, passing buckets of water, attempting to douse the flaming pyre that was once our short sail. The bow was a mass of confusion with men hacking at towlines with swords, attempting to slice them in twain. The ropes slowly unraveled, the blades weakening the hemp.

Kris and I rushed to join Sven, retrieving discarded weapons from the deck on the run. Armed with swords and daggers, striking deeply, slicing savagely, we viciously attacked the heavy rope. The hemp unwound, clinging by a thread, breaking at last.

The Scorpion's aft deck came into view. It was more than a foot out of the water. Her bow was completely under. The waves lapped higher up her deck, pulling her farther into the depths. Ropes stretched from her aft deck, half a dozen in all. Dangling harmlessly now, cut in half one by one. Only a single chain remained, stretching from her aft to our bow and wrapped around the maidenhead. It was as heavy and thick as our own anchor chain and pulled taut between the two ships with no slack in sight.

The Wolfsbane shifted sharply, causing the deck to tilt beneath us at an awkward angle. I glanced at *The Scorpion*. She was slipping even farther into the water, her death throes churning the water about us into turbulent waves.

"She'll pull us down with her," Vincent said.

"We only have one chance," Kris' gaze fixed on the chain wrapped securely about the wolf's head.

Vincent and Sven flanked the maidenhead. They were both holding onto a rope, keeping it stretched taut. The other end was tied about Kris' waist and beneath her arms. She secured the rope round herself and climbed the maidenhead.

A feeling of trepidation crept across me as I watched her, now perched between the wolf's ears, kneeling upon its head. *The Wolfsbane* shifted again, almost knocking Kris from her precarious perch.

Kris reached out, clutching at one of the wolf's ears. As she regained her balance, she took her sword out and plunged it into the maidenhead. Deeply embedding the steel beneath the chain, she lifted, attempting to leverage the chain off.

The deck rocked beneath us. There was a shout, a curse from Kris. She was suspended upside down, hanging precariously, saved from falling only by the rope fastened around her waist. She was red, the blood rushing to her face.

"Kris!" I shouted. "Hold on. I'm coming."

Sven shook his head. "You can't—"

"I have to." I said, moving toward the railing. "You're both needed to hold the rope."

"Then let another go," Sven said.

I glanced back upon the deck. *The Wolfsbane* was in disarray. Rufus and his men were at work, attempting to keep us afloat and the fires to a minimum. I knew there was no time to beg for another's help. I kicked off my boots, leaving them upon the deck.

"Alexis! No." Kris shouted.

I scrambled upon the railing, onto the wolf's neck and pulled myself up the maidenhead. I moved quickly, reaching the top and knelt between the wolf's ears. I leaned over, reached out, and struggled to pull her near. I lost my grip.

With an anguished cry, Kris slipped away again.

I lay flat on my stomach, fingers of one hand firmly gripped around the hilt of the sword. With the other, I reached for Kris, fingertips straining. She craned her neck, staring at *The Scorpion* from her upside down position.

"Forget me."

"Never."

"You have to. Focus on the chain," she commanded. "Do it now or we'll all perish."

I settled back upon my heels, using the sword as leverage. It was drenched with sea spray, slick to the touch. The metal was cold, burning my tender flesh with an icy chill. I gritted my teeth and pushed upwards.

As *The Scorpion* slid farther beneath the waves, the chain loosened somewhat, easing the tautness that had stretched between the two ships. I reached into my reserves and heaved all my weight against the sword, using momentum to leverage the chain off the wolf's ears. The result was instantaneous. It skidded off the wolf's head, crashing into *The Scorpion*'s aft deck as she went under.

I looked down, yelling for Sven and Vincent. "Pull!"

As they heaved, the rope holding Kris swayed, bringing her back in line with the maidenhead. I stretched, reaching out and catching hold of Kris' legs, guiding her in.

Breathing heavily, we lay braced against the maidenhead, seeking a moment's respite.

Kris abruptly sat up, fighting to undo the knot tied in the rope about her waist. The knot abruptly gave and Kris' elbow flung back, awkwardly connecting with my body.

We fell. Quick and hard.

I screamed, clutching blindly at Kris.

The landing was just as hard. We fell upon the deck, wood splintering, protesting beneath our combined weight. The impact rattled me to my teeth. We lay there stunned, a tangle of arms and legs.

"Are you well?" Sven rushed to us. He threw his end of the rope down and knelt beside us.

"Never better," I groaned out.

"Fine," Kris said. She lifted her head from beneath my leg and stared up at Sven. "Man the wheel. Get us turned back around. I want us as far from here as possible."

"Aye."

Sven ran off, heading for the ship's wheel.

Kris and I sat up carefully, working to disentangle ourselves.

A set of approaching footfalls echoed in my ear and trousered legs came into my field of vision. I turned my head, following the line of fabric.

Rufus McGregor held a sword, the tip pressed to Kris' throat.

She strained, attempting to inch away from the blade. Trapped beneath me as she was, there was nowhere for her to go.

Rufus looked from Kris to me and back again. His grip on the sword pommel tightened.

To the left, behind him, I saw Vincent carefully approaching, his own sword at the ready. His sword tip flashed.

My breath caught as Rufus raised the blade. He turned it around, handing the weapon to Kris, hilt first.

Visibly stunned, Kris took the sword, firmly gripping its weight in her hand.

Rufus nodded, turned and walked away.

I let out a breath and collapsed back against Kris.

We stared numbly at the destruction before us. *The Wolfsbane* was the worse for wear. Her deck torn up, small fires still burning here and there and only one sail left to operate under.

I felt the same. Battered and crippled, every part of my body aching. "Now what?" I asked.

"We limp back to the channel, make repairs upon the island. Get underway before anyone thinks to search for their missing ships."

"And then?"

"On to a safe port for supplies."

Her face froze; her eyes were watching me warily. "Unless you'd rather I return you to Fortress Monsarrent."

"You would do that?"

She shrugged. "I make the same offer Jackson did. To drop you on any shore you choose."

"I told you I would never leave again."

"You also said the one thing you desired from me was your freedom. I give it to you now."

Her words were brave. Only her eyes betrayed her fear.

"I have my freedom," I said. "And I choose to stay with you, my Captain."

I leaned forward, mouth at her ear. "For always."

About the Author

Del Robertson

Del Robertson lives, works, and plays in San Antonio, Texas, where, much to the disappointment of her twin nieces, she emphatically *does not* ride a horse to work every morning.

An avid reader, whose mom graciously looked the other way while she devoured Nancy Drew books beneath the covers with a flashlight every night, Del has been penning short stories since she was old enough to pick up a Husky pencil. Thanks to the encouragement of her partner and the coincidental/accidental breaking of her favorite pencil, she was eventually convinced to take up the keyboard. After that, it was years spent writing stories for the Web before having a manuscript accepted by Intaglio Publications. *Taming The Wolff* is her first published novel.

E-Books, Limited First Edition Print, Printed Books, Free e-books

Visit our website for more publications available online.

http://www.affinityebooks.com

Published by Affinity E-Book Press NZ Ltd

Canterbury, New Zealand

Registered company 2517228

Printed in Great Britain
by Amazon

17940092R00153